Pride of Paradise

Lane

Black Country Saga

Lydia King

Second Edition
Palm Tree Publishing
2025
ISBN: 978-1-0681583-0-8

Dedication

To the memory of Thomas Bentley, who fought in WW1

Grandad - who taught me to read, write and appreciate the joy of poetry. And for his devoted daughter Lilian Rose, Mom who was so looking forward to reading this book. I know she will be looking over my shoulder loving it all.

Lily Rose 14th February 1934 – 13th February 2025

Contents

Pride of Paradise
Copyright © Lydia King 2025
Dedication
Contents...
Reviews...
Chapter 1 1
Chapter 2 13
Chapter 3 25
Chapter 4 35
Chapter 5 47
Chapter 6 59
Chapter 7 71
Chapter 8 81
Chapter 9 90
Chapter 10 100
Chapter 11 108
Chapter 12 114
Chapter 13 118
Chapter 14 124
Chapter 15 138
Chapter 16 146
Chapter 17 153
Chapter 18 163
Chapter 19 170
Chapter 20 181
Chapter 21 190
Chapter 22 195
Chapter 23 205
Chapter 24 211

Chapter 25 226
Chapter 26 237
Chapter 27 242
Chapter 28 255

Reviews

This book is set in the Black Country during WW1. It reads authentically, the characters and descriptions ring true. It is an enjoyable read of 273 pages. Taking the pen name of Lydia King, Susan Jones, has written a book, the first in a planned series which please the many fans who know her other books. – Paul Newton.

Gritty, yet poignant at the same time; this is a story that is written from the heart. It is set during WW1 and is about ordinary people trying to survive in an extraordinary time. It is obvious that the writer, Lydia King, has come across the characters she has met in reality because they are so lifelike. It is also clear that the writer knows the setting that she writes about so well too. If you want a story that is a mixture of poignancy, grit and love, then this saga is for you. – Michelle.

Chapter 1

May 1915

'You've gone and done what! Have you lost your marbles, Issac Cartwright? Holy mother of God – tell me you're kidding!'

Molly Marsden swung round and glared; navy eyes flashing like jet as she pushed her stray dark curls from her face, fuming with upset and indignation.

He calmly pulled a bottle of brandy from the drawer in front of his desk.

'You don't drink. That's your dad's, you told me. He keeps it there for when he pops in, though he never does.'

'I know, and yes, I have enlisted. How can it be right for me to carry on here as if nothing's happened, when all the lads and wenches are doing their bit, tell me that?'

For once, Molly was speechless.

'It must come as a shock to you, I know, but you've been running this place with me for a number of years now, and doing a good job at that.' He drank his brandy. 'There'll be no difference, other than I'll be over there instead of here.'

Her boss had been pacing back and forth for most of the afternoon, the dark ridge across his brow growing deeper by the second.

'I know it's serious, us being at war with Germany, but you're not on the battlefield because you're a businessman, a good one.

There's too much responsibility here for me to take on running the place.'

She was in a panic. Her breathing was getting heavy; her voluminous breasts were heaving up and down. She wanted to grab him, shake the bones of him into reality, and carry on as normal. Placing her left hand firmly on her hip, she spoke more calmly

'You mean you're going away, need a break for a day or two? Cos that'll be a first, seeing as you eat sleep and breathe this place.'

Molly turned back to her work, not wanting him to see the effect his being so close had on her, besides, more chatter would mean a later finish and she'd promised aunt Violet she'd be home on time. She'd always spoken her mind with Issac and they worked together, with ease mostly. That's how she liked it.

Working her way through all aspects of the hatting manufacturing, to helping manage the Bloxwich & Walsall Hat Business had been her proudest achievement of her life so far; never one to shirk any extra hours or responsibilities that came with the job, she accepted all that.

Now Issac Cartwright was asking one of the daftest questions she'd heard in a long time. Run his blooming business for him? Talk about coals to Newcastle.

'I've enlisted for war duties, if they'll have me. I'm a bit on the old side for what they want. But they'll take me.' He encircled her gently with his arms, and pressed his hard-on against her bottom, gently moving from side to side, until she arched her back and murmured. 'You'd better stop that else you'll send me out of control.' She turned and gave him a seductive smile.

'I hope so.' He turned her around, and pressed up close where she ached for him. 'They're desperate for men on the front line. I'll have to do some training first, and then I'll be ready for off. I'll be back before we get posted overseas anyway. You won't get rid of me that easily.'

He brushed her lips with his, teasing until she grabbed his hair and kissed him back with more passion than she thought she was capable of. She stood back, and studied his face, full of longing and brooding with sex appeal.

'You really can't be serious? About going away I mean?' From the look on his face, she knew he was. She reached up and pushed her hands through those thick dark curls. 'If you're going to start something you can't finish, Issac, you'd better stop messing me around.' She tugged at his locks, and gave him one of her looks.

'They're all off to fight for England, help with the war effort, and here's me… What effort am I making - other than worry about preparing hats to be sent to men on the front line?'

Frustration etched across his face, before a roguish smile replaced his anguish and he fixed her with those silvery grey eyes. 'Make me happy, one more time, Molly.'

He was lifting her skirts, and hitched her up onto the huge desk in the middle of the office. Kissing her as he unbuttoned his breeches at the same time, letting them drop before he manoeuvred himself nearer, whispering her name as he pushed gently into her; like he had so many times before. The workers had all gone for their usual chippy dinner; he knew they wouldn't be disturbed.

Issac Moved slowly at first, making magic until she moved in time with him until they both went crazy to reach a great satisfaction, from each other, coming to ecstasy quicker than she would have liked.

As usual, he pulled out, making sure he wouldn't give her a child out of wedlock. They'd always agreed on that. Kissing her with a hurried passion like never before, he showered her breasts in tender kisses before she dressed herself. He used his large handkerchief to tidy up the evidence of their lovemaking.

His head rested on her shoulder as he gently kissed her neck before quickly shifting his mind back to the subject in hand.

'Even the wenches are going off to train up as nurses, or getting in the volunteering services in some way. Our Clara is doing her bit, now. She's joined the QAINS… for god's sake. Over here for now, but planning to go out and work on the battlefields, helping transport wounded soldiers to hospital. I mean, Queen Alexandra's nurses! Yet I bet she's sitting comfortable in one of the many royal carriages, or at the palace, reading a book.'

'You can't say that; she's doing everything she can think of to help, making sure there are enough nurses for a start, so why shouldn't she be relaxing over in Sandringham? Our new Queen Mary will take up the cause now. You've no idea how many have taken up the call. But we've got work to do here!'

'The country is in dire straits, Molly. I can't stand by and do nothing anymore. And of course, I love Queen Alexandra.' He turned and blew her a kiss, but not like I feel about you.'

'This is your livelihood, though, what about your great-grandad's legacy; surely you need to *be* here, in Paradise Lane?' Molly spoke quietly and clasped her hands together in her lap, trying not to panic. There was no way she would plead with him, but her own livelihood was at stake as well.

Her heart banged in her chest. If he walked out now, how would she manage? Yes, she practically ran the business already, but with him at the helm guiding her. She didn't want to think of him fighting, no matter how great the cause. Damn the stupid war! It wouldn't change anything, apart from lives wasted.

'My mind is made up. I want to make my family proud, it's what they'd expect deep down, and I know that. You're capable, that's why I'm leaving it in your hands. You'll do well and there's nobody else I trust; like you said, it'd be no more than you're doing already.'

Now he was pouring brandy, like it was a celebration. 'I'll have a few weeks training on Cannock Chase, then it'll be back to see everyone, you especially, then across the channel, here I come.'

'You'll be putting all your responsibility onto me?' She rounded on him, flinging her arms down by her sides. 'What about the workers?' Her dark eyes burned with all the colours of a midnight sky in a storm. That happened when she was annoyed, like now.

'They're asking for extra shifts on the press and in the finishing room. I've only got one pair of hands to train people up. Aunt Violet depends on what I take home to pay the rent, buy food and help keep us in a decent way of living. What if it all goes wrong? You haven't thought it through properly.'

She moved the batch of cloth hats she'd been stacking ready to be packed off the next day, silently thanking God that the other workers had now gone. Most of them would be in the Old Bush, the nearest tavern past the corner of the street on their way home.

If they had half inkling Issac was about to sign up for the war effort all hell would break loose. It was a hard enough job to keep the workers in hand at the best of times.

'I've thought of nothing else, believe me. Every time I read the newspapers and hear news of what's happening in Europe… We must act. I must.' He sat down on a chair next to her and leaned forward resting his forearms on the workbench.

'I heard the Mayor of Coventry has resigned, and him sending all them motorbikes out to Belgium for the soldiers an all. He's been pushed out more than likely with all the talk. He is German, but he's done so much good the city, you'd have thought he'd be left alone; which makes me know I must go. It's the only way. Otherwise, I'll not be able to walk through Walsall without getting the white feather treatment.'

He looked so sad she wanted to hug the man she'd worked beside for so long. It hadn't entered her mind he would want to leave her to go and fight. 'Tell me it's not the only reason, fear of being shamed, when you run a business supporting people and their extended families? We've done so well to build it up, getting orders from all the local shops, and even the big stores in Birmingham have shown an interest.' Her voice got louder as she tried to convince him how important his presence was to her alone, if not the others.

Issac shook his head and drank more brandy. 'I've already signed up, passed the medical, and they'll take me.'

Molly knew there was nothing more to be said. He'd told rather than asked her to keep the business going, and she knew everything he said made sense, but Issac on the front line?

When he finally looked up, he threw her an irresistible smile. 'Will you write?'

'Depends if I have any spare time seeing as I'll be looking after family as well as making sure we keep churning out the hats;' she fixed her hand on hip and refused to beg him to stay here, home in Pelsall, the Black Country, where he belonged. '

Men have gone from here already, and a few others left to take up jobs in the Triumph motorcycle business and the munitions factory over the border in Warwickshire. There's plenty of work there because the pay's better. Coventry's turning into a boom town, I suppose you've heard? Anyway, I it's time I got back. We're in the Black Country, its home for me, where I intend to stay. I'm known as the hat girl from Paradise Lane, not only that, it's my birthday today; they'll be wondering where I am.'

'You should have told me; I'd have wished you happy birthday, Molly, my love. How did I forget?' He lifted his eyes skyward, then smiled and she wondered if he'd kiss her again, and make love to her like he always did. Her hopes came to nothing; he was engrossed in adventures that lay ahead for him.

'And go steady on yer bike, up that Wolverhampton Road. I'd offer you a lift, but I know how independent you are.' He gave her a long hard stare… was this the moment they'd kiss and he'd ask her to marry him? Reluctantly she gathered her jacket. Of course, that would never happen. They'd worked together for so long and both were far too busy for serious relationships of that kind. She waited while he locked up then they left together, he in his motor car and she on her pushbike, pedalling her way home, to Victoria Row in Bloxwich.

***

'Make a wish; go on… I only had yellow and white candles, and there was only five in the pack, we'll pretend there's the right amount.' Aunt Violet clapped her hands, followed by a burst of laughter.

Molly savoured the wonderful spread laid out in front of her. A jam sponge alight with five lonely candles sitting proudly in the centre of the small round table in the parlour. Sandwiches with home-made bread cut into great door stoppers with thinly sliced cheese poking out of the sides. Sausage rolls, made earlier, golden and crispy, adorned with delicate lettuce leaves, no doubt from one of the back gardens along the row of terrace houses where they lived in Victoria Row.

Everyone grew something different then they swapped produce. Aunt Violet had fruit trees, goose-gog bushes and rhubarb aplenty. Those who grew salad leaves always dropped a dish in at times like now. The display made a mouth-watering sight. There was a huge home-made apple pie for afters.

'You must have spent all day, preparing this.' Molly swept her red, work worn hand over the buffet table then leaned forward, blowing the candles out, taking three tries, sending a great wisp of smoke trailing into the air. How her aunt afforded all this was beyond her; she must have been saving up for weeks, or else hoarding it away ready for today.

'Now you think on, our Molly and wish for something good, as all I've been reading in the paper is talk of the war to end all wars, only it's not, is it? It should have been sorted out by now, but here we are again. I wanted to make a special tea for yer twenty-ninth birthday. Now come on an' cut us a chunk of that cake.

It might be a while until we have a spread like this with talk of rations and supplies getting scarce. Half the shops are empty with the hob nobs buying everything up. Good job I'm on friendly terms with the butcher, and the grocer. They know I like to bake, so I'm stocked up with my cooking ingredients for now.'

'Issac is talking about signing up; feels it's his duty.' Savouring the jam sponge, she avoided eye contact with her aunt, though she couldn't keep the sadness from her voice.

'What about the business? Who'll keep the trade going? There's quite a few in this town depends on their weekly wage, how'll they get by? With this blasted war hanging over us *all* the men will feel pressured into going off to fight; though I wouldn't have thought *he* would. What'll happen?' Violet's voice held a quiver that couldn't disguise her fears that matched exactly how she felt.

Steadying herself to calm her breathing, she couldn't upset aunt Violet any more than she had to; she brushed crumbs from her dress then looked up. 'Half the men have left already. Gone to join up and this week we've had a couple more women asking for jobs. They're coming to Bloxwich and Walsall, from the small villages; the work is here, they're coming in bus loads from Birmingham and London. I think they feel safer over here in Pelsall, and a lot of the children have gone to the country, so they'll be closer to the little ones.

We've even had Belgian refugees calling in to ask for work as well. I'll work it out, don't worry, we'll get by. A bonus of being in the black-country, apart from the smoke and smog, there's work to be had. I intend to keep the business going.'

Janey sat eagerly glancing from one to the other of her older relatives, 'Happy birthday, Sis.' Her rosy apple cheeks and warm smile melted Molly's heart. 'I could come with you to work. You can show me. I've been with you lots of times. It's not that hard. I'm already busy with my sewing projects; we could put my curtains and cushions on show with the hats in the front room of the cottage.'

'Well blow me down if you're not thinking up ideas to take over already, and that's not a bad idea either, our Janey.' Molly laughed. The love and trust in her little sister's brown eyes made her whisper a silent promise to her mum and dad. It's what they'd have said if they'd been alive. *Look after your little sister* and she would; damn that storm causing the car her dad had just bought to steer off the road into a ditch.

It robbed herself and Janey of the kindest parents that ever lived. The doctor told them that if it was any consolation, they died instantly, and didn't suffer. It wasn't any help, if anything, made her sadder they hadn't had chance to say goodbye. She tried to be brave, most of the time. Only occasionally, like now, she wished they were back, to feel their arms round her once more, to ask them what to do.

She shook herself back to reality; now was no time to get maudlin. Feeling sad was usually kept for when she was alone, like in bed at night. That's when she'd cry quietly to herself, hugging her pillow. She wanted the best for her little sister who hadn't a clue how much of a struggle it was to keep bills paid and food on the table for the three of them. To keep smiling through when her heart was breaking, yearning for her mother's arms to wrap her up in love that would never come again was agony. She cried silent tears until her pillow was soaking wet, then eventually fell into a disturbed sleep, most nights.

Not to hear her father sing the old Black Country folk songs taught to him from his mother's knee was what she missed most. Nobody would ever know the depth of her grief, not even aunt Violet, her rock. There was no way she could begin to talk of her own worries; not with Janey, nor Violet; they depended on her too much.

'Thanks, Janey. Now how about me and you get in that scullery and do some washing up?' Plumping the cushions on her aunt's favourite chair as she passed Molly insisted that for the rest of the day, Violet put her feet up. 'We'll make sure and tidy the kitchen as well. There should be plenty of food left over for tomorrow if we keep it covered. We'll put some plates over it all and keep it in the pantry.'

Janey followed her big sister into the scullery and between them they made short work of the clearing up. Soon everywhere sparkled all squeaky clean and fresh while Violet snored like an Irish navvy, as her dad would have said, relaxing on her favourite chair.

'You know when you were telling aunt Violet about the workers all leaving the hat workshop? Janey turned to her sister, head tilted to one side and a great frown furrowing her brow. 'Well, I think it's time I came to work with you. I know you have too much to manage. I would do what you tell me, our Molly. You know how good I am at following instructions.'

'Haven't I been running up curtains on the old treadle for the neighbours? You know how pleased they are, with my work. I'm fourteen now remember. I can't depend on odd jobs forever. I could easily help with making hats. I go round the houses selling aunt Violet's pickles and home-made toffee apples; I could easily say I'm taking hat orders, what d'you think?'

Gathering her young sister close for a hug, she fought back tears then buried her head into her neck while they hugged.

'Now listen here missy! I'll have no talk of you going out to work, though your ideas are up there with the best, our kid. Just keep up the good work, and think on…

Don't sell all them tu-penny toffee apples; I haven't had one for ages. Make sure and save me one next time.'

Leading her to the back garden she hoped some sports-time might take her mind off such serious ideas. 'If you want to do something useful for me, keep studying and reading, in between your sewing and helping make jam and pickles. You know how the shop took as much as you could make with them pickles you did last year? Maybe one Saturday, we'll see about you coming to work with me, just to have a look, but not yet, our Janey.

The world is changing now for young ladies like you. Imagine if you learned some languages, like French, or Italian. You could travel, be a governess, teacher, anything. It's all in them books our dad collected for us. The encyclopaedias have everything you need to know.

The world is waiting and you can expand your horizons far away from Victoria Row in a year or so. There are boats taking people all over Europe, and why shouldn't you be one of them?'

'Now let's see who can score the first goal.' Molly ran with the ball, across the narrow strip of grass then booted it up against the shed at the bottom of the garden.

The moment of maudlin had passed. It usually did. Janey and her aunt kept her feet firmly on the ground. Niggling thoughts about how she'd manage kept without Issac kept coming back. He'd shown her he ropes, been a guiding light at the business from day one. Taught her all she knew about felting, dying the wool, shaping, stretching the fabrics.

How hadn't she understood before now, exactly how much he meant to her? It wasn't what she wanted for their Janey; she was young, and there were more opportunities opening up for young ladies, and she wanted her to have a better life than factory work.

He'd hinted at marriage, even though they made love whenever the chance came up, which was often if they were alone, but only then. It was those eyes, the way he looked at her, watched as she learned all there was to know about the hatting trade.

He hadn't a clue how hard she had tried not to fall into those silver-grey pools of gorgeousness, every time he came near. Now his mind was set. He was off to fight for England, while she had a fight of her own on her hands. If he wrote to her first, then she'd write back.

Tomorrow was another day, and all Molly prayed for was the workers be on her side in trying to keep Bloxwich & Walsall hat business afloat. It had to stay open, otherwise what would become of Janey and aunt Violet? And herself! She had to make it work.

Thoughts of her task ahead caused her a restless night. Throughout the tossing and turning, she saw Issac in her dreams, only for him to turn and leave her, bound for an unknown world much too far away.

Chapter 2

Crowds made their way down Park Street, pushing and shoving all heading for Walsall Station. It was Issac's last Saturday in the Black Country, until he returned home safely. Lovers snatched one last kiss; sweethearts everywhere, whispered lasting promises to keep each other going through hard times ahead.

For Molly, looking into his eyes, she wanted to tell him how she felt, but couldn't find the words. His leave-time at home had flown by, and the walks along the curly Wyrley canal they'd shared were etched in her mind forever. That day when he'd held her close and told her he wanted to marry her, but after the war was over, just in case he didn't come back.

He didn't want to leave her a widow; she'd pushed him away, in fun almost sending him hurtling into the cut. Turned out to be only the one foot got stuck in the muddy reeds. He'd clambered out, pulling her onto the lush green canal bank. There they'd rolled together and kissed until they were breathless.

Horse riding together, over the Fairy Fields common, was blissful, on evenings he'd asked her to spend some time with him, doing something other than work. The bag containing ham and lettuce sandwiches, with home-made dandelion wine to wash it down with, were the best food and drink she'd ever tasted.

He promised to love her forever, but she knew it was fear of the future, giving him more confidence and cockiness than his usual way of speaking. They almost got as intimate as they often did, until Molly, in fear of a barge coming round the corner, or folks out walking, reluctantly stopped him from taking their romp any further.

She stood and watched as he jumped aboard the train. He threw his kit bag down on the floor before shoving the window open to lean out and wave her goodbye. Raising her hand, Molly blew a kiss to the man she had known for so long, yet not had chance to put into words how much she loved him. She waved her lace hankie and almost choked on the lump in her throat. It felt strange, her emotions rising like never before, then hot tears streaming down her cheeks.

Doors banged, a whistle blew followed by screams, and then sobs from girlfriends and wives, mothers and lovers drowned out sounds from the train hooting a last goodbye, as it disappeared around the bend. Thick smoke curled through the distance between them… he was gone.

'My darling, Issac, take care… keep safe for me love.' She whispered into the space where the train had left a cloud of sooty smoke. She remembered how he'd held her hands tightly in his, before he left.

'Take care of everything for me.' He didn't mention that he cared for her; he was referring to the business he was leaving behind. She'd nodded and fought back tears she didn't want him to see.

He'd done all the training on Cannock Chase, though he didn't discuss details, so she didn't push him on it. It would be for several weeks, if not months, now before she would see him again, and at least he promised to write.

***

'Hey, Molly, have you seen Jack's neck? E's been eaten alive by summat in the night if you ask me.' The new labourer from Birmingham was quick to notice the bite marks covering Jack Solomon's neck, as if nobody else had, though it was obvious he'd tried to hide them with his checked scarf.

'Never mind Jack's neck, it's your mucky mouth I'm watching out for, and if yer can put a mind to getting on with yer work, we'll all be better off; now think on.' Molly glared as she pointed a finger in the direction of Bobby Reynolds. It wasn't often she had to lay down the rules at work; recently she had to.

'If all you Brummie lads think a lady boss means shouting and bantering takes priority over your work in this business, listen up…' She was in charge now and thanks to the suffragettes giving women a voice in the workplace and life in general, she made herself crystal clear.

'A good day's work will earn yer a good day's pay. I can't make it plainer than that.' From the day she'd waved Issac off to war she missed him with an ache that filled her heart and mind constantly. The business wasn't as big as the saddlers, or the steel nor nail works, and mostly it was the coal mine that employed the men, unless the threat of flooding stopped all work. Now the war had left everything in turmoil.

'Molly, where do you want me to put these, the packing bench is full already?' Rita held armfuls of cloth hats due to be posted abroad.

'Get them over there and do the best you can to make room. Squash them down; we'll get them off tonight.'

'Righty oh, and Molly,' she gushed. 'You're coming down the Old Bush later, with us, aren't you? Me and a few of the girls are having a bit of a do. It's Marlene's birthday; let's face it, you're only seventeen once.' Her laughter echoed around the room and bounced from the high ceiling.

Molly smiled. 'I might join you after I've sorted these orders out.' She crossed off the hats that were made and others to be completed by the end of the week. It was getting harder to source the materials for the individual orders, but so far, she'd only turned a couple of new customers down. Soon as she found time, a trip over to the rag market in Birmingham, would lead to a choice of quality fabrics; often deliveries changed what she'd asked for, and replacements weren't always to her liking.

'We'll be knocking back the brown ale, and if I know Marlene, she'll be the first one dancing on the table; unless you beat her to it of course.'

Molly busied herself and smiled though she didn't make any promises. She didn't mind having a laugh, but work had to come first. A letter arrived early that morning, from Issac. She recognised his handwriting, but wanted to save it for later, when she would have more time to read it. She'd give the Bush a miss for tonight; she wanted to get home and open the brown envelope.

The clip clop of old Mr Peacock's horse and cart echoed through the high window in her small office as it came to a halt on the cobblestones in the side yard. The weekly delivery was due - her usual hardwearing cloth material, buttons and lace from Nottingham. She set the kettle on the range, over the fire, in readiness for his chat and gossip from Robin Hood's County.

A younger man, more thick set than Mr Peacock was tying up the horse and cart. He stretched his arms above his head then on sighting Molly, waiting at the door, he marched forward pushing past, rubbing up a bit too close for comfort, and entered the small room.

'It's taken longer than I expected it to.' He rubbed his hands together and looked across at the kettle, singing to a boil on the rack over the embers sending steam upwards. 'Ah, you've got just what I need there, after that pot-hole jolting journey. I'd swear them roads haven't changed since the Roman's made them.'

'Mr. Peacock had to stay on in Nottingham; I'm his second in charge. And a bit of summat to warm me up would be good an all.'

Molly bent to tend the kettle. He grabbed her backside and pinched with both hands. 'Ouch, you hurt me!'

'How yer fixed for a bit of a tumble on the table then, love? Seeing as yer'm all alone and looking ready for it. 'I heard as yer gaffers away. We all know how the mice play when the cats away. Eh?'

His throaty chuckle gave her the creeps and now he was pressing himself up behind her, tugging her blouse open, grabbing her breasts and fondling as if he had a licence for it. Her stomach churned and the urge to throw up all over the kitchen floor overwhelmed her. The last thing she wanted was what he had in mind. She struggled to turn and face her attacker.

His braces hung down, now he untied his belt. Her cheeks reddened, heart pounding in her chest. Her mouth was so dry she couldn't swallow; the scream on her lips silenced – she couldn't let the workers find her with a man, half naked in her office.

He had her trapped against the wall. A burly knee kicked her legs open. Molly had to get control... No man could walk into her place. Now this one dribbled across her exposed breasts.

She hissed. '*I'm not interested*, never will be. Are you listening? I'm here to run the place. I'll tell Mr Peacock about you - doing this?' She was hurting from his earlier advances, but forced herself not to crumble.

'It's not for Mr Peacock to find out is it me pretty wench. How many men have been up here?' He pinned her to the wall with his bulk of body, then grabbed her leg above the knee and ran his big rough hand up the inside of her thigh and inside her knickers. His fingers reached for her intimate part – he stroked with his thumb, and probed with his fingers … she gasped.

'Stop it will you, I don't want this!'

'What's up wench? You never had it; don't know the pleasure of a stiff cock up inside here? He jabbed, not caring that she winced and bit on her lip to save herself from crying out. 'Word on the grapevine is that yer pleasure the boss, and he's gone away, so…'

His eyes glinted and took on a mocking glow. 'Different to the usual sluts I'm used to; more like a quality type of slag, eh?' He leered in her face. 'You want a bit of rough up here.' Again, he jabbed his fingers inside her and Molly flinched and shuddered.

Built like an army tank this monster wasn't going anywhere. His hard body pressed against her; Molly wondered how she could escape before he went any further. Shouting out wasn't an option; whoever came to her rescue would see her skirt around her waist and his hand, up her knickers, and her bigger than average breasts spilling from her opened blouse. It would make her the laughing stock of Bloxwich and Walsall.

His hot breath stunk; a combination of Woodbines, last night's ale, and meat pie. If he didn't let her go soon, she was in grave danger of puking all over him. He pulled her hand to where his opened breeches revealed the great hard length of dick that jerked as he forced her fingers to touch it.

She stifled a sob and turned her head as she endured the stuff of nightmares. 'If Issac was here, he'd kill you!' Her words fell on deaf ears.

'Well he's not here so stop complaining and suck it then, bitch.' He grabbed chunks of her dark curls, either side of her face and wound her locks around large sausage-like fingers and forced her mouth onto his smelly crotch then thrust his throbbing dick down her throat. 'Me name's Eddie by the way, so yer know who yer'm sucking' off.'

He rotated his cock round her mouth - she felt sick. 'Come on, swallow it down now, bitch woman.'

Molly choked and gagged; her mouth filthy from the taste of him. The almighty gut-wretch came half a second before she bit down hard on his knob as he withdrew.

'You fucking dirty cow, what happened to enjoying a bit of rough? Don't you know how to pleasure a man down here in the slums of the Black Country?' He threw her to the floor as he dropped to his knees.

She floundered, and then rose hastily, fastening the buttons on her blouse. Fingers shaking, she darted outside to the water pump on the yard. Spluttering and coughing she splashed her face then rinsed her mouth of the putrid taste.

Again, she washed her mouth and face, calming herself; from the stench of the brute she'd never seen until today. Standing tall, she looked to the sky and took a deep breath of sooty Black Country air. Nobody would faze her, nor do that again.

Jack appeared in the yard and lit up a woodbine outside the workshop door. He looked across to where she tidied her hair and straightened her blouse, where he'd groped her. She coughed and breathed steadily to calm herself down.

He stubbed out his cigarette then came over to check out the delivery horse and cart. As he held a bucket of fresh water for the horse, his frown in her direction showed concern.

Her shrill reply rang out across the yard, though she tried to speak normally, hoping he hadn't noticed what had gone on in her office only minutes earlier.

'Jack! It's not Mr Peacock!' She turned to where the unthinkable had just happened. 'It's his assistant - he's leaving as soon as that wagon gets unloaded. Come on, hurry,' she beckoned him to look sharp.

'We've work to do! Get that cloth into the storage; I'll put the accessories in the finishing area; she grabbed a couple of smaller boxes from the cart, knowing they would have ribbons and buttons in for adorning the wedding hats.

He patted the horse's mane, frowned then asked again if she was okay as he went round to the cart still loaded with material. 'I'll get this lot into the bay and then Mr Peacock's mate can get on his way.'

He gave a loud whistle. 'Hey, Bobby, giz hand with the delivery can you?' The lad humped a great bundle of cloth onto his back, and took it through the side door of the workshop. He didn't ask any more questions, to Molly's relief.

Straightening her skirt and pinning her hair into place, she took another drink in her cupped hands, from the water pump. A swift glance towards the kitchen window, showed the slob, helping himself to her tea and biscuits.

'You pig!'

'Until next time, then wench,' he turned and stood at the door, raised his mug of tea, and rubbed himself with his free hand. He'd caught her glaring at him. Turning quickly, Molly took great strides, marching swiftly to the workshop. If she couldn't deal with Mr Peacock directly, she'd cancel their order. The bully acted as if nothing had happened. Not only had he hurt her, he'd degraded the position she'd promised to uphold for Issac. That bothered her most. The afternoon would be difficult to get through.

That wouldn't have happened if Issac had been here. She pursed her lips and stood tall. Stay calm and keep going. Much worse was happening on the battlefields overseas, and in trenches. *Please God keep Issac safe.* She pushed the event earlier from her mind.

'Ee wants the money, for the cloth, Molly. Eddie's waiting for yer in the yard he said to tell yer.' Jack shouted up the hallway, where she was about to oversee the pressing machine.

'I'll deal with Mr Peacock next time he comes, like we normally do, Jack.' The trembling hands threatened to give her away, she steadied her voice. 'I'll send a cheque in the post, tell him. Leave the delivery note on my desk. I'm busy on the shop floor now. Tell him to go!' She didn't want to make a scene, in front of the others. It's possible they'd think she encouraged him - being alone, without a man.

How could she make advances to anyone, when the only man on her mind, was Issac?

The lad nodded. Molly watched him go to the door and called after him. 'Oh, and Jack… Make sure you watch him out the gate.'

The abusive toad had gone - out of sight and off the property. He needed reporting, but who would believe her word against his? The thought of standing up in court and seeing him again made her want to die.

****

As soon as she got home, she threw a bucket of coal on the fire before drawing a pan of water from the copper, in the corner of the scullery. Glad to see her aunt Violet busy weeding the vegetable patch down the garden, she carried it upstairs. Janey wasn't in the house, which gave her time to herself, in the privacy of her room.

She filled the jug that stood on her dressing table, put the empty pan on the floor, and then steadily emptied half the steaming water into her floral wash bowl. She closed her curtains and reached for a medicated soap bar from the shelf nearby.

With her clean face flannel, she scrubbed around her mouth and washed her face over and over until it stung… trying hard to rid her memory of the man who assaulted her, then she rinsed her mouth with antiseptic liquid.

No matter how hard she tried, nothing worked. Though she emptied the bowl into the drain on the yard, and got more water, repeating her actions, she didn't feel clean. She knew she'd never feel clean again.

When she'd brushed her hair a hundred times and dabbed rose water over her neck, she could still smell and taste him.

She lost all track of time. Her aunt, in from weeding the vegetable corner, had put dinner out. She shouted up the stairs.

'Molly! This supper won't be fit for a dog if yer'm up there any longer me wench, what you up to? Got a date with a good-looking feller or summat?'

Molly recoiled, wrapping herself up in a hug. Aunt Violet didn't miss anything. She needed to act normal. 'Down in a bit, just freshening up.'

Molly was applying a slick of Vaseline to hide the red soreness on her face and lips, when aunt Violet appeared at the bedroom door.

'Honestly, there might be a war on, but you've been up here ages. Janey's back from next door. Told me how she's been reading her latest book with old Muriel. We've eaten cos we were tired of waiting. I did shout up, its only lamb stew, it won't spoil. You alright, love?'

She placed a gentle arm around her shoulders. Molly couldn't hold back the tears, as she sobbed onto the older lady's shoulder.

'Aw, love, come on, what's up. Is it the Brummie lads giving you hassle?' It would be a get out for Molly, to agree, but she couldn't use the new lads as scapegoats. They were good lads.

'Just everything in general; daily routine, you know how it is?' She sobbed while aunt Violet held her close. 'Just feel like everything's falling on me, it's wearing me down a bit.'

'Well, nothing a shared cuppa then relaxing chat by the fire won't put right. Come on now, love, our Janey's wondering what's up.' She hugged her tight. 'You dry your eyes, and get yourself down for some stew. You don't think I chatted up the butcher for it to go to next door's dog now, do you?'

Violet always made things better. If not for she and Janey, she'd take to her bed and never get up again. She fixed a smile on her face and a slick of lipstick. They would never know what happened that afternoon. She hoped one day she'd forget all about it, though that didn't seem likely right now.

After tea she tore open Issac's letter, scanning every line for news of how he was getting on. She read quietly to herself.

My Dear Molly,

Hope this letter finds you well and managing alright. I know you'll do me proud, and keep the workers on their toes. Carry on making them quality hats that put our town on the map. Well, Paradise Row in Pelsall, any rate. I've been thinking back to when we were doing manoeuvres on Cannock Chase. I didn't get chance to talk about it much did I? It's lovely there; you should see it when the sun's shining, over them Staffordshire hills. It's magical; if it weren't for the war, it was getting me fitter than ever. I hope you noticed. We didn't get much chance for that did we? We were up and down them hills like teenagers.

Best news ever; one of the officers had his Alsatian dog with him - he sniffs around, and eats better than we do – the grub was alright though. Same as here, we get tinned beef, decent cuppa even peppermints, when we're not digging out trenches. The mining lads are expert at that; they make short work with their shovels. I've been doing manoeuvres with the horse and carts. You should see the size of them, horses and the cannons as well. There are no home comforts, but you don't need to hear me moaning. Being here makes me proud, and glad I got involved in this dirty war. If I can be here to help keep you and my family safe; that makes it all worthwhile.

I'm going to be a gunner in the RFA. That means Royal Field Artillery, working with the horses. Don't worry about me, we're in France. I'll be leading my men in the fields. We're going into the Battle of Loos.

Hopefully we'll do our best, and then be straight back home. We'll have a proper chat when it's over. Keep safe and write again soon, address top of this letter.

Yours faithfully,

Issac. Xxxx

P.s. We're pushing forward tomorrow – hope the ground will be easier, a little less muddy for the horses, it's tough going, but the lads keep each other's morale going. There's a couple of Walsall lads with me, they're bostin' to keep a man cheerful. I will write more news soon. With a bit of luck, they'll all be running away fast, when they see us coming and I'll be back before you know it.

Fondest Love, Issac xxx

Chapter 3

'Hurry up, get yer hat and coat on else we'll be late for church.' Molly cleared the breakfast table and ushered her sister to get moving. They had a fair walk to the All-Saint's Church up Bloxwich town, with weather looking promising; the exercise would do them all good. 'Instead of going short cut, we'll take the Field Road way, past the gardens, let's try and guess what's planted in there.'

'What's the rush? Let's make me-self decent. With a bit of luck, volunteers have planted cabbages.' Violet was fixing her best hat in place, in front of the hall mirror, and checking her make up. She poked her head around the door.

'Those suffragettes have been at it again. You have to admire them, speaking up for the cause. Not that I agree to all the damage they're causing mind. Set a bloody post box on fire yesterday for god's sake. They'll get injured one day, with that behaviour. At least they're getting themselves noticed, making their voices heard, in a man's world.'

Giving a shudder, Molly was reminded how much of a man's world it really was. She pulled on her cloche hat, one she'd designed herself coordinating well with her green jacket, then she pulled a pair of cream-coloured gloves out of her pocket.

'I've been chatting to one of the girls, she's organised a march this afternoon and invited me to join them. Janey, get yourself together; we need to be leave in a minute. I've never thought about it up until now. I think it's time I got involved… they need all the help they can get.' A quick glance from each of the threesome, in the hall mirror, and they were finally ready for off.

One by one, like a row of soldiers, they left the small terraced house. Molly had been out of her mind worrying how she'd manage to keep Janey safe and carry on working when they'd lost their parents in the car accident. Aunt Violet, their mum's sister, hadn't given it a second thought and stepped right up to the plate.

'Now listen up!' she'd said. 'If our Nelly was ever in a fix, wasn't it always me she turned to eh, tell me?' Never in any doubt as to where they would live, she'd insisted from the start.

'No nieces of mine will go knocking doors looking for charity and depending on good folk to help. Even though half the folk round here *would* take you in. I wouldn't have you going skivvying, living in some posh house where that little wench would be treated like a slave, an all. No, you're coming 'ere and that's all there is to it. You'll be company for me and you'll be able to keep yer job on at the hat business.'

From that day to this, she'd stuck to her word, and treated them like her own daughters. Violet was insistent; It made sense and Molly helped pay for food and shared the bills. Uncle Arnold hadn't come back from his war.

Violet never mentioned it other than to say she hoped in her heart he'd turn up one day because *missing presumed dead* only meant they hadn't found him yet.

Janey linked arms with her older sister; her captivating smile melted Molly's heart, letting her know exactly how much she always needed her, even though she was becoming more independent lately.

'We'll go and see the nuns after, for a chat. They always look forward to seeing you. It's good how they give up their time and help with Sunday reading class as well.' No need to look at aunt Violet, who she knew, was throwing enquiring glances across at her.

'They told me your English and geography studies are coming on a treat.' Smiling at her sister, she squeezed her hand tight. God forbid she would ever face anyone like that creep the other day.

'It'll come in handy for writing letters or if you work for a newspaper one day. You'll be able to travel, especially if you know other languages than Black Country twang.'

Molly smiled. 'They, dawnt all talk loike what we do rewnd eya ya know.'

'From how I see it, there'll be plenty of jobs in the midlands with the saddlers getting busy in the leather business, and all them weapons being sent to the front line, and over Coventry where they make them motorcycles; they're all the rage now with the young chaps.' Violet was in full flow.

'And there's getting more motor cars about now; they seem to have caught on, for them as can afford it any rate. You'll be getting one of them next. She'll be able to pick and choose what job she wants if she's not fussy.'

Aunt Violet had all the news from gossip from shop queues, and snatched conversations over the garden fence with neighbours and delivery men.

'I read it in the paper yesterday. Surely our little wench will have a job in the hat place with you? You'll be surprised how quick time flies, she's old enough now, and 'er's got the brains to help, you have to admit.'

She didn't want to think about Janey getting work, though it was clear aunt Violet had it in mind. Molly hoped to move out of Victoria Row. She had her eye on the smart houses with big windows, nearer to Walsall. And there were some houses she liked over Pelsall, though things might change when Issac came home, she'd have to wait and see.

Nothing was the same without Issac. She would write and tell him, without sounding too needy. All she could dream of was being Mrs Molly Cartwright one day. Before she had chance to reply to her aunt, identical twin boys ran across the road to join them followed by an older girl with their mother and a woman who looked like their grandma.

Francesca Murphy was one of the Irish immigrants whose husband had moved over to Birmingham looking for work on the canals for a while. He'd found a position in the Bloxwich nail works, after that, and moved his family closer to his work; Now, along with so many other Bloxwich lads, he'd been sent abroad to fight in the war effort.

'I remember seeing you on Walsall station, waving him off, it wasn't a time for talking though was it?'

Molly smiled and glanced at the woman's third finger where a band of gold glinted in the morning sunshine. 'I know, it's hard, but worse for you… you know.'

She couldn't put into words what she was thinking without upsetting the woman who had fallen into step with them in the weekly walk to church.

'Oh, my Lionel is a brave man, so he is. And I've got my mother to help me, isn't that right, Ma?' She immediately linked arms with the woman who was yelling at the twins to stop jumping around in the road.

'What about you? Have you heard from your young man yet?'

'Issac has written; that's because he's a work colleague, not anything like a husband or sweetheart.' She blushed at the thought of him being either of those. To most people, they kept their private life to themselves. What happened between them was secret for now. It would have only complicated things otherwise.

'He's keeping in touch as a way of knowing what's happening in Paradise Lane,' she smiled. 'I'm running the Bloxwich and Walsall

Hat Company, or trying to, more like, over in Pelsall It's a small concern, but we do quite well, considering.'

She explained to her friend how Issac's great-grandad, William had started up a back yard concern, and eventually bought the house next door, with enough land to create a yard in-between, then take on a few staff.

Since then, it had grown into what it was now. Still a cottage industry, that expanded with stables for the horse, and storage space for stock and supplies they used.

'I'm looking for work.' Francesca's shoulders drooped. 'The kids are good, and Ma takes no nonsense from them, so I'm lucky really, I am; the allowance his work place gives us is barely enough to feed them, never mind fuel bills and all. Good job he showed me how to get coal the alternative way.'

She put her hand to her mouth. 'Oh, listen to me; you don't want to hear all that on a Sunday, when we're off to pray for our boys out there on the front line. Sorry I spoke out of turn; typical of me and my big mouth.'

The group turned left into Lichfield Road, heading for Bloxwich town centre, and their place of worship, All Saint's Church, opposite to Pat Colliers, ground where he held the annual wakes week, every autumn.

Molly smiled, and dismissed her apology. 'Don't be daft, if you don't ask, you'll never get. That's what my old mom used to say. I'll keep in mind that you're available. Call in sometime; it's over in Pelsall,' she turned and waved her hand in the opposite direction.

'Go along into Wolverhampton Road, you can't miss it, then turn right when you see Foundry Lane, then head up the Old Town. We're in Paradise Lane. Issac had a new sign put up; you'll see

Bloxwich and Walsall Hat Company on the front of the building. We'll have a chat and I can show you round.'

Francesca nodded. They followed the growing crowd through the gate into church. Issac's letter was deep in her pocket. She curled her fingers round it for reassurance. Not that it helped her much. Already news of men from Bloxwich and Walsall being brought home with life changing injuries were talk of the town.

The service was a sombre reflection, remembering loved ones far away. How the efforts of women here at home were crucial, and are proud if you could get work in a local factory. The vicar mentioned work being more readily available and wage packets swelling was no excuse to be frivolous, going out drinking and dancing.

Aunt Violet raised an eyebrow and shuffled in her seat, giving side eye to Molly. Looking up at the stained-glass windows her mind wandered to when Issac came back. They'd have time together; explore the local bluebell woods and green hills of Staffordshire.

She'd ask him to show her where he'd been training on Cannock Chase. Maybe even go dancing or ice skating when the lake froze over like other couples did. He might think about taking her around the jewellery quarter to look for a ring. Now she knew her imagination was going into overdrive.

She could make a difference. Not only joining in the march with the suffragettes, demanding women got the vote, but if she employed women to get Issac's business – that was now her business – into a better position she could grow the hatting trade.

They'd get more sales from word of mouth. A warm glow flowed over her as the congregation stood for the final hymn, 'abide with me' letting her know she would do her best for Issac, and herself and their future together.

Molly Marsden, you will stand strong and never ever let a man degrade you again. She held on tight to Issac's letter in her pocket, as she made a silent promise to the man who had given her the greatest responsibility and the greatest compliment of all rolled into one that she'd ever faced in her life so far.

***

The stroll back from church was more peaceful, after singing hymns, and reciting prayers, to remember the lads doing their bit had a grounding effect. Janey and her new friend, Nadine, walked in front, linking arms, chatting about what they could do this afternoon together.

Twin boys, Patrick and Oliver, had calmed down, by playing hop scotch on and more off the pavement, which got them both a cuff around the ear-ole from their grandma.

'You pair want to get run over by a motor or trampled under a cart-horse or summat? Keep on the pavement like the girls.'

'Ooh, but we ain't girls, so we don't walk up the street like they do.' An exaggerated feminine gait followed from Patrick. Oliver was more practically minded.

'We can run errands if you want anything from the shops or the Offie.' Eager faces were trying their best to get round their grandma, who often asked them to fetch a bottle of brown ale at the weekend.

'Be good the next few days, and we'll see if I can find you some pennies for sweets to share.'

Francesca turned to Molly and raised her eyes to heaven, whispering that her mother couldn't spare even a penny for the kids to have sweets. 'I wish she wouldn't promise. It falls on me then to find money out of nowhere.'

Looking at the children walking ahead, Molly quickly opened her handbag and gave a few pennies to her friend. 'Don't be offended, it only adds up to a tanner, for some sweeties. They might get scarce as time goes on.'

'I couldn't really.' Her friend looked horrified, embarrassed and uncomfortable. 'My mother needs a talking to. I am sorry.'

Pushing the pennies into her pocket, Molly put her finger to her lips. 'No need to say anything, please take it. They can get some sweeties for themselves, during the week.'

The girls were deep in conversation, Janey shouted over her shoulder. 'Nadine wants to come round and see my scrapbook, is that okay?'

Molly felt the kids were testing the patience of the adults, yet they were all getting on so well, it was a breath of fresh air during these frightening times. She had forgotten all about talking to the nuns. It would have to wait until a more private visit to the church.

'Ask aunt Violet, she's in charge of who comes and goes.'

One look of sweet innocence from Janey and she heard their aunt telling them that of course it was alright, and turns out Moira, Francesca's ma, was calling for a cup of tea as well.

So, if Grandma Doolan and Nadine were calling in for scrapbooking and tea, it made sense for Molly to ask if Francesca and the twins, wanted to come round and join them too.

'Maybe another time, thanks anyways.' She was quick to answer. 'Don't mind me, only with mam and Nadine being kept busy, gives me some time to get the ironing done. You can't imagine the amount of clothes they get through.'

Indicating to the twins, and her daughter; her face lit up at the thought of getting some quiet time on her own.

'No, I get it, but we'll catch up with some time of our own when we can. Maybe go and see a film one night. There's usually a classic on midweek. It's great to see Janey with a friend. She's a bit on the shy side. They're getting along great guns, aren't they?'

'Oh me and my tongue, that's a bad choice of words. I can't bear to think of our boys out there having to … Well; let's not think about all that. We'll hope and pray they'll get through, and come home safely.'

'Do the hatters have a certain uniform or anything?' Her frown that was a permanent fixture on her forehead grew deeper.

'Keep hair back off your face, obvious reasons. Come and have a look and see for yourself.'

'I like to sew, and knit, it's a case of having to with the kids growing so fast.' Her face became serious. 'Are you looking for qualifications? Only …'

'A willingness to work hard, learn and be loyal to me is what I'm looking for.'

She was so certain this woman with her three children and mother to think about would be perfect for the job and someone she could talk to as well. But she wasn't going to take her on without seeing her in the actual workplace and how she responded when she saw how hard the work could be.

'It's not a job for sissies, more of a man's job some of it, but there's more women there now, so let's see how it goes. It's Sunday, time off, we can talk more about it tomorrow.'

They'd reached Victoria Row, and Violet and Moira were chatting about how to use beetroot in recipes. Janey and Nadine were heads together talking about their favourite animals, the twins raced ahead to their house planning a footie match in the back garden.

'Wolverhampton Wanderers will whack your Man U any day brother,' teased Patrick, who pulled a face and held his fist high. 'We'll see who gets the most goals, and then we can decide shall we?'

He held up his right hand, and shouted after his brother, 'five nil and Man United can whip Wolves any day.'

'Stop scrapping you two, and see who scores the most goals, eh? She turned to smile and confessed she would be reading her copy of Vanity Fair she'd found in the red-cross charity shop in town, in-between ironing. A quick wave and she hurried along home.

Chapter 4

'Give women the vote… We – want – the – vote! – And – we – want – it - now!'

Molly waved her placard in time to the chant as she marched with the suffragettes through the town of Walsall.

Christine, the organiser was handing out posters with colourful wording on, for anyone strolling through town to see. They were practising for bigger marches, later in Wolverhampton, Birmingham, and London when the momentum got going.

For now, they were on their own town streets. They'd gathered on the bridge, by the sister Dora statue, just like the soldiers did, who'd gone off to war. 'C'mon ladies, let them know what we want…' She led the march, and spirits were high.

Issac was over in France, up to his knees in mud and slush. She was glad of her freedom, and let her voice be heard to show locals who stood listening exactly how important a women's place in society was.

Aunt Violet and Ma Doolan were settled for the afternoon, giving her chance to join the march. They were having Sunday dinner later; they'd eaten a snack of bread and cheese for now.

She'd been walking through Bloxwich Park, when she heard a talk of sexual assaults happening to women which had shocked, her then, yet mirrored her own experience lately. That was happening in the middle of London town; when all the ladies were asking for, was to be heard. The story rang truer for Molly now. She still could hardly believe she'd been assaulted, at her own workplace. The last meeting she'd been to, had taken place in the Walsall arboretum, on the bandstand. She happened to be walking through, helping plant potatoes for the war effort, when she caught the end of Caroline's speech.

She stayed behind, and took a note of the time and place of today's march. Attitudes had to change and men would realise; if women can run the country while they were away, they should have equal rights.

She knew full well Issac would have heartily approved, and encouraged her to go on the march. His sister was a modern woman. He supported her all the way, much to the disapproval of their father.

'How can women have their say, without being given a vote?' Christine shouted through her megaphone. People were stopping to listen. Some nodding in agreement, others shaking heads and turning away. The march proceeded around Walsall town; the turnout far better than expected.

Flushed with excitement - Molly's jaw dropped when one of her 'comrades' climbed atop a wall shouting louder. It attracted attention from the local bobby.

He'd been keeping a watchful eye from a distance, now he needed to get this unruly mob under control now. He ran toward the front of the crowd, blowing his whistle, cheeks reddened with the exertion as he came up close with the more vocal ladies at the front.

'Come on now, ladies. Move along, you know this'll get yer nowhere. I do understand yer reasoning and all that. Nice and steady now, get yourselves home, eh?'

'Home...What for? You mean stand at the sink washing up? Cooking your dinner, is that it?

He didn't bargain for what came next. Two well-built women on the front line handed him a banner, hoisted him shoulder height, laughing all the way along the road, shouting …

'He's a jolly good fellow, yes he's a jolly good fellow,' followed by some probing questions. Or you mean like in the bedroom, waiting for you? Is that what you think P.C. Rowley?'

The noises she made after that were rude sending the crowd squealing with laughter as they gently dropped him back down earth.

In a matter of seconds, the high-spirited crowd decided they'd made their point, with no hard feelings, on either part, he had his whistle and truncheon back, and the march dispersed.

Local butcher, Danny Glover watched on with interest. He was locking up after a bit of stock-taking.

'I wouldn't have thought you'd be involved in harassing the law?' He caught up with Molly as she walked away heading in the Bloxwich direction.

'I'm showing my support. Manhandling the local Bobby wasn't the intended plan.' She sucked in her cheeks, trying not to laugh and wondering whether he'd tell aunt Violet. Of course, he would.

'We have to get the vote; it's the least they can offer us. Let's face it, we're all doing our bit for King and Country, don't you agree?'

He walked with her, eyes raking her up and down.

'Well, it's not for me to decide, I'm only the local butcher. Must look after the ladies, and your aunt Violet is one of my favourites. She always gets her bit of extra sausage if there's nobody else in the shop at the time.'

He winked and gave Molly a feeling he was being dirty or flirty, or both. She cringed and walked a bit faster.

'I'd appreciate if you didn't mention the bobby episode to aunt Violet.' She threw him a sidelong glance.

'Depends what's in it for me.' His eyes took on that familiar glint she'd seen only the other day. 'You know how juicy gossip spreads around here though.'

'Danny Glover! What d'you mean, in it for you? You're our family butcher. Surely, you're on the side of the suffragettes? Only this morning Violet was singing the praises of our girls. That's why I had to join them. I'm running a business on my own after all. She practically encouraged me to go.'

'Well, that's what I was referring to, you daft wench. If you need any help with balancing the books, or advice on profits and loss, how to make your budget stretch further. You know where I am.'

He tapped the side of his nose, leaving Molly feeling guilty of jumping to conclusions. She shouldn't judge Danny on the actions of an old creep who'd taken advantage.

'Thanks. I'll bear that in mind and giving Violet special offers is appreciated. She keeps me and Janey well fed and that's something that can't be said for everyone.'

A large hand waved away her comments as if he wasn't used to getting compliments and Violet knew she was joining the march - so even if he did tell her, she wouldn't be surprised to hear of the afternoon's events.

She caught the tram from Walsall, back to Bloxwich, and dropped off at the crossroads, by the Bell pub at the bottom of the High Street, then took the short walk down Lichfield Road, glad there weren't many folks around leaving her deep in her thoughts, so she could plan what she'd tell Issac, when she wrote.

It would have been quicker to take the short cut to Victoria Row, but she wanted time to think, about Issac. Most of all, she'd tell him how women all over the country were closer to getting the vote, for one thing, and all was well as another.

She needed to ask him if he'd let her borrow his Ford Motor car to drive herself over to Birmingham to look in the rag market. He'd often told her to have a ride, but she'd always said no. Now things were different.

She had the horse and cart they used for deliveries and doing the rounds. Only Dolly their faithful four-legged transport wasn't used to going further than Bloxwich or Walsall. If this was the age of women gaining independence, what better way to start?

He'd urged her to use it before he left, insisting that it would be parked outside his parents' home and not used. It never occurred to her she'd need to use it.

As the new owner of Bloxwich & Walsall Hat Company, she could use it as the business vehicle. She'd need to get some practice in, and he'd paid the licence fee and it was just standing there, doing nothing.

She could see from the corner of Field Road, how the vegetable plots at the back of the houses were bursting with rows of runner beans, carrot tops ruffling in the wind, and canes held the beginnings of colourful sweet peas ripening in the pods.

Jack Wilkins was bent over weeding his bedding plants. He glanced across when he stood up then removed his cap and wiped a dirty hand across his brow.

'Young Molly, how're yer doing?' He took a slug from his hip flask and ambled over.

'I'm doing fine, Jack. How about yourself? The plot's looking good.' Feeling the breeze in her hair, she held her face to the sun then looked over to where he'd been working among his rows of flowers and vegetables. He mixed them up, and you couldn't tell the flowers from the cabbages at times.

'How's Madam Bovary, and her piglets today?'

'Bostin' little porkers, they'm growing bigger every day. And me old sow's loving the potato peelings your aunt sent along yesterday an all.

The old gel needs to keep her strength up with all the little squealers feeding off her. Hang on a minute, there's some baby carrots and spring onions ready, you can take some home if you've got time.'

He limped over to collect the crops. Never one to moan, everyone knew he'd been shot and wounded in the last war. Now he wasn't the age to go off to fight any more, but he made use of his time growing and helping at home.

His war wound didn't stop him from living a full life. It seemed so unfair that he'd lost his wife to pneumonia while he'd been away fighting. And in the same year, Violet had got that fateful telegram about her Albert.

They were good friends; often he'd pop by to share a pot of tea with her aunt. Neither of them was able to move on from the loss they'd been through, but at least they could find comfort from sharing thoughts and chatting over old times.

Molly wondered if she and Issac would ever see each other again. She prayed every night for him to stay safe. It wasn't as if they were married or engaged even. Both were free to live and love even though she knew her love for him would always be there.

The future was so unsure, yet things were happening in the Black Country. Folks were arriving for work every week in droves, by rail and omnibus, some on their bikes.

She needed to take on a couple more trainees, as well as find someone she could trust to keep an eye on the business while she travelled in the motor car to fetch more supplies.

'Here, send her these with my good wishes. An tell her it'll only cost a pot of tea and a large slice of her jam sponge next time I'm passing.' He handed over a generous crop of vegetables before pushing his cap further back on his head.

'Thanks, she'll be glad of these. You're welcome round at aunt Violet's any time, Jack, I'm sure.'

Molly was confident her words were true. Often, she'd come back from work or from chatting with the nuns on a Sunday with Janey to find them, enjoying each other's company, laughing away, which was good to see.

It crossed her mind that Violet had quite a few admirers, what with Jack here and Danny the butcher; yet for all they looked out for her aunt, nobody replaced the space of her Uncle Albert; she knew that for certain.

'How are things at the hat works - you managing alright then? Violet told me as how you're in charge now.'

'All going fine Jack, thanks.' Molly gave her brightest smile. 'Only one thing bothering me slightly though Jack.'

'What's up our kid? Anything an old soldier can help with?' His face crinkled into a smile.

'Can you teach me to drive?' The idea was growing roots in her mind and filled Molly with a rush of excitement.

'It's only starting the thing up and getting to where I want to be, turning the jalopy round and getting back here. Can't be too difficult surely; please say yes.'

She willed him on, with crossed fingers behind her back.

Jack took a step back in surprise, and cleared his throat. 'Yer sound as if yer'm got it all planned out, wench. And where might I ask are you going to get this here motor from? They might make and send 'em out from Coventry, but you'm doing better than I thought if yer can afford to get yerself one of them already.'

'Listen, Jack…' She looked up and down the road to check no-one was listening in, which was usually the case. 'I don't have to buy one! That's just the thing, Jack. Issac told me, I could use his before he left, honestly, he did.'

Pressing the point, Molly, was in full flow. It's getting harder to wait for deliveries that might or might not come, and then it's not always the cloth and items I ordered. It's high time I got behind the wheel and went to look at the goods and fetch my own supplies. This is the way of the future. So, was that a 'yes' to teaching me?'

'As long as Violet's alright about it. I wouldn't want her getting upset. Have you spoken to her yet?' Jack pushed his flat cap back, and ruffled his fingers through his thinning hair.

'I'm about to now, and as soon as you've got some free time, we'll start with a few runs up and down Issac's folks' driveway. Oh, that reminds me. I'd better have a word with them about it first. I'm due a visit to keep them up to date with business news.'

With a wave of her hand, she was gone; on her way full of ideas and buzzing with the expectation of getting behind the wheel of Issac's motor car.

She sprinted home, veggies stuffed under arm. Her black ankle boots were getting worn, though she'd have to make them last a while longer yet.

Janey was fast growing into a young lady, needing clothes for outings, even though she was making her way with the sewing machine.

Getting an education for her sister was one of her main priorities, to give her a better chance in life than herself.

Molly wasn't complaining. She'd gone to the hat works as an apprentice, and fast learned all the jobs. Even paperwork and ordering stock they needed was something she could do now, from the office.

When Issac was around, there was plenty of loving going on as well. How she missed those special moments with him. Her smile at the thought of him spread wide across her face.

From the apprentice to being under manager, she was now able to use her own initiative and make plans that would grow the hatting business. She was confident with all the jobs now.

Lately she'd even been doodling designs that had come to mind and she would cut out the patterns when she had a spare moment.

'I'm back.' She burst in through the front door of Violet's terraced cottage.

'Jeepers, girl you gave me a fright.' She'd just come in from pegging undies out down the back garden. 'What's got into you this afternoon, you look as if you've won a ticket to Buckingham Palace? I take it the march went well for you then?'

'Better than that aunt Violet, you'll never guess what?' Grabbing her aunt's hands, Molly waltzed her around the small parlour. 'I'm going to borrow Issac's car, and Jack is going to show me how the thing works. Isn't that just grand?'

'Hey wench, who told you you could use it for a start?' I don't think his mam and dad will agree to that, do you?'

'It's alright, aunt Violet, don't fret yerself. He practically forced me to agree to use it if I had to - while he was away. Behind her back, fingers were crossed at the tiny white fib. Molly spoke gently.

'Listen, if you like, I'll get him to write and tell you himself. You must believe I'm speaking the truth. I'd never just go and take the blooming motor if he hadn't said so, would I? Let's not waste more time. I'll go and see his mom and dad.'

'Not before you've had something to eat. I've got liver and onions on the go. And not today now, it's too late to go visiting. What's that you've got there?'

Violet reached for the bundle of vegetables Molly had dropped to the floor.

'Oh, sorry I forgot to mention, presents from Jack. He's sent us carrots and spring onions fresh from the garden. I must say you've got some good connections - with extra liver from the butcher, vegetables from Jack. If I didn't know you better, I'd say you were a bit of a girl, aunt Violet.'

Before the sentence had left her lips, Molly felt the back of a tea towel whacked around her ears.

'Listen up you! Just cos you'm in charge of the hatting factory and got yourself a motor lined up - don't give you place to stick yer conk into my business our Molly. Pass us them carrots ....'

'If yer'd come back a bit sooner, we could have had 'em with the liver. Give Janey a shout; she's gone for a walk with the little Irish wench down the road. They won't be far away. Do her good to get out on her own for a bit with someone of her own age. Makes a change from all that reading and writing you keep nagging her with.'

'It's all for the good; you always encouraged her to read as much as I do so don't make me out to be a tyrant. Any education has to be good. The nuns have such patience with teaching her. And Muriel, next door has spent hours, going through her grammar, and spelling.'

'She, being a teacher, back in the day has been a godsend. She's made a real difference to her handwriting.' *What rattled her cage just because I mentioned favours? Maybe there is some truth in here after all.*

'I know, love. Take no notice; it's just how everything is so up in the air these days. We get along well enough now, don't we?'

Violet reached for the carrots, wiping away a tear.

Molly went to her side; their mom's sister who had willingly taken them in. No question, and always food on the table. Whatever aunt Violet had to do, maybe if she was in her position, she'd have to talk nicely to whoever would supply what they needed. She really should try harder not to judge.

'I'll sort those out. Go and get some fresh air. Janey won't have gone far, and I'm sure her new friend's grandma will have her eye on them. From what I see, it's she who keeps them all together. A bit like someone not too far away.'

She gave her aunt a nudge to get herself outside, and find the two girls who she knew would be sitting on a wall nattering away about all and everything under the sun.

Molly went to the back door, and rinsed earth from the carrots under the tap in the yard, then placed a pan full of salted water on the hot plate ready for the vegetables.

She topped, tailed then chopped the carrots into slices before throwing them in the pot, along with a few chopped spring onions. She threw more coal on the fire then rubbed her hands, looking forward to Jack's fresh vegetables that would go nicely with the liver and onions, in gravy with mushy peas. The potato with mustard mash was set to one side in an oval crock dish, keeping warm.

Molly busied herself putting the finishing touches to the tea that had been so lovingly prepared earlier. Putting the discarded carrot tops and roots to one side, she gave them another swill under the tap, in the back yard, knowing her aunt would give them back to Jack, to feed his eight piglets and, of course, Madam Bovary, his prize pig.

Violet sometimes let him bring his piglets along the row and down her side alley to get into her apple orchard for a root around. Their long back garden was a haven, with windfalls and other leaves and greens, for the growing piglets.

That's before butcher Danny got his hands on them. It completely put her off bacon and any cuts of pork, but like her aunt always told her, times were hard; folks had to do what they could to keep going.

She remembered to appreciate everything they had, and the sacrifices Violet was making having both she and her sister living here.

Who knew what she had to go through to keep heads above water? One thing was certain, she depended on her hat business wages, so whatever it took, she would keep her job safe. She owed that to her aunt and younger sister … Brighter days were ahead, she really believed that.

Chapter 5

'Looks like our boys are wearing their hats out on the front line with the size of this lot they've ordered.'

Molly turned see who was speaking from behind the mountain of cloth being heaved from the store room towards the workshop. Bobby popped his head round the heap of fabric. 'Hey, wouldn't it be a lark, if our boss ended up wearing one of his own hats?'

Bobby, blissfully unaware of his comment denting Molly's feelings, trotted off with his load, whistling away as if he'd lost a penny and found a sixpence.

'For your information, let me remind you Bobby Reynolds.' She shouted after him. 'It's me who's your boss, so less lip and more action, if you can manage that!' Her mind was down in the dumps; she was in no mood for flippant remarks. The war was too serious for jesting, even from the young lads. It was ages since she'd had news from Issac. Tonight was the night she'd go and see his parents.

'Yes, on to it now. And will you be getting your usual Nottingham delivery this week? Only I was wondering after last time…'

'No! I've made new arrangements with Mr Peacock,' Molly lied. *He didn't miss much.* 'I'll be using the automobile from now on so no need to worry about deliveries.' She didn't wait to hear any more comments, and when the knock came on the door she jumped a mile.

Her nerves were all a jangle at the thought of unwanted visitors coming through those double gates leading onto the yard. She quickly straightened her white blouse and smoothed her waistcoat down before she marched confidently to open the door.

'Francesca, you found us, come on in, I'll get a brew on, it's almost tea break time anyway.' Molly reached for the kettle and then whispered. 'Don't tell them lot in there, any excuse to down tools; they're due their break in ten minutes.'

'I heard our Janey called round for your daughter. I hope she didn't make a nuisance of herself? Tell her to clear off and get home, if she did.' Molly was glad to see a friendly face. Waving off their loved ones at Walsall station, gave them a common bond. She couldn't remember feeling such a connection with someone, who wasn't family. She wondered if Francesca felt the same.

'You have to be joking; it's the first time our Nadine has laughed so much, since moving here. She's a shy girl and doesn't mix easily. Me Mam worries;' she tutted. 'Fusses over her too much; she means well, just over protective, it's stifling at times.'

She raised her eyes. 'Still, I didn't come here to tell you about family, sorry; though it's grand, really it is, to chat and share things; Y'know, them little things you can't say to those closest, but you were saying you might be able to find a bit of sommat' for me, work wise?'

'Well, first off, our Janey is similar. I'm glad she's found a friend in Nadine. Let's hope it does them both good. She's usually got her head in a book, when she's not on her sewing machine, but that's not a bad thing, is it?'

Francesca smiled. 'Not at all, maybe she'll help our girl with her reading. How're you getting on with running the business, since whatsisname, y'know?'

'His name's Issac, if you mean since the main man left me in the lurch?' Molly smiled then shrugged. 'It's alright; let me show you round, put you in the picture, show you the basics of how it all works, and then you can decide if it's for you.'

After tea and more chat, Molly gave Francesca a tour, showing her the different stages of hat manufacture. Jack and Bobby gave her a wave in passing, but carried on working on the pressing machine. After that, a quick look in at the girls laying pattern pieces and cutting, some using machines, others by hand, who looked up and nodded but then put heads back down. All focused and dedicated to their own particular job that was each an important part of compiling a hat as the next.

The decorating and finishing room smelled of glue and lastly the packing area was near the back door. That made it easy to get parcels up onto the cart for delivery, or taking to the post office.

'That's about it. Obviously, the store-room's separate, over there by our Dolly's stable.'

Taking it all in, Francesca nodded and judging from her expression; she liked what she'd seen so far. They took the short walk, back over the yard, heading for the office also used as kitchen.

'What kind of work did you do before? Back in Ireland I mean.' Molly pushed through the door leading them back into the office.

'I was brought up on a farm, so it was mostly outdoor work, hard slog as well. We had livestock, vegetables, crops, while it lasted. Our Lionel, my hubby, well he moved in, y'know when we got married; helped out with everything. We all had jobs on the farm, pulled together as a family but it got too much.'

'I'd had the kids by that time; it was a bit crowded anyways. Then one day, my dad got us all together, and told us it couldn't work anymore. The rising rents put a toll on his health, meaning we would lose the farm. His health took a turn for the worst. Suddenly one morning, he was gone.'

Francesca's face clouded, showing the hardship she'd endured; she swallowed hard. 'Having to give up his farm, it's what finished him. I could never leave mammy alone. We come as a family.' She smiled. 'The landlords had other ideas of what to do with the land.

We were pushed out, yet looking back, it's given us a new life here, and now I've met you. Always a silver lining as my dad used to say.' Her smile was bright and genuine.

'It must have been difficult for you, with having the little ones to look after as well as your ma?'

'It was tough after he died. We travelled over by boat, and Lionel got some work in the docklands, up Liverpool. We didn't stay long, as he found work down here, in the midlands. My man followed where work with the best pay, took him. On the canals, moving cargo on the barges; he was a cut rat at first; we all were, living on a barge while he did deliveries, from the pits, anything he could get from all around the Black Country.'

'That was until he found a more permanent job at the nail factory, over Walsall, closer to home. He'd made sure we'd got the house in Bloxwich by then, so we could see more of him; more settling for the kids and me ma as well. Seeing as he wasn't away travelling so much all the time. It worked out well, until he signed up. Now with the war in full swing, it's come down to me to be the bread winner.'

'I've been volunteering at the red-cross shop, over in Walsall; keeps me busy and an ear to the ground with the job situation. They were looking for someone in the brush works, up Bloxwich… it had gone by time I found chance to go round and see them. Sometimes I wonder where it'll all end, but mam's a great help, there's always someone worse off as she keeps telling me.'

'I put my name down at the saddlery, but it takes a while to learn that same as everything.' She forced a smile, and Molly decided then she was the right person for what she had in mind.

'It's grand to have someone nearer my own age willing to take on what I'm asking.' Reaching for the biscuit tin that was now half empty, Molly chose her words carefully. 'Have a go at all of the jobs, but if you can run your home and family and keep a roof over your head, I'm quite confident that you'll soon be my right-hand woman on the shop floor. It's good to know we're not alone. If it weren't for our aunt Violet, goodness only knows where me and our Janey would be.'

She shuddered. 'In the workhouse at the end of the road I wouldn't be surprised. So, let's be grateful for what we've got, and talk about when you start as my new assistant.' Molly beamed.

'What, you mean you'll give me a go? I'd be really grateful, so I would. I'll do my absolute best to help keep the business working well. Aw, Molly me love, you've given me hope. You'll never know how I've hardly slept, worrying how I'm going to keep finding money for everything a growing family needs. I don't reckon this government have a clue what it's like to be poor.' Francesca was close to tears.

'Hey, come on. I'm hoping you grasp the hang of things, then I can go and get supplies with you keeping charge, but we'll take it steady. I'm in no rush to run the show alone just yet. My next move is - go and visit Issac's parents. They need to get involved, lend a hand. I'm sure they'll be willing to come down and show their faces. We'll be a great team. The workers are a reliable bunch; mostly friends of friends who got the job from knowing someone who knows someone.' She smiled.

Molly felt safer with people around her, especially if it was Issac's family, and her new best friend Francesca. If that monster, bragged over a few pints, to his mates, how she was alone, at the hat works down Paradise Lane, and up for a frisking, she'd be a sitting duck, even though she wasn't up for anything, apart from keeping herself safe until Issac returned - equally as safe.

Francesca nodded. 'Must be hard for them, especially if his sister has gone volunteering, you told me, with the VADS was it?'

'Yes, they miss them both. Still, she's only in Bloxwich Hospital for now, they've converted it to a recovery home for the soldiers, so not far away. They'll both be worried sick though, you're right; it's time I had a chat with them anyway. I'm glad you came and found us.'

As Francesca stood and made her way out, she turned with a smile. 'Look forward to seeing you in the morning then, Molly love. And thanks ever so.'

Molly waved her off with a glow in her heart, knowing she'd found someone she could share a cup of tea and biscuit with, and have help discussing the hatting trade. Often she'd asked the workers if anyone wanted a more senior role, supervising. Nobody ever had. All happy to pick up their packet on Friday night then off to the Old Bush Pub up the town.

The girls would keep each other going when the reality of The Great War threatened to get them down, when worries of their men out there, fighting to keep them back home safe took a hold.

She made a mental note, to pick up a pack of mixed Huntley & Palmers, next time she passed the grocers along the road so she could top the tin back up. Nothing lifted the spirits like a biccy and a cuppa.

***

'You've taken on a new worker then, it makes sense and if she works as hard as her mother, then you'll be well blessed.' Aunt Violet dished up the sausage and mash while giving her tuppence worth on Francesca starting work with the hatters.

'She's a likeable sort … I'm looking forward to setting her of, working, getting to know everyone, tomorrow morning. There's something I need to do after tea. Been on me mind for a while actually.' Molly scooped up her food enjoying every mouthful, knowing if the war didn't end soon, food would become scarce.

Already Violet was secretly stashing tins under her bed, as if she didn't know. 'I'm popping round to see Issac's parents. Thought I'd ask them about the motor. And if Jack calls by, tell him I'm ready for that driving practice he promised me.' Jumping up and rushing to the kitchen sink, Molly quickly rinsed her plate and knife and fork in the bowl, throwing a wink in Janey's direction, she reached for her coat and escaped through the door before protests from aunt Violet reached her ears.

She scarpered down the road as fast as she could, feeling the wind in her hair and full musky scent of summer in her nostrils as she ran, gathering her skirts around her knees to avoid occasional puddles accumulated from recent rain.

If Issac's parents' agreed, she would be able to write and tell him how she was using his motor car to fetch supplies from Birmingham rag market, and lace from Nottingham, giving her more variety of materials. Providing all went well with his folk. On top of that, she planned to visit Cousin Isabella down on Dudley.

She hurried along the two-mile journey across town; a fleeting thought crossing her mind was she making a mistake? She stood in front of the large black wrought iron gates of 'Oak tree Grange,' home to the Cartwright family.

One thing kept her focused. She had to get behind the wheel … here goes, she told herself.

With head high, heart pounding from the excitement, she strode through the gates, up the gravel drive and gave a confident rap on the knocker. A dog barked towards the back of the building, to the left stood a field and a paddock, with stables nearby. Two horses were grazing in a further field. She took in her surroundings.

Issac came from a wealthy family, though he'd never made her feel lower class, yet clearly her life was a million miles away from what he was used to. To the right of the house a concrete shelter held something the shape of Issac's motor covered in a tarpaulin. She felt a warm glow. In her heart she wanted to run and uncover the contraption, then announce her intentions. Her manners knew better, and she'd remember to ask if they'd heard from their son first; and keep her own news until they told her what they knew.

He'd told them she was running the Hat Business, and they had met a few times, a while ago, but her little knowledge of Issac's family was that his dad had fought in the same war as aunt Violet's Albert, like all the older war hero's, he didn't speak much of it, same as Jack.

When the door opened, a small woman with hair tied back a thin, serious face answered. She looked her up and down. 'Yes, what do you want? They've just had tea and don't normally take visitors of an evening.'

Getting to speak to the Cartwrights' wasn't proving to be as easy as Molly envisioned. Issac hadn't warned her they employed a body guard - even if she was only doing her job as family protection officer.

'I'm Molly, the lady running Issac's business while he's away, fighting in the war.' She forced a smile, raised eyebrows to encourage the body guard she was no random intruder. Waiting for a little human response after a long pause, the little lady lightly nodded, instructing her to wait.

'Well, I'll tell 'em who it is then, that's disturbing their peace. Don't get your hopes up; they like to keep themselves to themselves, and won't take kindly to being reminded about Issac being gone either.' With a swish and a bustle of her skirts, she turned leaving Molly in the hallway.

A few mumbled words exchanged, who, what and other questions, ended when a man the double of Issac, but older version, came through the hallway and beckoned her through to the room where she could see they were finishing their evening meal.

'I'm sorry to disturb your evening; I could come back… make an appointment?' Her apology was dismissed as quickly as it was accepted. She came face to face with a neatly dressed woman who looked far more elegant than anyone who worked in the factory. Now was the ideal time to get to know Issac's parents, although they weren't complete strangers to her, she hardly knew them at all.

'I'm Molly; it's grand to meet you both again. You've heard I'm running the business for Issac while he's… away?' Clearing her throat, she waited for their reply.

'We think it's a noble thing for you to take on.' His dad was the first to speak and wiped his mouth on a serviette then pushed his plate aside, before glancing at his wife. 'Don't we dear?'

Issac's mom nodded and shook Molly's outstretched hand. 'No need to stand on ceremony, love. We're ordinary folk only tend to keep a quiet life these days. The day to day worries of the works was too much for us in the end, and Issac wanted to carry on with it, like you know. That leaves me time to do the charity work I always wanted to pursue, and Stanley here keeps an eye on the land and buildings. We always knew when war news came out things might not go to plan for our Issac.'

'I trust you've had word from him?' Issac's father stood in front of a roaring fire, back to the flames warming his behind. He nodded. 'Of course you have, it's the romantic thing to do, write a letter to the girl back home. Yet let the parents know you're still alive, oh no… far too much trouble that would be. Ha! How is the old lad then?'

'Stanley, keep your thoughts to yourself will you. The lass might have news for us. Any news is better than nothing, so they say. He is still alive and well, please say he is?'

The worry etched across his mother's face pulled on Molly's heart strings. *How could he be such a twerp and forget to write home?* She chose her words carefully. 'Yes, I have heard, to do with the business mostly, you made a mistake about the romantic girlfriend notion. There's nothing like that going on with me and Issac.' Her cheeks reddened. 'Well, nothing set in concrete, we're taking it steady.'

The memory of his love making flashed into her mind, as she added. 'It's more of a business relationship,' she smiled. 'He did ask me to pay a visit and reassure you he's fine. With the day so full out there in France, the boys only have limited time and paper and pens to write home with. She hoped her eyes didn't give away the little white lie she'd told to ease their worry and made a mental note to give him what for in her next letter and tell him to make sure and drop them a line.

'You're managing alright with the business then? Call me Doris by the way, Stanley won't bite, come and sit down.' Issac's mother took a seat on a wide easy chair to the right of the glowing fire and beckoned Molly to sit beside her. 'There's room for two, now tell us all about things.'

'It's all going well, and I've taken on a new worker to help me run the business. I'm looking to fetch my own supplies from Birmingham rag market, and Nottingham and Dudley market, where my cousin works. I'll take a look on Walsall market as well, there's a new cloth stall been standing recently, I heard they're selling fabric remnants, at bargain prices.'

A glance at the family gave Molly a reminder of why she was there. 'Which brings me to ask, and it's something Issac was keen for me to do before he left. He might have… mentioned it…' She couldn't get the words out, and found herself twirling her hair round her finger, an old childhood habit.

'Gaah, spit it out wench, one thing I will not abide is a woman gabbling on and expecting me to know what she's on about. For the life of me, how do we know what he was keen for you to do if he doesn't even drop us a line, let alone tell us where his future lies?'

This had turned horribly wrong. Stanley was a man after her own heart, a bit like her dad… There was only one way to do it, so she spat out the words that had been on her mind all afternoon.

'The motor car… He wants me to use his motor car to help with the running of the business. Fetching and carrying, or running to the bank, other errands. I really wished he'd mentioned it to you first; I hope you don't mind me pushing for this, only it would be a tremendous help.'

Doris looked at her husband. Clearly talk of motor cars was too far out of her comfort zone. Both she and Molly waited for Stanley's response.

'Can you drive?' He rasped out the question, at least it wasn't a 'no' he was wondering if she was capable.

'I'm a quick learner, and a friend of the family is willing to come and show me what to do and which levers to pull and how to stop and start.'

'No need for that, I'll teach you how to drive. Come every night for a week or so and we'll soon have you driving around like you were born for it.' He puffed out his chest, as if looking forward to getting the motor out of its hibernation.

The lady who'd answered the door came in with a pot of tea. 'Thought a pot of tea might help.' Her face managed a smile in

Molly's direction, as she placed the tray on a low table. 'Seeing as you're a friend of Issac's.'

'Business partner, and her name's Molly, Gertrude; so you know what to call her, next time she visits. Stanley's going to teach her to drive.' That sour old face just got a bit more serious; she gave a little bob and scurried from the room.

'Don't mind Gertrude, she likes to protect us.'

From the look on his face, Issac's father was quite capable of looking after himself. And now she had two men willing to help her get the hang of the jalopy. Life was looking up.

Chapter 6

'Take it steady, like this.' Stanley cranked the jalopy into gear and chugged across the gravel drive. 'It'll come easier as you go on – the steering is self-explanatory.

Molly wasn't so sure, her only go at driving was when her friend from school, asked her to go and look at her dad's new car and she sat behind the wheel for a couple of minutes and jiggled it like crazy until she was worried, she'd break it and she quickly jumped out.

Another time, was when the circus came to Wolverhampton and they had a little bubble car for the audience to have a ride in. Neither could compare to Issac's sporty little number.

Mrs Cartwright, looked on in trepidation, hands clasped in front of her. 'Oh, it's good to see the old motor back in action, isn't it our Stan? We've avoided getting it out, since Issac went. It feels odd,' she sucked her lips inward, blinking fast. 'Kind of strange, watching it moving and getting started up again, do take care, dear… then again, if he promised you could use it…' She stood level to Molly watching her with a suspicious sidelong glance.

She wasn't feeling overly brave, but this had to be done. The only way she held onto some courage, was to imagine Issac right there; standing in front of them, willing her on. Maybe he was thinking of her, right at this moment; wondering what she was up to, picturing her driving his motor car, up and down round the huge driveway at his parents' home - from his post far away. Whether he was or not, it gave her the confidence, and surprising inner strength to get in and give it a whirl.

'Sometimes it's quicker to get the pony and trap out. We've been lying low like my wife said.' Stanley turned the car, pulled up beside them and beamed in his wife's direction. It was startling, how like his son he was. Her stomach clenched at the very thought of seeing Issac again, and how different things would be next time. It felt like a year since he'd been gone, even though it wasn't, and when she began to realise, she was running the business alone; it got scarier as time went on.

'You ready to get behind the wheel, wench, or am yer here to be daydreaming the day away?'

'Better now than never, if ever!' Jolted from her thoughts, she put on a brave front; her lightness of tone belied her real feelings. Truth be told, she was nervous as heck, but couldn't tell the protectors of the shiny untouchable motor contraption that. They were more than kind, yet she couldn't help think they would rather keep it in storage with the cloth wrapped over it.

Stanley busied himself turning the handle to crank start the motor, telling her that bit was a man's job. Then it was ready for driving. She might as well get stuck in and behind the wheel, she heard him shout.

Quick as lightening, she climbed in, door secured then tucking her skirts underneath her, she took the wheel. Placing her foot on the pedals, as he'd explained and shown, in great detail, she whispered a silent prayer to the gods of lady drivers, and so, began her first lesson in driving.

Her passenger held on to his hat and tipped backwards; the kangaroo jolt and speed she took off at was rather a shock to them all. Doris ran after them - as if she could slow the drive away process down. 'Where's the brake?!' Molly shot him a glance, and took her hands off the wheel to indicate him tell her quick.

'Hands always on the wheel, foot on the pedal, girl, like I told you that one there.' He stood up out of his seat and leaned right over to show her, then shouted … 'Grab the handbrake!'

She did – engaging the severe emergency stop sent Stanley launching himself over the windshield. 'Phew!' She stopped the motor just short of the rose border. Too bad that her newly found driving instructor had landed head first and was up to his neck in the pink English rose bushes. He was fast getting himself upright, so luckily, as far as she could see, no physical harm done.

'Oh my, Stanley, are you alright, love?' His wife rushed to help him, turning to Molly who was by now, red faced and gasping for breath. 'You need to get a bit more practice in, on the straight before taking off.' Doris was flapping around her husband, checking he was still breathing. Thank goodness he was.

Quite the robust kind of man, he brushed himself down, and shouted. 'No damage done, and now you've had a lesson in finding the brakes. They're highly sensitive and better to go a bit slower if I was you to start with, eh love?'

He tutted, 'what did I try to tell him? Only would he listen to me, eh?' Speaking to his wife, he muttered about the perils of getting a car named after a German prince. 'If he's going to get a C-10 Prince Henry, what can you expect? Hardly going to have reliable brakes is the darn thing? That's what you get for keeping up with the crowd, but I'm only his dad, why would he? Out fighting the Germans, and here we are driving a bloody car named after one of the blighters. The world's gone barmy.'

Coughing slightly, she needed to remind them she was still waiting there. Not wanting to be in the middle of a family debate all because of her clumsy driving efforts. 'Erm... Should we call it a day? I'm sorry about that, wasn't what I had planned ...' It was the best she could do; to gesture to his prize blooms, flattened with a Stanley Cartwright shaped space amid the bushes; his hat was squashed into itself. 'I'll make sure you get a new hat.' She pulled it out of itself, and gave it a pat with her hand, placing it on the dash, hoping he could make do until she could get a replacement.

'Baloney; never heard such codswallop spoken in all my life. I'm not that decrepit as a tumble into the rose border would hurt me. There was a time, me and the missus…' He went into a coughing fit at the memory of what he and Doris got up to among the roses.

'Stanley. Back behind the wheel, this chatter won't get the girl driving. Let him show you a few more times, love, before you get behind the wheel, hey? And for Christ's sake Stan, tell her where all the different kinds of brakes are, and when to use them, etcetera!' Her voice got louder as she went on. 'The motor is not a toy, its Issac's pride and glory. Let's keep it in one piece shall we for him to come back to!? I'll get Gertrude to put the kettle on; terrace garden, for tea and cakes - fifteen minutes.'

Stanley brushed his hand through his hair, and adjusted his shirt, gave her a wink and jumped back in, indicating for her to join him in the passenger seat. He obviously wasn't going to listen to what Doris had instructed.

'Right, promise full attention! Sorry about that.' Molly cleared her throat willing to get it better this time.

'Tch, could have been a lot worse. At least you didn't crash into the house, eh?'

'And you haven't booted me off the premises.' She listened and watched with great intent as he began to roll the car forward – in the opposite direction of the rose borders.

'Gently down on the throttle -. And it's a great car. Trust him to get the best. He usually does. One thing about our Issac, he's got an eye for quality.'

Thank goodness his launch had left him uninjured and his tone had mellowed. She hadn't a clue on the type of car it was. Only that it looked fabulous and with Issac at the wheel she could imagine them driving around Brocton and Abbot's Bromley going for picnics and fishing trips along the canal.

She wondered if Stanley meant Issac getting the best where girlfriends were concerned. He'd never been engaged, she knew that, and he didn't seem to have time to get involved with anyone in that way. Same as she didn't. They were two of a kind – both obsessed with work. Yet here he was – gone so far from the ones he loved, putting his life at risk to keep them safe.

'Are you listening? Yer'm a right old dolly daydream?' His booming voice brought her back to earth with a bump.

'Oh, I'm sorry. I think I could do with that cup of tea if you don't mind, Stanley.'

With a giant 'harrumph,' he came to another emergency stop and shut down Prince Henry. 'Cup of tea it is then. Lead the way.'

Settled on a raised terrace, adorned with colourful hibiscus, hydrangeas and huge urns filled with red and white geraniums, like she'd seen in her encyclopaedia's, tea and biscuits were served. Gertrude hovered, checking there was enough seed cake to go round, and making sure they had enough milk and hot water for the drinks. Keeping an eagle eye on the group, and an ear to the conversation, she was ferociously protective to Issac's family, which was touching to see.

'How're you getting on with running the business then, Molly?' Gently sipping tea, the question came as a surprise, seeing as the little lady in front of her looked as if she wouldn't have a clue about the business. Her eagle eyes didn't leave Molly's face, daring her to tell the truth.

A heat rushed to her cheeks; Stanley sat opposite, also giving her the look. She reminded herself … These were decent people, Issac's parents, and she could strangle him at this moment for not making better plans. She wanted to run and hide; tell them she'd been molested by someone who should have known better.

She cleared her throat. 'I'm having a bit of a struggle with it all, if I'm honest.' *Phew, it was a relief to speak openly to them. She couldn't lie, as it was hurting her head not to be able to talk about how she was feeling.* Whatever followed would be her doing. She flicked a glance from one to the other, knowing in her heart she had to be straight with them.

'There, what did I tell you?' She gave a knowing glance and nod of the head towards her husband. 'I knew it.' Doris looked kindly, not patronising, like she might have expected to hear this. Her eyes softened her tone, one of understanding. 'I bet you miss him as much as we do. Blasted war shouldn't be happening. Telling us it wasn't going to last long, well; that was over a year ago now and still no sign of it ending. The last one did enough damage and took too many. Oh, can't bear to think about it.' A great sigh escaped her lips. 'No wonder women want the vote to get involved in politics and run the country. Sort the men out and get things back on track.'

'Hey, we'll have no silly talk like that under this roof. He should have spoken to me, and told us what he planned to do. That way we could have taken control and given you a part time job. Save you the effort of having to keep up full time.' He finished the sentence with his usual harrumph.

Reality washed over her, before she quickly put them straight. 'I was only feeling a bit low. Issac put me in charge, and I have been working closely with him for the last few years. He trusts me to work every day, apart from Sunday, unless we have an order to get out. Everything I earn goes towards keeping my family warm, and fed. They only have me.' She twiddled her fingers and held her hands together, fingers entwined in her lap to stop them shaking.

This was going horribly wrong. From needing a bit of sympathy, she'd all but talked herself out of her own job. She would fight tooth and nail if she had to. The hat business was in her capable hands; she needed to learn to drive, take control of everyone and the business around her then be there for the ones who needed her most. They always came top of her list. That was all she had to do.

'It's good to talk, but *really; I am managing alright.* It's just getting my new employee trained up so I'll be free to fetch more stock; when I can afford it obviously. There's no way the business will ever go into debt while I'm here.' She sat tall, pushing her shoulders back, defiantly lifting her head, chin up, looking them both straight in the eye. If her parents had taught her anything, it was, be honest and thrifty and don't waste hard earned money when you can save a few pennies.

'I thought he had the stock delivered; that's what Issac always did; as far as I knew any road. That gave him more time so he could be there on hand, and not out gallivanting.' Stanley stood up and prowled like a jungle tiger on the hunt. 'Peacock comes down - brings us all the stock we need - on the cart.'

'Yes, but I worked out the delivery cost, against me fetching it; I think we can save lots over the space of a year when you add it up. And I've noticed how they've gradually been putting a lower grade of cloth on the waggon when they deliver. We've lots of competition from the bigger factories over in Coventry & Warwick. They're getting more orders than us. They're cutting the prices all round.' She glanced from one to the other hoping she hadn't gone too far with her thoughts and ideas. Issac should be here to back her up.

'I've got the solution. And I'll have no more suffragette talk, but we need to pull together here. This is what we'll do – Doris, you can hold the fort at the works on buying days, with thingy ma what's er name, new apprentice girl. You did it all back in the day, we both did

– and not a bad job either. Me and you will go in the C – 10 to find the best priced and quality felts and fabrics you need.'

He nodded in her direction, looking mighty satisfied with his instant solution to her dilemma. 'Well? And I agree, you have to feel the cloth with your own bare hands and check on the shades as they want the very best, even if they can't afford it, you'll be surprised what they'll spend if there's a wedding or christening in the family. We have our pride us Black Country lot, don't we? It's how we started out, fetching our own materials.'

'I vote that's a great idea, my love.' Doris had a cheeky glint in her eye as she threw a sideways sneaky wink in her direction. Between them, they'd convinced Stanley it was his idea all along. 'We'll all pull together, but *you are* still running the place, Molly, it's what Issac wanted. He trusted you. It's his business, left to him from my father, and his father before that. My old grandad started in a shed, down the bottom of his garden, in Paradise Lane. He expanded until he had all the space he needed then created the yard, and the property next door.

He always wanted Issac to carry it on, even get a shop on the premises for people to try on and buy from there. We aren't getting any younger after all, but there's a war on. It needs a full-on effort from all of us. Don't you agree Gertrude?' Doris threw her voice to be heard by someone they couldn't see.

As always not far away, she came in and nodded, then gave Molly the old up and down as if she'd been sucking on a lemon; still not quite sure what to make of her. Perhaps she fancied her chances with Issac, who knew?

Having the promise of help, especially on buying days would be a god-send. Travelling on her own wasn't something she'd been looking forward to – even if women were supposed to be more independent.

'So how did it go up at the mansion then?' Aunt Violet had stayed up later than she normally did. Knitting in her favourite armchair, up the corner, and she'd banked up the fire with extra coal and a log; another reminder how much she needed to keep her full-time job, and make a success of the hatting business. How she afforded so much luxury was a miracle.

'They were friendly, really nice. Even when I sent him hurtling into the rose bushes, he didn't send me packing; I think I've made an impression.' At the thought of events earlier, Molly couldn't help the giggles that she'd been holding in all that time. She leaned back in her comfy chair and let rip with laughter that had been missing from her life for a long time.

'You didn't get the old man in the bushes? Oh, my lord that's terrible.' Violet shrieked; laughing fit to burst. 'Oh, lord, our Molly you're making me cry.' She wiped her eyes with her handkerchief; stop it!'

Their belly laughs followed by more shrieks had Janey running from her room, to join in the catch up from the grand house. 'Oh Janey, you should have been there. He's such a sport, if you'd seen the way he launched himself over the windshield. If he'd had a parachute attached he'd have took off.'

Another round of screaming belly laughs rang out having Violet reach for the huge tea pot on the aga. She poured three welcome cuppas. 'Oh, lord, I'll be wetting me self if I laugh anymore. I've got a bag of crumpets for supper to go with that. Janey, pass us the toasting fork, we'll have a couple each.' They took turns holding the long fork into the glow of the fire, turning the crumpets around until they were brown on either side. They shared the tiny dot of butter on the little rounds of delicious tasting snacks which went down a treat.

Violet settled back with her knitting, more socks and balaclavas for the boys overseas. She was counting stitches, and engrossed in her latest pattern.

'Thanks, they were smashing. I'll take this up and have an early night. She grabbed the latest envelope with the familiar writing on the front. Even though she was tired, the truth of it – she wanted to read Issac's letter in private. Her face would give away how much she missed him. How she searched every word for a sign, some little hint that he was hers. If only they were engaged, she'd feel more secure, but he'd trusted her with his most precious endeavour. That was enough to get her through.

'Alright love, night night. I'll pop a water bottle up in half an hour. It's getting cooler now the autumn's getting closer. I've got wool and patterns, keeping my hands busy with these.' She waved her latest olive-green craft work for Molly to admire. 'The nuns gave me the idea, last Sunday at church. They're busy working on these as well. We have to try and do our bit haven't we? There's plenty of wool in the basket if you want to keep your hands busy.'

'Thanks, great idea. I will get some done for him. A bit of knitting helps me relax as well.' She waved Issac's latest envelope as a goodnight before leaving the room.

Eagerly, once alone, she tore open the envelope, holding it close, imagining him writing as he grabbed a few moments between watching for the enemy; Praying for good news, or at least nothing bad. It was his own handwriting, so he must still be well enough to write.

My Dearest Molly;

Hope this reaches you and finds you well. It's not the best place I've ever been, and thinking of home keeps me going. Please say hello to my parents, and sorry I haven't written. There's limited time and essentials we need to write home, so I trust you will reassure them I'm thinking of them, and hope all is well at Paradise Lane. Hope you're using the motor for your convenience.

We're moving forward again soon. Pressing on into the next area and the boots are giving me gip, but the lads keep the morale up with singing and we play footie in-between digging trenches and marching.

Did I tell you that we did some training on Milford Common? The last time I was there was a few years ago now, with the folks; they took me and Clara over for a jolly - Sunday afternoon. Brought back memories of walking on Cannock Chase, and the fun we had picnicking there. Tell them that if you could please, Molly, love.

Didn't think for one minute I'd be training in that same place years later, for going into war! The difference the years make. All the time, training over Brocton and rural Staffordshire, made me know – when this damn dirty war is over. We'll go there together, you and me. I'm not good with words, but we'll have some private time, and get to know each other properly, and I'll turf out my fishing rod and we'll catch some tiddlers. Don't worry, I'll throw them back.

You've been there by my side for so long. But this is something I wanted to do; then we'll be free to roam those hills, and enjoy the fairground when it comes, together.

How's the driving coming along? Please write, and let me know.

All for now Molly- love.

Yours, faithfully,

Issac. Xxxx

She held the letter close to her chest, pressing it to her heart – kissed it once and then again before reading through it one more time. Scrutinising every word, she whispered to herself, *Molly, love.*

He wants to spend time with me, special time. Slowly, she pushed the letter under her pillow. Tears streamed down her cheeks, but she could only sniff and wipe them away. He was pouring his heart out on the page, and now she knew as soon as they possibly could, she wanted to marry her Issac.

She'd call to see his parents, after work tomorrow, and tell them he was remembering to them. About the times on Milford Common with his sister Clara; how he trained there before moving across to France in Europe. They were good people, and with them helping, she would build the business up to being the best in the midlands.

Saddlers and iron mongers in Walsall were thriving. The steel works, cutlery and nails were the up-and-coming industries in Bloxwich and the brush industry; though everyone wore a hat. From paupers, to poachers and preachers, rich or poor, they wore a hat of some description, and Paradise Lane, would be the place they'd come to. She would be the best in the area – and first thing tomorrow she would get up early and write to Issac with her news. She was fast asleep by the time aunt Violet tiptoed in with her hot water bottle.

Chapter 7

'It's Memorial Day! Janey; get your best coat and hat our lift will be round here soon. Danny Glover's picking us up in his new van.'

Aunt Violet, powdered her nose in the hall mirror, and stood back to check she was presentable. The butcher had offered her a lift and she didn't refuse his kind gesture; times were getting hard with food rations and the girls needing a full square meal and Danny was more than happy to help out.

There was a time when she resisted his charms, and nobody would ever replace Albert. Still, never look a gift horse and all that. Nobody would find out about their little arrangement; she didn't even kid herself to think she was the only one, though he insisted she was. As long as the bills were paid, and they lived as best as they could in these dire times, that's all she cared about now.

'We'll meet our Molly round there, she left early, with Francesca. The new girl's learning well about the running of the works, according to what she told me. She's going to show her how the office work is done; some of the workers are going in even though it's a Sunday: all part of the job running your own business. Now let me look at you.'

She brushed a few hairs from Janey's collar. 'You'll do,' we mustn't ever forget the miner's memorial, all those lives lost, to think all for the sake of the flaming coal mines. Death traps if you ask me. Just glad your mother had two daughters and not lads, otherwise who knows? Come on our Janey.'

Her nieces were her world. No matter how much she teased and urged them to stand up for themselves, she protected them fiercely; all too aware how quickly the younger one was growing up.

Changing into a young lady; and Molly was a fine young woman now. Well into her prime and a real catch for any man.

All this women's independence wasn't such a good thing – men and women are built different. Why would they try and be the same? How couldn't they see it was better to keep the home clean and tidy and look after the nippers? Gone was the day when you knew your place and stayed there. It was more natural back then, and now for that matter. Why try and compete with men, when they were the providers? Everyone knew that was the way it was, if they had any sense.

It was as plain as the moon in the night sky to see Molly was in love with her boss, Issac Cartwright. Why they hadn't got engaged or married by now was beyond her. If they couldn't spot a good thing when they had it; she wondered if they ever would. Allowing a moment to remember her one love; she smiled and knew he would never be replaced.

She had friends who tried to play matchmaker with her and Jack Wilkins. He was a true friend, sending vegetables and often just calling in for a cuppa and chat – whether she wanted to talk or not, he was full of local news and gossip and always left leaving her laughing at some silly joke and feeling glad he came by.

They often spoke about a time when the four of them, newly married moved into Victoria Row, when the world was a better place, and they enjoyed the simple things in life; drinking home-made dandelion wine, picnics in the park, or over Cannock Chase. Back when days were warmer, skies bluer. Men earned the money, and women nurtured the family, and kept a welcome for their men coming home… she sighed.

The butcher was always trying his luck, and keeping him dangling on a string had worked for only so long. Now was different; his weekly afternoon visits, trying to be discreet couldn't last forever, yet they weren't doing anyone any harm. They both knew it was all in fun, and only flirting; now those games had turned into regular bedroom activities, which involved her spreading her legs like a whore on the game. A small sacrifice - considering how he kept her in fresh meat for the stews and other tasty meals she managed to eke out over several days for them all.

Along with the pile of notes he left on the dressing table before he left. It added up to a lot, that she wasn't proud of, yet now she was caught in a roller coaster of a trap. Especially now he'd added a few sacks of coal and logs to be dropped into the coal hole once a fortnight for her; just when she worried how she would ever keep them warm...

Molly ordered coal often, but had no knowledge how much they really used. She prayed neither of her nieces ever found out. It would be the end of her if they did, but there wasn't a way out she could see for now.

'He's here aunt Violet, pipping his horn! Hurry up he says.' Janey hung out of the front door giving a high wave to the waiting chauffeur. 'He's got a new van, with his name on the side and everything. Come and see.'

'As if I don't know he's here, flipping heck, who'd want a man who keeps honking on his hooter every minute as if I'm a bloody imbecile!' She slammed and locked the door behind them, following her niece up the garden path, knowing she'd be pulling his other hooter one afternoon next week.

Jostling into the front of Danny's van, they settled down for a meaty smelling ride to the Pelsall memorial site. Proudly holding her small posy of chrysanthemums, Jack had provided, Violet tried hard not to be sick and wrinkled up her nose instead.

'What dye think of my new get about, getting up in the world, eh?' He gave her knee a squeeze and Violet smacked his hand off.

'It's just fine for a lift now and again, thank you. It'll get your orders out faster than that old bicycle you've been getting the lad to drop deliveries off in.' She teased, and gave him a warning glare. No touching when the girls were around. That was established long ago, and she wouldn't compromise on that. Her beautiful nieces would be known as kids from a brothel if word got out. She knew full well, Molly would disown her, and Janey would be devastated.

Danny put his foot down on the accelerator, taking them racing driver style in his small van to the miner's memorial in Pelsall. There was a good turnout, at the church, as always, and they had only been there five minutes before Molly joined them. Pulling her collar up, she shivered. The wind had picked up, most of the villagers were chatting but the atmosphere was sombre.

It was more than 40 years now since the 1872 Pelsall Hall mining disaster, but Violet always showed her support. Her Albert's dad was a miner, at the time of the accident. The mine had flooded, men and boys, drowned while they toiled to earn an honest crust. He had nightmares for years after, telling of how the men were shouting to be rescued, and they could only get a couple at a time in the bucket lift leading down the mine shaft.

He never went back to work after that, and vowed he'd never allow Albert to go underground. He had the blasted Boer War to deal with instead. Now she'd never know what he'd been through, over there.

The Vicar led the prayers and each man who had lost his life in the tragedy was named, and flowers laid for each and every one. Violet and her nieces linked arms. Danny kept his head bowed throughout. He'd brought a homemade wreath of laurel and greenery from his garden. He quietly placed it down as the names were called out, and prayers were recited.

Not a dry eye among the many who attended. Mutterings … lives wasted; and them only kids; it should never have happened. A candle was lit and placed in a jar to avoid it blowing out in the wind. Violet reflected on her own loss, and the parents of the two girls encircled in her arms. She glanced over to where the butcher had his head bowed in prayer. *Praying for forgiveness if you've got any sense Danny Glover.*

Things were changing all the time. If only Albert was still here, it would be so much easier. Part of her never gave up hope of him being found. Often in her dreams, she would hear him climbing the stairs and pulling back the sheets, climbing in beside her then feeling his arms circling her, holding her tightly as she slept, loving her, as only a proper husband could. Caring and sharing their life together. The only trouble was, he was never there when she woke.

'I'd better get back up to work and see how they're going on.' Molly broke from the comfort of her aunt's embrace, and then hugged her sister. 'Will you be alright?' She turned and asked aunt Violet.

'Hey, you get yourself back over to the hat works, I'll take Janey home and make sure the fire's lit and get us summat good to eat. On you go love, don't worry.'

She waved her goodbyes, trying to get her head straight to face the workers who had kindly turned up that morning. The buzz of conversation greeted her through the airways among the smell of glue, steam and hot felt as she entered the shop floor. She slung her coat over the usual hook, behind the door and walked into heated chatter of where they would have the market stall.

'Has to be Walsall,' the handsome blond, Birmingham lad gushed. 'I know the Toby; he's the feller who collects the rent. I can put a word in there.'

'That sounds good.' She put her head around the door, made her presence felt, before they said something she might not want to hear. 'I think we can mark that as a possibility. What about Bloxwich?'

'It's probably too small, but we can enquire, yes, that an all, and then there's Wednesbury, there's plenty get round there. We want somewhere with plenty of folk walking round, though, you'll sell more hats that way.'

Positivity ran rife among the workers, giving her an immense pride filling her from head to foot. If only Issac could see the loyalty and dedication – that was the minute she knew, his business would be safe in her hands with the help of this team.

'We need to start close to home first, so Bloxwich.' She gathered up her note book and pen. 'The town is busy most Saturday's, and if we could get a stall on there, establish ourselves, then branch out. I'm not taking on all those pitches until we know we can sell on a market.

'Bobby, you said you know the Walsall Toby; how do you feel, about Bloxwich?' She looked over to where the Birmingham lad was counting over his pieces of work completed and noting it down. His head shot up on hearing his name being called out.

'Oh, er, yes. Just keeping my records straight,' he pushed the paper to the back of his workbench. 'Well, thing is, I know there's a lot trying to get on there, and if you turn up, wait and see if some of the regulars don't turn up, then you might get on, or might not, depends.'

'You're saying we might turn up and not get a stall?' Molly wondered if she could stand the uncertainty of waiting only to be turned away.

'It works like this…' Obviously a street wise lad, she listened with interest. By the time he'd finished explaining, he'd told her you go and queue up with anyone else wanting a stall who wasn't a regular, as what they call a casual; then when they get to know and like you, that's when you get a regular place. Molly understood, and looked at Francesca, who was nodding and looking admiringly in his direction.

'Seeing as you know so much, how d'you fancy trying to get a casual stall then, say next Saturday? Francesca, will you go with him? Seeing as it was your suggestion in the first place.' She had a feeling the wily ways of these two together could make a good team.

'I definitely will. Maybe when we get to the regular stall, I could bring one of my lads with me. They love helping, and another pair of hands is always good for running errands and suchlike.'

She knew it was more about childcare and not leaving her mom with too much to handle, though it had to be business first. 'Maybe you could when we get established; but not until then.' She threw a sympathetic smile in her friend's direction. She didn't want the worry of the children getting under their feet. She wasn't even sure if Francesca and Bobby would get along – working together.

'Of course, that's what I meant. How do you feel, Bobby? Having a woman show you the ropes?' Francesca was teasing, and the crooked grin of the Brummie lad showed he revelled in having a partner to banter with.

'As long as you can hold yerself back from grabbing me while I'm busy selling the most hats. Don't want any hard feelings if I sell out, and you just stand there looking like the hat stall model!'

He turned his head away from Francesca, trying to control the laughter, until he could contain his curiosity no longer. Slowly turning back to give her his trademark grin, he looked coy... 'Well?'

'I'll try my best to resist yer; to be jolly well sure I will definitely try my best.' She raised her eyes to the ceiling. 'As for who sells the most hats, we'll see about that. I'll bet you a pound it's me.'

Molly knew between them, if and when they got a stall, they'd be trying so hard, they'd likely as much completely sell out of hats and accessories.

The sound of hooves clip clopping on the yard gave Molly a start. Her insides felt like a hundred butterflies were trying to get out. Her mind went right back to that day. With a deft move, she pulled the netting to one side that hung against the window. It was the Cartwright's. Almost fainting with relief, she ran to welcome them in.

'We were at the memorial. Didn't want to interrupt you when you were with family, only we thought it's a good chance to pop in, when we saw you heading over to the works.' Stanley cast his eyes round the small office kitchen, making himself at home filling the kettle from the huge copper over by the wall, and setting it on the hot plate. He reached in the top cupboard and pulled down the tea canister then spooned out four teaspoons of leaves into the teapot warming on the side; 'One for each of us, and one for the pot.' There was something quite comforting about his behaviour. He was a man in charge, and she didn't mind his attitude, as long as he wasn't going to change things around, he could brew up anytime.

'Now then, I'll get stuck in here, have a look at the ledger.' He smiled as the two ladies drank their tea, leaving him to continue his quest to find out how the business was going.

'You do that dear, Molly can show me around the workshops, it's been ages since I've been here.' Doris finished her drink, and whispered to Molly, checking she was happy to leave Stanley rummaging through her cabinet.

Nodding, she gestured and led the way for her to come and see the workers. 'It's great to see you both, and yes, of course, the ledger is up to date.' She bit on her lower lip, knowing the sales weren't as healthy as they should be. Also, a couple of regulars had asked if they could pay next month. 'Follow me…' She led Doris through to where the few Sunday staff was catching up on work left over from earlier in the week. Finishing touches were being added to complete hats ready to be posted out.

'As you know, we don't always come in on Sunday's these are my loyal workers who want to catch up with the orders. Also, there's a venture we have in mind, we're going to try out. I really need to come and have a chat with you. But we'll certainly be going ahead, what with one thing and another.' She couldn't go into detail here, more likely when they were sitting, back at Oak Tree Grange, comfortably in their own home; that would be a more sensible place to talk about the nitty gritty of what she and her workers had got planned. Back in the office Stanley was scribbling away.

'Where's the petty cash kept?' In his glory, with the ledger spread out, his notebook and pen laid out on top of it, figures and notes filling the page jotted down in columns, Stanley enquired. His huge feathery eyebrows rose higher than before, and his eyes boggled.

Only glad it had been them paying a visit and not that monster, she pulled the bottom drawer of her cabinet open. Reaching out a purple box with embroidery on, a present from her mother when she was fifteen, she placed it on the desk. 'We keep the petty cash in here. We always used to keep around fifty pounds, in notes and change, but lately twenty is more than enough for odds and sundries.'

She came closer to where he was racking over the figures. 'Is everything alright?'

He didn't answer her, but opened the box. It was empty. They all stood perfectly silent for a minute or two. Molly froze on the spot. 'I always keep this office locked. There's only me, and Francesca who come in here. The workers have their own rest room, where they eat and have their flasks. Everyone is honest, I can be sure of it.'

'I wouldn't bank on that.' He sat back and wiped his hand across his face. 'We need to have a discussion about the state of the business. Not interfere, only get to the bottom of where that money's gone, and how we can get this business back on track.' He looked at Molly as she steeled herself not to break down. That money was in her box last time she looked. And though she knew he'd never believe her, in a million years, yet she trusted her loyal workers.

'I'll get to the bottom of this, and not only that, we have plans to get out of the slump we've gone into. I know this looks bad, and you think I'm incompetent, I'm not. Your Issac taught me everything I know about the hatting business, but not how ruthless and cruel people can be. As soon as it's convenient for you both, I'd like to come over and have a proper business chat.' Molly managed to speak without crying. She was shaking with anger, but she wanted to keep a cool head in front of Issac's family.

'We'd like that, wouldn't we, Stanley.' Doris gave her a watery smile. She clasped her hands together, and looked as if she would break down in tears.

'I'll send a note with Gertrude; say in a week from now.'

'That suits me…' She watched as they climbed aboard the horse and carriage before it made a wide turn around the yard, leaving her feeling more alone than ever.

Chapter 8

'We'll go and see the nuns; you can tell them how well you're getting on with your sewing. I'm out this afternoon as well, remember?' Trying to sound far jollier than she felt, she packed a bag with the latest book her sister was reading. She'd had the note, delivered by Gertrude, from the Cartwright's, inviting her to go round and see them next Sunday afternoon, which was today, around three o'clock. They'd added that she could have afternoon tea with them, as well as the business talk.

Molly needed to speak with the elders; they always gave her a feeling of calm and peacefulness. Every day was becoming a struggle, to keep her head above water and make out things were going well. Stanley had opened up Pandora's Box by asking her about the figures and why she'd cancelled her abuser (though he wasn't aware that he wasn't the usual delivery man) into the private space of the hat business.

'You're not putting a shift in this Sunday then?' Aunt Violet stood in the doorway, scrutinising her every move as she wiped her hands on a tea towel. 'Must say I'm glad; there's a bit of brisket I managed to scrounge from Danny. It'll go nicely with some carrots and potatoes. What time are you coming back? I'll give the church a miss for today.'

Flicking a brush through her hair, she smiled and shook her head. 'We'll only be an hour, maybe a bit more.' Giving Janey a gentle shove, she made her way towards the door. At this rate she was never going to get away. Affectionately, she put an arm round her sister's shoulder. 'This one wants to show Sister Dorinda how good her sewing is coming along, and I need to discuss what type of flowers Sister Margareta thinks we need for the church arrangements next week. They've volunteered me for creating the vases along the windowsills.' Molly pulled a face. Floristry was something she enjoyed doing at home; she just wasn't sure about the entire church. More at home with a cabbage patch and digging up potatoes from the arboretum was more along her line of expertise.

'Mm, I'll have it ready for then. As long as there's nothing else you want to see her for?'

Nothing got past aunt Violet who was sharp as a blade and twice as bright. This was something she wasn't going to share with anyone, unless she could think of someone she could trust.

Violet watched her nieces stride up the garden path and out the gate, a frown etched across her brow. Something was wrong; she could feel it in her bones. Their Molly was a bonnie girl, and she had a certain bloom to her cheeks these days, yet she couldn't hide the sadness in her eyes. Wasn't it such a pity the man who'd put that glow on her face was so far away, and she knew how that felt only too well.

Every day she prayed he'd come back for her, same as she never gave up hope of her Albert appearing. Though as time ticked along and this war went on, everything got worse. She felt it was an impossible dream to ever see him again. She put the kettle on the hob. When there wasn't an answer to the questions on her mind – a lovely cuppa usually settled her down. Then after that, she'd peel some potatoes and prepare a hearty meal for the three of them.

***

Issac chewed the end of the pen Walter had pushed into his hand. 'You sure you want me to put that?' He blushed at the eager expression of his comrade waiting for him to pen the words letting his sweetheart back home know what he had a mind to do with her when he returned. The cheeky glint in Walter's eye only added to the affirmation he was nodding making sure it was exactly what he wanted Issac to put in the letter. 'Becha penny for a pound it'll get censored. Remember last month when she hadn't got a notion of what you said before? It would be better for me to find you a dictionary, that way you can write your own bloody letters.'

He was only joking, but it made him think of home, who if anyone would be thinking of him. His parents, obviously and he really needed to pen them a few lines. But his mind drifted to the one who was filling his thoughts more than ever recently.

Why had he been so blinkered on the job? Fair enough, it was his life's work, and lots of people depended on him and the hat making work for a living. For one certain lady, her entire family depended on her. He was tinged with guilt, though he was knee deep in mud most of the time, doing what he wanted to do for king country and his nearest and dearest.

Only now he realised he hadn't really thought this idea through as well as he should have, just as she'd told him in no uncertain terms. His Molly was a feisty one, she wasn't half. That's why he loved her so much. The passion in her eyes whenever he went near her. How he missed their lovemaking, and why had he been so stupid not to make her his wife a long time ago.

'Have you gone to sleep on me or what?' The Walsall lad's voice boomed in his ear, cutting through his thoughts of Molly, the way her hair curled around her ears, her steely determination in those eyes to get the designs just right for the customers. She was one in a million, and he had taken her for granted, he knew that now.

'What? Oh, yes you were saying, I want to kiss you on the neck and work my way down to the pleasure point.' Issac scribbled away, chuckling as Walter added more x rated promises. He couldn't blame the chap and now he might have some ideas of what he and Molly might get up to when he got back.

***

It wasn't easy to talk to Sister Margareta as she'd hoped it would be. Often, they'd asked her about her worries, the usual things were discussed. Like how to manage with looking after Janey, and whether or not she was doing the right thing working full time. The latter wasn't an option. If they weren't with aunt Violet, she'd have to be working nights as well as days and surely wouldn't manage to look after her sister so well. The best she could manage was…

'What would you do if a man you didn't know or didn't like made a pass at you, Sister Margareta?' Holding her hands clasped in her lap and avoiding eye contact, Molly hoped her flushed cheeks didn't give away her embarrassment.

'Well, I have had one or two such as you mention, as you're prone to do, walking round Walsall after dark. I'd advise you to give 'em a hefty kick up the balls like I did!' She sat back, almost relishing the memory licking her lips in delight.

Molly collapsed off her seat, unable to control her laughter. 'That's it then. I did the right thing. Just needed to make sure it was the normal thing us ladies would do.' Smiling at her friend opposite, she let out a much-needed breath of relief, and wiped imaginary sweat from her brow.

'You've not spoken to your aunt about this… unwanted attention? Sister Margareta enquired. She politely turned her back and adjusted a bouquet of flowers arranged in a huge pottery vase covered in oranges and lemons, holding flowers of the same colours.

'On my life, I can't talk to anyone, and its erm, not something I want anyone else knowing about if you're able to keep it to yourself. I'm so embarrassed and goodness knows how I've had the guts to even tell you now.' She glanced across to where Janey sat with her latest cushion she'd made and her books, beaming at the attention the nuns were showering upon her as she turned the page of Wuthering Heights, reading to them, with great precision. Those extra hours she'd spent helping her were paying off, and she was glad her sister read anything and everything she could get her hands on.

'But you have, and I'm glad. There's no point in keeping things to yourself that's no fault of your own. Was it one of them cheeky new workers? You told me you'd taken on some Brummie lads. And can you be certain you're not… you know, up the family way?'

'Lord no!' She looked upwards. 'Admitted, it was at work; someone who came to deliver - and from a firm we've used for years. This would never have happened if Issac had been there. Imagine if he or his parents ever found out!' Placing her hand to cover her face, she groaned. 'Oh, no, I've just remembered, they've invited me over for afternoon tea today, and they're asking why I've stopped a certain someone coming to the business. What can I say?'

Molly spoke in a terrible impression of an upper class voice lifting her skirts. 'Did you know, your highly respected firm, you've used for centuries? Yes of course you do, well, the other day, they sent a letch that stuck his cock in my mouth and tried to get inside my knickers and would have done if I hadn't bitten his knob.'

She looked glum. 'I shouldn't have told you. Now there'll be more trouble. I can't have Janey and aunt Violet finding out.' Her eyes begged Sister Margareta to keep her secret.

'Hush hush, love it's going to be alright. Nobody will know what you've told me. It stays between you me and these four walls.' She opened her arms wide, holding Molly close for a moment, allowing time for her to be confident – her secret was safe with her.

Hugging wasn't something Sister Margareta made a habit of, but the situation called for some down to earth love and understanding. She wanted young Molly to know there was a safe haven for her to turn to. Even just to talk and have a listening ear, get some reassurance, that's why they were here. Everyone needed someone to listen and be there for them in times of strife, grief, or whatever else these dark days threw at them.

Hadn't many a girl come to her, after being abused, left with child and not knowing where to turn? Incidents like this were unfortunately not uncommon. They may be marching and demanding the right to vote, but women's liberty was far from the freedom to voice their opinions they wished for. She'd make a purpose of watching out for Molly and check nothing like what she'd described in great detail ever happened again, and was only a one off, even if it meant making a visit to Mr and Mrs Cartwright herself. If only they knew the truth, they'd surely be on her side, and more supportive than she imagined.

***

Afternoon tea began with dainty sandwiches of spam, cut into triangles, with plenty of tea and small slithers of cheese. A delicate green side salad with a small slice of tomato garnish made Molly feel she was in some posh hotel in Birmingham, rather than a house in Pelsall.

'We'll eat, and then go to the business in hand after that.' Stanley gave her a broad smile; it reassured her a little. They weren't about to eat her and throw her to the dogs, for the moment, anyhow. Doris fluffed up her skirts and reached for her tapestry out of a bag beside her.

'I'm working on a cushion… peaches and peonies. It's going rather well; don't you think dear?' She placed the canvas on her lap and instructed Molly to examine her work. Glad of the distraction, she ran her hand over the neat stitches, and gave Issac's mother a nod. 'You've got some patience there, and what a beautiful cushion it'll make. I'll tell my sister about your handiwork, she's a sewing genius as well.'

They ate more sandwiches and Gertrude appeared from the kitchen to pour tea all round, then gave a little bob before leaving them to enjoy the afternoon tea. Almost half an hour later, Stanley cleared his throat.

'Let's start at the beginning. Are we any closer to knowing who took the petty cash?' Quickly putting her craft work to one side, Doris instructed Gertrude to clear away the tea things.

'I've spoken to the workers, they're all trustworthy. They know about the petty cash, even ask me for some when we need food for Dolly, our horse, extra sundries and such that they pick up in town.' She flicked a glance at her two elders, willing them to believe her. 'I'd have known if someone had been in there from the workshop.' She leaned back in her chair, lost for what else to say.

'Well, someone's been in there, and we do aim to get to the crux of the matter.' Stanley huffed and sat upright, waiting...

'There was an occasion.' She shook from the roots of her hair, uncertain of how this was going. 'I haven't mentioned it to anyone, other than close friends at the church. It's quite personal.' Now was the time to come clean. This wasn't going to be easy. 'There was a man, he called with a delivery.' Her face flushed and she bit on her lower lip. 'He brought different cloth from normal - knowing Issac was away.' She flicked a glance at Doris, wondering if she would pick up on her vibe, though no way was she going into details, not in front of Stanley.

'He was acting a bit strange from the off; domineering.' Doris's was nodding in a knowing kind of way. 'It's hard to put into words and I wish I'd mentioned it earlier, but not wanting to worry anyone...' She couldn't say anymore.

'Have you spoken to anyone about this, your family, for example?' Doris tilted her head. 'Did he harm you in any way?' She looked down, allowing her time to think it through.

She'd got the gist, without hearing any more. 'I didn't let him do what he wanted to do.' Tugging on her handkerchief on her lap she screwed her eyes up to shut out the event she'd never get out of her head.

'That's awful, for you lass, and he can't get away with that. But was he alone in the office at any time? This so-called bully, because I've dealt with Peacock for years, same as our Issac has; he's always been alright with us, for all the years we've known him. I can't understand…'

'It wasn't him.' Molly turned, snapping a little more than she intended to. 'They'd heard through the grapevine about Issac, signing up. They knew I was on my own, he thought I'd be fair game to use, and abuse but he got what for, then I ran out of the office to get away from him. That would have given him chance to look through the drawer. He helped himself to a cup of tea as well, so it really wouldn't surprise me, if it was him.' An almighty relief swept over her now they knew the truth.

Stanley sat with his head in his hands. For the first time, Molly wondered how he was coping with his son leaving them. What she'd told them was serious stuff, they would take time to digest that they'd been robbed, and she had been abused.

'You do believe me?' They had to; otherwise, she was in deep trouble. There was no way she was having her work force accused of stealing, when she knew full well, they hadn't.

'We'll get to the bottom of this, and I will be writing to Mr Peacock personally to ask who it was he sent with the goods, why they were inferior materials, and how he thought intimidating the business manageress was acceptable?' He looked tired now, but satisfied that he had the information, to push forward with a complaint. 'Let's leave it there for now, shall we?'

The abusive attack was worse than she'd let on. A side glance to Doris showed her that she knew there was more to be said; but not today. If Issac got to hear about it her world would end. She reminded herself, it was time to get back to her family.

Chapter 9

The day wasn't going well for Issac. Overnight rain had filled the trenches, not looking to stop any time soon. His feet were soaked, boots leaked and altogether he just wanted to be home. Molly's smile haunted him. Every time he closed his eyes for a second, she was there, with her warn smile, and loving nature, the comforting smell of primroses.

How he wished he could hold her close it would make everything right. For him, and all his comrades, it was a scary place to be. It never truly entered his head, that pals either side of him could be blasted to bits before his very eyes. It wasn't good. They'd all marched out, thinking they were invincible. Nobody could stop them, as they marched off to make a difference.

His nerves were shredded a little bit more and each day. He didn't let on, nor mention it in his letters home. He couldn't face being thought of as a coward and a conchie if he really expressed his feelings about not wanting to kill his fellow men. Whatever race, religion or cult, in his mind, humans were all the same under the skin. Up until now he hadn't given it all that much thought. His dad had been a war hero, and now happily living out his retirement, knowing he did his bit. Out here, with weapons built to destroy, and seeing his comrades dropping like flies was his worst nightmare.

He thought of his poor gentle mother, she'd be worried enough without giving a detailed sketch of what was going on in the battlefield. His job as a gunner on field duties, gave him access to the horses, one consolation. Without the animals, carrying the tackle, and pulling the guns, none of it would be possible. The image of her knitting him warm socks, like Molly had told him in her last letter, kept his mind full of goodness among the horror of war. Imagine! He thought he could make a difference. Now he was getting maudlin and that wasn't why he was here. There were younger lads than him around and the least he could do was set an example, be strong on the outside even if his morale was being severely tested.

Only yesterday he was talking to his mate from Walsall, who was looking forward to seeing his new baby when he got back. A recent attack had left him slumped, dead next to him. Now that baby would have to grow up without his daddy even seeing him. He made a silent pact to himself; he'd go and let Walter's family know how much he'd spoken about them - the way his eyes twinkled whenever he mentioned the name Betty. He knew it would make things worse, but the least he could do was reassure his wife, her name was on his lips constantly; same as it was for him, with Molly. The days couldn't go by quick enough for him. Now he was on a mission to get home in one piece; he'd seen horrors a human should never have to see. He wondered how he'd keep it all together before he got back.

The march into the battle of Loos they called it had already taken more lives than it was worth. Now they were calling for more soldiers to replace the fallen comrades. He felt sick inside except when he was with the horses. Trying to make it more bearable for the animals was part of his job. New men joined them every day in what was turning out to be a suicidal mission.

Now they'd had news of gasses being used in the trenches. It happened unexpectedly. A stray dog wandering on the front line, should have been bringing a message, but got stuck in a mud lake.

It was middle of the night, hours before dawn; he'd heard it floundering, whimpering. His instincts were to save the dog - a German shepherd - with a box attached to his neck. Not only was it his duty to save the dog and retrieve the message, it reminded him of his own dog, from when he was young, his pal, Jasper. They'd had him when they were young, and the pain of losing him after ten loyal years almost prevented his parents from ever getting another dog. Only lately, they'd got a sheep dog, for company and as a guard dog more than anything. Here was a similar one and he knew he had only one choice.

He crawled nearer to the lake, covered in mud himself, and he hadn't got anything to throw towards the dog, only some rope, that he planned to use somehow. The mud was beginning to suck the dog under.

'Hang on little buddy, I'll get you out, just keep holding on a few more seconds.' He wriggled towards the edge of the swamp area. Just then a voice from his right hollered out not too loudly.

'You will drown – along with the dog, let me get him…' It wasn't one of his men. Nobody he recognised – this fellow with a German accent, wandered over from the front trenches, over yonder. *Had he come over to surprise and kill them? Or trying to help him save this distraught creature same as he was? Holy Moses, was he about to take his last breath?*

His eyesight became clearer in the dark of the night, and then he saw it was a German soldier, crawling on his belly, just as he had done, the squelch of the mud became louder. Either one of them could disappear into the swamp, dog included; though the four-legged friend was silent now, having two companions, talking, encouraging him to hold on for dear life. The dog barley made a whimper as they encouraged him to hang on.

'I'm Fritz, here little feller, climb onto this.' Issac watched as the other man wriggled out of his jacket and threw it towards the dog. He looked in his direction and nodded. This might work and it might not, Issac prayed with all his heart. These dogs risked their lives every day searching for dead soldiers, carrying messages to the front line, and back again, providing small comforts to all men, whatever rank or nationality. The dogs had neither prejudice nor hatred in their bones, only service.

He made a noose with his thick rope. Tossing it in the right direction, but landing short, he cursed under his breath. The dogs were intelligent, but this one was stuck fast. Fritz wriggled towards his jacket, now getting wet and muddy. He used it to wriggle a little further forward. Issac took his off and threw it forward from where he lay sprawled across the ground. Inching forward, it gave some kind of support.

'Keep going Jasper, come on pal. You can make it.' They spoke gently to the dog and managed to ease the rope over his neck and loop it around his back end; pulling gently at first until it felt firm and taught. Jasper yelped. More soothing words and then gently but firmly, Issac began wriggling back the way he'd come, Fritz remained beside Jasper, his hand tucked under the rope round his neck, checking he wasn't about to strangle himself.

As the rope became more taught, between them, they eased Jasper out of the mire. He gave a low growl as the rope snagged against his fur. 'It's the only way this can be done little buddy.' Fritz grabbed one hand on the rope, and one hand on the back of the neck of Jasper, and shouted his instructions. 'Pull, I have the dog, pull – I will too. We can do this, together now, pull.'

Heaving and gasping, knowing this would end badly otherwise, the soldiers tugged with all their might, into the cold dark night, working together, as mates trying to do the best for their four-legged friend, who was on a mission to deliver messages to the men.

A couple more soldiers joined them, from both sides. Amidst the bleak night of war, German and British men routed for the hero dog that'd have disappeared under the swamp without their assistance.

One extra tug and Fritz hurled Jasper across onto a dryer patch of land than he'd known for the last half hour. Panting heavily and cautiously eyeing his rescuers, huge brown eyes looked forever grateful as he lay down his head, closed his eyes and stayed still for a while.

The soldiers fetched water and a little chopped ham for the dog, who ate and drank gently at first, then hungrily; obviously he hadn't eaten for days. Worse for wear, Issac and Fritz wriggled out of the mud exhausted themselves, exhilarated to see the dog, safe and alive.

'Now what happens?' Fritz watched Issac stroke Jasper's ears. Issac pulled out a brandy flask, offering it to his comrade of the task completed. He drank, and then offered Issac a smoke. He didn't smoke at home, but he needed something so joined the German, feeling a connection, yet knowing any minute he could open fire on him.

'We need to read the message, could be important for both sides.' The soldier buddies either side of Fritz and Issac, gathered round, ignoring they were enemies and had been sent to war to kill each other.

Issac read out slowly. *'Prepare to use nerve gas on the enemy. Tear gas and following that - mustard gas… Nobody will survive this, keep in mind you will win, and nobody of the opposing side will live to tell of the gassing in the trenches. It will happen too fast. Latest news… Over and out!*

Issac put the note down and wrapped his mates' overcoat around the creature they'd saved, only for him to bring such awful news.

'Can I keep him with us?' Holding his breath, he knew he might be killed by these enemy soldiers before he had chance to get back to the bunker, full of rats and other awful critters.

'I would have fought for him, but you look after him. And let's get this bloody war finished before that killer gas gets chance to be used on us. My wife and kids would love him, but you look like you need him more. Good luck, and let's try and remember what we're supposed to be doing eh?' The German laughed, and shook Issac's hand.

Other men did the same – a moment of humanity among the fighting that would stick with him forever. His eyes filled with tears. Nobody wanted this war. All the men wanted were to be home with loved ones, curled up in their arms. Making love to their women and hugging their children. Issac wanted to marry Molly, and tell her how Jasper united the enemy on a cold dark night in France, even though he was a German shepherd. He was a loveable one at that and wouldn't stop licking his hand.

He hunkered down. Another night of mud, cold water around his ankles, yet comforted that the dog was safe, their mascot and pal. He drank his ration of weak tea and began to look forward to far away, in another land, another time when he could tell the woman of his dreams just how much she'd always meant to him. How he would hold her tight and never let her go.

The only thing keeping him going was asking Molly to marry him; more still, trying to stifle the regret that he hadn't asked her to be his wife before he signed up.

Jasper had found a dry patch on the next man's blanket. For now, life was that little bit better. The mascot was a sign. Issac had only one mission in his mind now… getting back to Molly. He pulled out his broken end of pencil and a scrap of paper to write and tell her about the new camp member. He'd leave the bit about the German's and the Brit's coming together, as the letters were all read and dissected, then censored.

He didn't want to get into trouble now he had his mascot to take home to his love. His dog would be the start of the family he could only dream of that he and she would have one day. For now, he began as he always did these days. Time was ticking by; surely there would be a ceasefire soon. Christmas was just around the corner. *My Dear Molly...*

***

The mere effort of getting out of bed and going to work was becoming harder each day. To make things worse there was a letter waiting for her on the mantelpiece when she got home half way through the following week. Normally the sight of a letter made her heart leap, news from Issac was always welcome, even if he was not feeling hundred percent, just to see his handwriting was a tonic. This wasn't one of those; it was the writing of someone not nearly as literate as him. She didn't recognise the handwriting, and it definitely wasn't her Issac's.

'There's a note on there for you.' aunt Violet was stating the obvious, as usual, and being inquisitive at the same time. She looked on, eagerly, but there was no chance of opening it here in front of her and Janey. Something gave her a bad feeling about the scrawl. There wasn't anything friendly about it and she wouldn't be a bit surprised if her aunt hadn't already steamed it open to have a peep.

She waited until after eating her sausage casserole. 'That was really delicious, thanks Aunt Violet.' She gave her a peck on the cheek and coaxed Janey towards the kitchen.

'Aw, do I have to. I'm studying for my exams; you said I had to concentrate on them and let nothing get in the way. No distractions, remember.'

Glad of the interruption from talk of the post, she chided her little sister. 'Hey, that's not to say we don't get to with the washing up when we've had a lovely meal cooked for us; less of your cheek milady.' Between them they made short work of the clearing up, and as she gathered the missive in her hand to take it to her room, she noticed there wasn't a stamp on the envelope. She had to look at it privately, it wasn't every day she had mail.

Aunt Violet looked under her lashes, as if she was only watching as an afterthought. 'Delivered by hand it was. Not long before you came actually. The morning post is always here early. Whoever dropped that off, must have come late, after work maybe. Don't tell me you've got an admirer. Would be a shame, because it's plain as the nose on your face you're carrying a candle for Issac.' Violet sat back with that look on her face, as if she knew exactly what was raging through her mind.

Molly left the room. Lifting her skirt, she ran up the stairs two at a time and escaped to the privacy of her bedroom. Ripping open the envelope her heart began to beat. There weren't many lines and the words were few.

I have seen what happened. And I think your fancy man and his lot might be interested to know what you get up to while he's away risking his life!!!!

She dropped the sheet of tatty paper, looking like a piece ripped out of any old notebook. Whoever wrote this did it in a hurry. No care to write properly or on decent paper. Her heart pounded; her mouth went dry immediately. Nobody saw what happened, who could have heard about it? She began reliving the whole sordid experience all over again. Her skin crawled, she put her hand over her mouth to stop herself from retching – trembling all over, she felt physically sick. Just when she thought she'd got over the situation; talked it through and put the ordeal behind her; now this!

She scrunched the disgusting accusations into a tiny ball and chucked it right behind her bed. That's all she could think of to do with it. How could she tell anyone without going over the whole damn thing again? She didn't sleep a wink that night. Tossing and waking up shaking like a jellyfish. She woke breathless knowing it was time to get this sorted. A handkerchief over her mouth helped block out sobs that threatened to keep her family awake.

Breakfast next morning was tense, after aunt Violet asked who was writing to her. She expected her to ask, and her only reply she could think of was… 'Only a note, it's just a friend.'

'Oh, and what did they want then?' She was nosey but the last thing she wanted was for her to worry.

'Oh, some ramble they're planning we'll make a day of it - get some fresh air, keep busy and talk politics, state of the country, boring stuff like that. It's around Cannock Chase, and that's where Issac did his training, did I tell you?'

'No, you didn't, but I know that's where they do manoeuvres and such like. So will you go?'

'Yes, I think so. I need to talk to others my own age, swap our thoughts about the future; you know the kind of thing?' She hated lying but to tell her or show her the contents of the disgusting letter would be much too much for her to have to explain and what good would it do for all that to be out in the open.

This was her problem, and other than Sister Margareta at church, nobody else knew. Only now someone else did. She had to find out who it was and talk to them, make them realise she was assaulted before this came all out in the open. She wasn't prepared for that to happen, and lose everything she'd set her heart on for a very long time.

***

Getting through the days at work now became harder. She watched everyone, suspecting them all. Even Francesca gave her a sideways glance and she wondered if she'd heard something. Were they all gossiping? This was getting out of hand. She had to do something. After work that night, she made excuses to her aunt that she felt a bit queasy and needed some fresh air. You sure you ain't coming down with some funny bug our wench? You've been looking pale for a while now. You can't be pregnant, as the man you're in love with isn't around. Don't think I don't know.' She drew in a sharp breath.

'I have to get out, don't worry about me, and no, how would I be pregnant without a boyfriend, honestly, what are you thinking?' Without waiting for another word, she slammed the door behind her and hurried down the path and out on to the main road. She picked up her skirt hem and ran to the end of the street, and out onto the main road, going as fast as her feet would take her. She kept on going, and found herself headed to the house of Issac's parents. What she was going to say there she hadn't a clue, but she needed to get this sorted; speak out before someone else did and ruined her reputation, and any chance of a relationship with the man she loved, and who she hoped loved her back.

It was getting late, they would be ready for bed, and aunt Violet and Janey would be worrying about her. She about turned and followed her footsteps back home, taking time to think things over. Tomorrow, she would ask them if she could take the car out, after opening up and leaving Francesca in charge. She had to start sometime, and the way she felt now, Molly wasn't sure she could carry on anymore.

Glad they'd both gone to bed when she got in, Molly brewed herself a cup of cocoa, and sat watching the flames dying low in the fire. When would things ever be normal again? And how long did she have to wait to feel the warmth of Issac's arms wrapped around her once more like he'd always done, since as long as she could remember? The way he kissed her neck was such a distant memory, yet when she closed her eyes it felt like he was standing beside her.

'How can I get by without you, my love?' She whispered into the night, before she turned out the oil lamp which stood on the round table in the middle of the room. Taking herself up the wooden stairs, she drowned her sorrows with another gulp of her cocoa.

Chapter 10

The Staffordshire countryside was looking mellow as the summer turned to autumn. Francesca had been only too happy to keep an eye on things at Paradise Lane, and driving along on her own was the most liberating feeling for Molly. She'd told Issac's family she was going to the wholesale fabric centre in Birmingham. When she pulled up on the rough car park at the bottom end of Cannock Chase, she knew in her heart, she'd chickened out.

She'd asked if it was alright for a run in the car, and told them she really wanted to get out and about on her own. *It was the only way to learn*, she'd heard herself saying. They were perfectly understanding, helping her take off the tarpaulin and checking while she did a few rounds of the driveway. When she made her way steadily out of the grounds, praying she didn't crash before she got out of sight, it was as if she'd been set free!

Now she was sitting where Issac had told her, in his letters, he practiced for war duty. The encampments were still there, empty now of men.

She bought ice cream and sat in the car enjoying her cone, watching other walkers and trying to imagine him with his comrades, learning how to attack and stop the enemy. Men too young to be sent off to fight; besides, Issac wasn't the fighting type, any more than the other hundreds of men from Bloxwich and Walsall were.

Part of her wanted to feel proud of him, yet he was a gentle man as far as she'd known him. Not designed to kill. He wouldn't harm a fly, let alone an oncoming attack of German soldiers. She hadn't heard from him for a while. Often, she lay in bed wondering if he was still alive. It was hard to talk to anyone about him, as they'd kept their private life together just that.

How could she tell her worries to aunt Violet, when she was still grieving quietly over her missing husband? She could talk all day about how he might come home, 'one of these days, just you wait and see. He could walk in through that front door and say, there didn't I tell you I'd never leave you?' But somewhere deep down, they all knew he wouldn't.

Maybe that would be her, in a year from now; hearing nothing and refusing to believe her love would never return.

Pulling on her reserves, she wrapped her woolly scarf around her neck and jumped out of the motor. She needed to burn off some energy - get rid of this maudlin feeling that threatened to swamp her thoughts.

Climbing the nearest hill to get a view on the surrounding area, she immediately felt connected. She visualised Issac and his colleagues, running through the white and purple heather, and fading bracken; full of vigour and patriotism.

She'd read in the newspaper, about Rupert Brooke, the Rugby poet. What a waste of life and talent that was. Edith Cavell, the Nurse from Norfolk was helping wounded soldiers get over the border to home. She'd been arrested was the latest news, accused of being a spy. Please God, if Issac gets wounded, let it be Edith's team who looks after him and not someone awful.

Rupert Brooke wrote his poem, telling how; if he died abroad, a corner of a foreign land would be forever England. As if he knew his own destiny. He was laid to rest in an olive grove, just as he predicted.

The newspaper reported, Winston Churchill, first lord of the admiralty gave a speech and read out his poem, If I should die think this of me… She shivered and pulled her coat tighter around her body as she walked on, not wanting to think about death and war Hero's. What was the point of being a dead hero? She wanted him home, taking care of the business alongside her. Even if he wasn't as strong as before, and full of beans, at least back, so they could talk, like he'd mentioned in his letters.

She turned her head to the sky and shouted into the open air – 'Damn you, stupid war! And while I'm at it, go to hell you old crones dishing out white feathers to working men who are needed here. I hope you all drop dead! You wouldn't go, would you?'

Never for the life of her would she find it right. Her sobs racked through her body as she walked across the open heather covered pathways, not seeing anything, only tasting salty tears, as they streamed down her face. She walked and kept on walking until her legs ached and she knew it was time to go home. She hadn't seen the man and his dog nearby, peering at her as if she was a total maniac…

'Are you alright dear? Well, I can see you're not but anything I can do to help?' He looked so full of concern; her tears fell all the more.

'It's alright, just missing someone, you know how it is?' She wondered if been in the last war, or knew someone in this one. He looked as if he understood.

'Oh, trust me I know. Our daughter is a nurse, out in Belgium. We don't hear from her, she told us it's too dangerous to write. Now some say no news is good news, but for me, well…' He stroked the dog's velvety ears, as it put a paw on his knees to reminding him she was there. 'You know don't you, all about our Julie, doing her good work out there; we all miss her don't we?' The dog let out a whine, and then ran to retrieve the ball he'd thrown across the heathland of the Chase.

'I'm sorry to hear – you know, that you don't hear. I do, he writes, but not nearly enough, so it's a worry, hard to carry on sometimes.'

She stifled a sob, and reached in her pocket for her hanky. How could talking to a stranger about her feelings be normal? Then again, nothing at the moment was how it should be and she wouldn't see him again, so it felt alright speaking openly.

'Still, we can keep hoping and praying every day.' Pulling herself out of the doldrums, she lifted her head and smiled. 'That's what we have to do isn't it?' Sounding more convincing than she felt, she owed it to the elderly gent to lift his spirits.

'Hope you get news soon, even if it's – Y'know, from someone else.' They parted ways after reassuring one another that hope and keeping a positive frame of mind was the best way forward. He threw the ball again and the bundle of tan fur ran off, not a care in the world, apart from getting the ball back to its master.

***

All the crying and walking in the world couldn't ease the pain inside. Molly was glad she hadn't blurted out too much personal stuff with a complete stranger; but she needed to talk things through with someone and sooner the better before she did something stupid that she might regret forever.

With a heavy heart she turned and made her way back through the long grass and shrubbery to the car.; now to get it back to Oak Tree Grange in one piece; all thoughts of Birmingham and the rag market completely gone from her mind.

***

It was over a cup of tea with Francesca, she couldn't keep it to herself any longer. In between sips, she blurted out. 'I've been assaulted, abused, groped, oh my god, handled.' She gulped down some more tea to help the words come out. 'Like, in a way I didn't ask for.' A heap of worry left her shoulders, for the second time recently.

Francesca sat as still as a statue, hardly moving, eyes wide and her mouth drooped open.

'Well, are you catching flies, or what? Don't say nothing; for Christ's sake. Call me a tease; tell me I was leading him on, say anything but silence… that's worse than calling me a dirty slag who asked for it. Please speak to me. I can't bear it.' She held her head in her hands and sobbed.

'I spoke to his parents.' Blowing her nose, she looked across at her friend. 'There's money gone missing from work, they wanted to know more. It was him; I know it. Only I had to say he was a bully, abusive, but I didn't go into the sordid, gory detail. They would have been disgusted. And who's to say they wouldn't think it was me who led him on.' Molly sniffed. 'I didn't, not for one minute; didn't even smile, wiggle me bum or nothing.'

'Hey, love. Come here.' Did he actually, you know, do the full intimate business?' Francesca put a reassuring arm around her shoulder. 'It's not your fault he's a dirty bastard… only that you'll need to know if he's put you in the family way. My old man only had to look at me and I was up the duff.' She gave her a squeeze. 'You'll need to see a doctor love.'

'He tried to, do the full thing, only I put my knee up his privates. That's when he grabbed at my hair, and made me push his horrible cock in me mouth.' She shuddered. 'It keeps coming back to mind, even though it kills me to think of it. I hope he's got a mark where I bit down hard on it. No, absolutely no chance he got me in the club. More likely he's got a nasty little rash.'

Francesca covered her mouth yet couldn't help laugh. 'Listen, he'll get his come-uppance, and if he doesn't, then he'll go on doing the same to others. Though I doubt he'd try it again with you. Imagine if it was our Nadine, or your Janey.' Now it was Francesca's turn to shudder.

'We'll get you through this, and if needs be, you can speak up, to his parents. I'll be with you every step of the way. They'll be on your side. I bet they think he just smacked yer backside or summat like that.'

Molly chewed on her bottom lip, and then shook her head. 'I'm not sure about that; the way they looked at me already, I don't think I can go into any more details. I don't want Issac to find out about this. He'd never speak to me again.'

How long before everyone found out? Nothing was kept secret around Paradise Lane for long. It would be the talk of the Post Office queue sooner or later.

'Keep this to yourself, Fran, at least for now, please, eh? The delivery man hasn't been here since that day, and now there'll be either you, or Issac's parents around. I don't think it's fair to keep adding to the worry they already have. I value your thoughts, and deep down I know you're right, I'm just scared of how they'll see me. That's all.' She smiled at her best friend who always made things seem not so bad.

'Ey, Molly, love… What do you take me for?' She was up and by her side in seconds, arms round her shoulders, giving the hug they both needed. 'It's awful; of course I won't tell anyone. Does your aunt Violet know?'

Her face, so full of concern was too much for Molly to handle. She sobbed on her friend's shoulder relieved to share the unforgettable experience before shaking her head.

'You must be bloody joking, I'd feel dirty – it's hard to get the image of him out of my head. I'd have gone round the bend if I couldn't talk to you. I mean, like earlier today. I took Issac's jalopy out, meaning to get to Birmingham for fabrics and accessories, and ended up on Cannock Chase of all places. It was somewhere Issac's been, for his training. Walking where he and his mates were – I needed to feel close to him.' She was rambling, and then sniffed then looked gingerly at her friend.

'Molly love, I didn't realise, but it all adds up, how sad you were at the station when they left; the effort you're putting in at the business. You love him, don't you?' She held her close, and rocked her back and forth. Sharing their sorrow made them both feel better.

'Have you thought of going to the police, telling someone in authority?' She genuinely meant it, though deep down they both knew how ridiculous the idea was.

'I've spoken to one of the nun's, at church. She's been a help, listening, you know, like you. But really, do we stand a chance of being believed?' On top of it all, there was a blackmail letter, but that wasn't for anyone else to know about. She really had to keep quiet on that – it was beyond serious.

'Trouble is, with all that on my mind, it's letting the business slide. We need to press on with getting a stall on Walsall market. I asked around, there's a bit of a wait, that's for a permanent pitch, or we can turn up as casuals, then wait and see if there's a vacant stall for us.'

'We've got it organised… me and Bobby. I often go and get the last cuts of meat off the wagon. Like scrag of mutton, or belly pork, when there's nothing much else left. They give you a bag of scrag for a shilling. Does us the week, and the veggies that drop on the floor, me ma's a champion at knocking them off the stall then kicking em along for the lads to pick up.' She hung her head. 'Oh, lord, I hope you don't think that's stealing, it's only an onion or a turnip for the stew. And usually, we get caught and pay a few coppers anyways.'

Molly conveniently ignored her friend's unique way of gathering the weekly groceries, and wanted to know more about the stall on Walsall market. 'You've organised all that, for us?' The news of having their own place on a market to sell a range of hats drove the blues away for the time being. 'Well, let's get planning what we can take and where we can get a tarpaulin from.'

'Welcome to my world…' Francesca winked. 'Beg steal and borrow.' She tapped the side of her nose. 'I know a chap who fixes motorcycles, lives up Brook Street. He helped my hubby get a few quid when he gave him a hand with some dirty work. He told my Lionel, if ever he wanted to borrow tools or such, let him know. I'll pay him a visit tomorrow and see what he's got in the way of a market sheet. Tarpaulin, consider it covered. Or the stall will be. Leave it with me.'

Chapter 11

'Woah, girl steady down now – here we are then.'

The morning sound of hooves clip clipping on the yard gave Molly a reassurance she'd lacked before she'd spoken to Issac's family. Hearing Stanley at the reigns, shouting his orders made her smile. He wasn't such a savage old stick as she'd first thought he was. Now she peeked round the net curtain to watch him helping Doris as she climbed down from the trap that had transported them both across town to Paradise Lane.

'Good morning!' He shouted and waved his hand over to a couple of workers in the yard. They'd been fetching extra water for the steam room, sweeping the yard and tending to the work horse, Dolly. Now he'd made himself comfortable in the office. Doris filled the copper kettle, busying herself, stoking the fire, and making tea.

'Let's see what's on the agenda today then.' He pulled the day book towards him, checking on the orders needing completion.

'It's all in hand, Stanley. And Francesca's on to the extra stock we're making for the market this week. We're hoping to stand on Walsall.'

'Oh aye, and have you got a place to pitch up?' The frown across his brow getting a bit deeper than it usually was. He looked slightly worried.

'Bobby's sorting that for us, he's been out on the market in the evenings, helping them pack up away and such, so he's put in a word for us. According to the Toby, money collector, if we go and get in the queue, then there'll be a spot for us, but we have to get there early. We're aiming for this Saturday. Francesca's on the job.'

'And how much is it to have a stall, does she know?'

'It's a shilling, until you're a regular, then it's a bit less. I've got a cousin; she does the market in Dudley. Uncle Tom's daughter, Isabella, 'I'm planning to go and see her; she sells curtain material, and dress making fabrics, as well as remnants and scraps. It's because of her, I got the job here. She's always been interested in different materials, same as our mom.'

'We used to sew together, making our own clothes – I talked about that during a visit here, from my newspaper job, which turned into Issac knowing I'd be interested in the hat making. And he was right. Anyway, I'm drifting, if I pop along to see her. Next Thursday is market day there, but they have traders' other days as well. She'll help with details on rent prices for us and then we'll know how much we have to pay, and other little bits of useful information. I'll take a note book with me and jot down any other questions you'd like me to ask her; see what she comes up with.'

'Sounds like you have it all under control then, Molly love.' Doris patted her husband's shoulder, sending a warm smile in her direction. 'I'm off to see who wants tea before I have a pep talk with the workers to let them know we're going to be here more often. Well, me at least…' she knew Stanley would rather be out on the road, making business deals, buying and selling the goods and chatting to folk, rather than being stuck in the heart of the cottage industry world of hatting.

Stanley's eyes followed Doris as she bustled through the door, and off up the corridor. He smiled. 'She'll be like a mother hen, clucking around her chicks now.' He raised his eyes to the ceiling. 'Misses having the family home, you see.' He took the brandy bottle out of the desk, and poured himself a large one.

***

The evening was dark, cold and miserable and didn't do anything to lift Molly's mood as she made her way home. The roaring fire was

109

a great welcome as she pulled up a chair and rubbed her hands to get warm in front of the glowing coals in aunt Violet's front room. Janey was sitting nearby, head in a book. She only glanced up when her big sister entered, a smile and nod was all she could manage. Aunt Violet was more talkative.

'How's yer day gone then, love?' Tilting her head, she was all ears.

'Brilliant, had Issac's folks in – they're getting a grip on things – lets me off the hook a bit you might say.' She pulled a face.

'And…' Violet put a tongue in her cheek. 'Don't tell me, they're interfering with you being in control, just a bit.

Molly burst out laughing; even Janey took her head out from her reading for a moment.

'That'll be a yes, then.' Satisfied, she reached for her knitting and sat back with a look of smugness on her face. 'I've got a mutton stew warming on the hob, that'll make it better, you'll see. These things come to try us, and you know what they say… Anything the lord meant for us, he won't let it go by us. You don't despise them trying to help though?' Needles clicked ten to the dozen; Violet gave her a look.

'Not really, they're good people, you have a point though.' She flapped her hand on the side of the tapestry chair. 'I'm just feeling a bit inadequate, at the moment, if you must know.'

'Oh, love, let them do what they have to. You can always step back, go and help the workers, they'll need you to muck in with them if you get more orders coming in. What with the market idea and all…'

'Oh, that reminds me. Do you know if your Tom's Isabella is still doing Dudley market on Thursday's? Only, the gaffer, Issac's dad was asking about the price of having a stall and things. I had an idea to go and see her, get some general info on how to get on with being a stall-holder.'

Violet nodded, then put her knitting to one side and bustled around the scullery getting a chunk of crusty bread on the table for Molly - then dishing up a bowl of hot mutton stew keeping warm on the stove, in between telling her; 'Yes, Isabella always stands on Dudley,' and she'd heard through her older brother Tom that she'd been doing a roaring trade lately, with everyone creating their own clothes, keeping kids in smocks and trousers, as well as getting black out curtains ready, to prevent drawing attention to the homes along the rows.

'She's looking to get help sewing work clothes and dungarees for the factory workers. I'm sure she'd put a word in towards getting you get a stall on there, if you asked her.'

'Oh, I need to talk to her about my home sewing work then.' Janey was all ears, and they both agreed, it was a way forward for the younger member of the family.

'I wasn't thinking of a stall there just yet, but you could be right.'

'Usually that's the case.' Violet smiled, and gave her a wink, reminding Molly how young and vibrant her aunt still was. To be left on her own, responsible for two grown up girls to feed and care for, was hardly fair. Not once had she moaned, apart from that, she always wore a smile and her trademark red lipstick, whatever the weather. She reminded herself to take a leaf from Violet's book; remember and make more effort to be like her resourceful aunt.

'I don't know how you do it.' She dipped bread in the broth and instantly felt warm and comforted inside; a true feeling of home. 'I mean though, delicious food, a warm cosy fire; you being here, for us – not having to go out to work and leave Janey and me, having to make our own tea, like plenty of doorstep kids do. We're lucky… we could have been…' She was cut off mid-sentence.

'I won't hear another word. Let me tell you, it's a pleasure to have you here, and you're growing up. Who knows what'll happen when he' – she nodded her head sideways, 'You know, comes home from the - front line. You might settle down, who knows.' She'd shushed her up and then more or less told her she might move out if and when Issac came back.

She honestly hadn't thought that far ahead. Was aunt Violet getting tired of keeping them? Fair to say, she gave up half her wages for housekeeping, then put the other half into saving or often she bought things Janey needed, like underwear, shoes or boots in the winter, and hair ribbons. It always baffled her how she managed, maybe now was the time to ask the inevitable.

'I'll start giving you a bit more; our nest egg can wait now there's a war on. It was for mine and Janey's future.' Digging into her stew, she was glad of the tasty meal; she listened to her aunt's reply as she mopped up the remains in the bottom of her bowl.

'I wasn't suggesting that, and you paid the last coal bill so let's have no more mention of money. You keep saving what you can, and I'll keep begging and borrowing and scrounging where I can. Who knows, we might be respectable one day.'

'We already are!' Molly realised she'd snapped a bit more than she intended to. Talk of not being respectable made her hair curl. With no idea who could have penned that note – it was now time to get her thinking head on, and turn detective. After her evening wash, she'd study that writing and somehow find out if it was anyone from her workplace. It looked that way, but she just couldn't see any of her co-workers being that spiteful. Time would tell, and for now, she wanted to find out how Janey's day had been.

'Fancy a game of patience, our Janey, or are you going to have your head in that book all night?'

Blinking, her younger sister, looked up. 'What? Oh, a game of cards, alright, you're on; are you playing aunt Violet?' Janey pushed her book to one side, and pulled up a chair at the table.

'Go on then, as long as it's Gin Rummy yer playing. I'll get some pennies out of my stash, we'll bet for a penny a game.' Her laughter filled the front parlour and for that moment, all was well with their world.

Chapter 12

Rushing to get ready for work, Molly had retrieved the spiteful note from down the back of her bed where she'd tossed it that fateful day it arrived. Smoothing the wrinkled piece of paper, she studied it for a few minutes before folding it and putting it deep in the pocket of her pinafore dress. She had a plan; to find out who the writer of this hate mail was.

As far as she knew, half of the workers at the hat business didn't read nor write. Something she intended to help them with. She had a passion for reading herself, that's why it was so important for her that Janey learned her words, sentences and how to understand grammar and how to construct a sentence.

Her father had shown them his volumes of encyclopaedias. He had a routine of going through them, with her after school and at weekends. They had come with them to aunt Violet's bookcase in the back room where the piano stood and contained all things worldly; from penguins to Kings and Queens of bygone centuries. The sisters had no excuse for not being educated after studying those.

She only had time for a quick cup of tea, and left in a hurry, just in time to catch the early morning tram at the end of Victoria Row.

No Francesca today; she'd be along later. Glad of the moment to prepare her plan of action in finding the anonymous letter writer, she went over the ideas in her mind. She handed tuppence to the conductress, and jumped up when the Pelsall stop came into view. The early morning staff was already busy, tending to Dolly, leading her over to the field opposite for her morning exercise. Another getting the gallons of water needed ready for the busy day, into the steam room. She loved the sound of the works bursting into action. Hissing, and clattering, the chatter and gossip from what they'd heard in the pub the night before. Who was sleeping with whom, and which drunken bum beat his wife. Often a black eye was hidden with powder, yet she didn't see that too much, thank goodness.

Today, she got herself into the thick of the business end of the works.

'Listen up, team…' She tapped her teaspoon from her early cup of tea on the side of the hat block where they steamed felt that shaped the hats. 'Can I have your attention all?' She waited while all workers from different departments were gathered. 'I know you're the early shift, and I'll be asking everyone. Thing is, we're going on the market this Saturday, casual like. Bobby and Francesca will get everything ready before then. What I'd like is, for any other ideas you might have, to grow the business, can you put it down here for me.'

She placed her notebook on the bench nearby, and patted it, leaving a pencil to one side. Every lunch time, they gathered round and shared a sandwich, meat pie or cold faggots and mushy peas. Some took turns to bring a fruit loaf in to share out, or bread pudding, and they brewed up a giant-sized pot of tea.

'There's no hurry, only if you have a brilliant idea, I want to know what it is.' Met with blank looks, she smiled. 'Don't worry if you have a job putting it down. Tell Francesca when she gets here; she'll help you write it down.' Satisfied, Molly returned to her office in the kitchen and made notes of her first thoughts towards getting to the bottom of who the letter writer could be.

Francesca arrived half an hour later. Molly told her she was looking for more ideas on how to improve sales at the business. Like open a shop front on the road side of the cottage industry, where folks could walk in and try on hats. 'I've left a notebook and pens for the workers to jot down ideas.

'Well, we're making a start with the market idea, aren't we?' Francesca's frown told Molly she wasn't impressed, and they were doing all they could to help. 'You do know half them workers can't read nor write for a start?'

'Look, I'm not trying to rub people up the wrong way.' Her grand plan wasn't going the way she wanted it to. The last thing she wanted was to alienate her new friend.

'You'd be better just letting everyone choose a free hat, for themselves, or a friend. Francesca looked irritated, and she herself had come up with plenty of ideas. 'I like the idea of making a shop at the front of the place though. If we opened it up, and you got a big window put in. They have to see what's on offer before they'd be tempted to walk in, don't you think? Otherwise, it's just like a warehouse.'

'How come you have all the brainwave creative ideas?' Molly chided herself for toying with the idea that any of her trusted workers would push a deluded note through her door. Most of them didn't even know where she lived. This was getting out of hand. Now she was pushing her overworked pal to do above and beyond what she needed.

'Listen, Fran… I'm sick with worry about Issac. His parents are pointing out where I'm going wrong; it's all getting on top of me a bit. And I know you must feel the same with your hubby away all the time, and there's no mention of them coming on leave is there? I bet the kids miss him as well.'

'They do.' Francesca bit on her lower lip, face ready to crumple, looking as if she would burst into tears any second. 'I try not to think about my Lionel if I'm honest. That sounds bad; I think about him of course. Miss his arms around me and the – you know, the other.' She gave a watery smile.

'Sit down; I'll get the kettle on. Can you go in the workshops while I brew us a cuppa and tell them you've had the free hat idea, one for everybody, they can choose; and that's enough ideas for now. They would get a free hat if they talked about the business to everyone they know. It'll give them something to smile about.'

'I wouldn't worry too much, they're happy enough when they leave here, I saw Rita arm in arm with Doug last night. They were off to the flicks, and from the way he had his hands all over her I daresay they didn't see much of the film.' Laughing together, Molly was reminded how dull her own life had become without Issac in it.

'I'll pop along one of the days, and have a chat with our Isabella, can you hold the fort?' She had full faith in Francesca, and they had to get out and find a way of selling the stock that was piling up in the business.

'I'll be fine, just leave the biscuit tin out.' She turned and walked towards the main production area of the business, to let them all know they were doing a great job, and they could forget everything about writing in the book.

Chapter 13

The tram across to Dudley didn't take long. She was soon taking the brisk walk to the open-air market where her cousin stood every Thursday, whatever the weather. They were a family brought up to know that if you wanted good things in life, like a meal on the table, and bills paid. Then working hard was the only way.

Molly had always been a dreamer, but she knew now, dreams were only helped along by a day's hard graft. Her dad's words stuck in her mind. Other than marrying a prince like in the fairy tales she and Janey read when they were younger. Their cousin was made of the same granite stuff as she and Janey. She turned down the first aisle, and there on the corner spot, she heard her before she saw her.

'Come on now ladies, you know this is quality fabric. Get your cloth here, feel the quality, trust in the best.' The slight figure of Isabella turned to drink from her tartan flask. Interested to see how the wandering public drew near as she cried her encouraging banter, same as her mom and dad before she'd taken over the stall.

Molly drew her jacket up around her neck, and pulled her scarf tight round, over her ears. She didn't want to interrupt a sale, so for a few moments, she stood aside and let her cousin cut and wrap the wonderful paisley print fabric she was selling to the lady with the rattan basket.

She could imagine Issac's mom would be a customer here, from how richly furnished her home was. Now she was free. 'Hey, Isabella…' She greeted her cousin with a brief hug and peck on the cheek. They weren't overly gushy with each other. Both had grown up much too tomboyish for that.

'Hey, our Molly…it's great to see you. What're you doing round here? I thought you'd be out delivering those hats, or piling up the orders for overseas, with all the men in Europe and other exotic places.' She shook her head. 'Hark at me, don't take any notice. They're a brave lot aren't they? I'd rather be here on the stall than anywhere else to be honest.'

'That's what I've come to see you about, have you've got time for a chat?' Molly wriggled her backside onto the small stool Isabella pushed towards her.

'Oh, plenty of time, but I'll have to carry on serving in-between; I need the dosh, not cuz I'm ignoring you cuz.' The wicked glint in her eye told Molly that she was doing well here, no matter how she protested to need every penny. Working hard was how she'd got on so well.

'How long have you been on the stall now?' Molly wished she'd kept in touch, a bit more than the usual birthdays and Christmas's.

'Well, dad still comes if it's going to be busy, like, and mom watches the stall if I have to go and get stock, but it's mostly me now. Only a few years, yet it's as if I've been here all my life. Well, I have when you think of how we'd be here with dad when we were nippers. Do you remember when we used to hide under the stall and tickle the rows of legs, making the customers shriek out…?'

Of course, Molly had spent lots of her childhood on the market, and had some fun… 'I know we were always begging after a threepenny bit for some aniseed balls, or peppermints. And remember them sugar coated fruit flavoured fishes?'

'Oh, don't remind me… my teeth with them aniseed balls. They were never the same after that.' She frowned as they recalled the little bullet sized sweeties that were so hard they didn't disappear for hours after they'd started sucking them.

'I'm thinking of getting a stall, for the hats.' Molly hoped her cousin didn't think she'd only paid a visit because she was going through hard times.

'Oh, blimey, that's a great idea. What took you so long to come back on the markets? Wouldn't have thought you'd come over here though. What happened to all the contacts you had with shops you were supplying? Hat buyers like to browse, don't they? Try on, and imagine what they'd wear them with, look in the mirror and strut their stuff a bit. Not that it's a bad idea our Molly. It's Bostin! Chance to bring hats your hats directly out to the people.'

'Glad you think so.' Molly beamed, knowing her cousin was a kind hearted soul and would back her up all the way. 'I'm running with the idea of a retail shop on the premises as well, but that's further down the line, when Issac comes back.'

'How's he getting on? Didn't think he was the forces type, he lived for the business, or he did last time we spoke.'

'He was doing alright last time I heard, though it's hard to know whether they're just telling us what we want to hear, rather than the real war news. Still, I'm doing the best I can.' She took a deep breath, and then knew she couldn't fool her cousin. They knew each other too well, even though they didn't see each other day to day. She came straight to the point.

'I've been undercut. Cheaper hats, and they look crass, but they used to buy from me, big orders as well. Now it's gone more like a dog fight among the retail shops. It started with one, cancelling mid order, when we were half way through making them. Now others are following suit. Apart from the abroad trade, that's going well. But the classic shops are cutting back. It's because I'm a woman. They always dealt with Issac. He's off to fighting, so I to have a fight back of my own.'

She took a breath, and pulled her jacket closer against the cold wind that blew across the market square. 'I wasn't thinking of standing on here. We're looking at Walsall, or Bloxwich that has a green near the church, but not officially a market; its barrow boys touting for work. I don't fancy going round with Dolly and the cart shouting. They'd think I was a rag and bone woman.' Molly tutted and raised her eyes skywards. 'Probably throw their old hats on there.'

Isabella laughed hard. 'You have to shout on the market our Molly, love. You'll have to learn fast. And I do a fair trade in rags, which have to be collected from a street hustle. Speaking of which, hold yer hands over yer ears. I need to do a shout out.' She gave her a second before hollering across the row with all her breath she could muster.

'Come on now ladies, get your fine quality fabric; nothing like it anywhere around. Make your home fit for a king. Come along now. Feel it before you buy… Come and get it here, ribbons and rags fill yer bags, don't miss out now, all gorra go.' She reached for her flask of broth, offering Molly a sip.

'No, you need it to keep warm and in good voice. I can get some chips off the wagon later.'

'There's a lady in the terrace, over there.' Isabella pointed to the dingy row of houses, where a woman in an overall, busied herself, parcels in hand visiting another stall. 'Go and ask Iris, she'll do yer a penne'th of chips if you ask her. I'll have some if you're paying as well.' She winked.

'Well, for the advice, how can I refuse?' Molly made off in the direction of Iris and ordered two penny bags of chips, and when Iris asked if she wanted a couple of tin mugs of Rosie-Lee, to go with the chips, she agreed.

Happy to spend a bit more time with her cousin, Molly knew she'd have a wealth of information to take back to Paradise Lane. The chips were surprisingly good. Cooked well, hot and crispy, but the tea was more of a treacle colour, but warming, so they both washed the chips down with the strong taste of Rosie Lee. Molly took the mugs back when they'd finished.

'So, you're thinking of standing on Walsall, then?' Isabella scraped scratchings from the bottom of the chip bag.

'All being well, they'll go as casual first, Bobby and Francesca, then after a week or so, hopefully get a permanent spot.'

Isabella nodded. 'That's how it works. We pay a shilling here, but you have to start early, and there's always a late rush; punters looking to root out a bargain, mostly it's the food stalls they head for. My day can start any time after seven o'clock, and ends late afternoon.'

That's when Molly noticed how tired her cousin looked. 'It's a long day, but the rest of the week, we sell from the back yard. Weather permitting. It all goes in the van, and then it gets unloaded at home, and piled back up in the old stable. It's better than when we used the horse and cart; it doesn't stop our dad moaning about the cost of running the van though.'

'I've got a good team, and his parents are back involved now.' Molly couldn't hide the disappointment in her voice.

'Oh; how come?' Isabella didn't miss a trick. She waited… 'Spill the beans.'

'I had to go and ask them for help really.' Tutting and shaking her head, Molly felt herself colouring up. 'There was an incident; I got roughed up a bit.' She didn't want to elaborate, as it might get back to aunt Violet. 'Since then, there's some kind of vendetta, that's what I feel anyway. But me and the team aren't going to take it sitting down.' Although she was sitting down, Molly banged her fist on the wooden slats of the market stall.

'We will overcome!'

'How d'you mean, roughed up?' Isabella squinted, studying her cousin, hands on her hips legs apart, looking ready for battle.

'Sexual assault, grabbing where he shouldn't have, trying to do things he ought not to, you get the picture?'

'Oh, do I ever…' Isabella shook her head, and pursed her lips in distaste. 'It's common place around here.' She folded her arms across her chest and looked angry on Molly's behalf. 'They expect us to go along with it, but we have to let them know, we will not stand there and take it anymore. It's not the dark ages; it's a new century for god's sake.'

She looked angry. 'You'll soon toughen up. We have to if we're going to survive in a man's world.' Isabella looked as if she'd had similar happen to her.

'You didn't?' Molly gasped, blinking, shocked at how often these assaults on women were happening all around her.

'Oh yes, but I put a stop to it, before he could get away with it.' She gave a smile, and showed her long nails, poking out of her fingerless gloves, letting Molly know she'd put up a fight.

'Get yourself one of these if I was you.' She pulled a knife out of a secret pocket on the inside sleeve of her jacket. Showed Molly, and then tucked it back in place. 'Keeps them at bay, and I have a few good trader mates.' One look to the stall opposite, she shouted over. 'How're yer going on today then Baz, alright or what?'

'Ar, cock, not bad, am yow?' He'd been watching them all the time Molly had been talking.

'Bostin' kid.' She stuck thumbs up to him.

Molly smiled, and knew, their Isabella was quite capable of looking after herself, not only that, she had heavy muscles on hand if anything dodgy took place. She needed to step up on her self-defence, though she'd still rather have Issac there by her side.

Chapter 14

Back in Paradise Lane, Molly updated Francesca about her visit to the market and how she had a good feeling about their new venture.

When she'd finished relating all the happenings, her friend shot her a warning look. 'Glad it went well for you. There've been developments here as well, since you left.' Francesca bit on her lower lip. 'I'm sure everything is okay, only Clara, Issac's sister, called in. She's gone through there.' She nodded towards the workshops.

Molly stood upright. 'His sister! What's happened? Where is she and why didn't you tell me straight away?' She was babbling her words, running up the corridor, round to the work rooms searching for the woman who loved Issac even more than she did. Engrossed in conversation with the workers, Clara turned when Molly skidded to a halt in front of her, crashing into the hat boxes.

'Ey up, steady there, where's the fire?' As casual as her brother! Dropping in without any warning, no tears, perhaps a good sign.

'It's a great welcome, but honestly, Molly… You don't change.' She gave her a warm smile. Impulsive and excitable as ever; haven't seen you for ages.'

'I know; how're you getting on?' Desperate to hear news, she jigged from one foot to the other, shaking like a child at Christmas…

'I'm doing alright thanks, driving ambulances, and already working overtime, they need all the help they can get.'

Molly nodded, and couldn't help getting to the point. 'Any news from Issac?' not wanting to give away her feelings, she was only showing interest as he was her boss. She held herself so tense she couldn't speak properly.

'We're struggling along without him, though we've got plans to get more trade in, and get the hat company back, how it used to be. Have you spoken to your mom and dad?' She tried to keep her voice calm, but failed miserably.

'Yes, to the first question, and yes again…'

Now Molly was almost jumping up and down. 'Tell me, he's safe. Please say he's not hurt.'

'You need to sit down Molly. Can we have a private chat?' She turned to walk back towards the kitchen office where all official business took place.

Now she sounded serious. Without saying anymore, they both took strides to the comfort of the cosier part of the hat works. Francesca had a clipboard in her hand, and gave a polite nod to the girls, leaving them alone to chat; she shut the door behind her as she left.

Molly gulped. Her body stone cold. Clara could do the talking. She was afraid to ask.

Clara, hands clasped in her lap as she spoke quietly. 'He's got a dog…' She was perched on the edge of the desk, keeping a close eye on Molly's every move.

She tugged her hand knitted shawl closer around her shoulders. 'Oh, how did that happen? I mean, that's good, isn't it?'

'He's always loved dogs, but been so wrapped up forging ahead with business in these old grey walls, he'd forgotten how to live, and what he liked doing, hobbies and interests. Almost like being buried alive in the old place.' She screwed her nose up and looked around the walls where mould and damp was plain to see. 'No wonder he wanted to get away.'

'Was that it? He was trapped, couldn't wait, to get away. No wonder he was in a hurry to get the training done, on Cannock chase, and head off across the channel.' She felt a chill go down her cheeks like icicles had appeared there. His sister didn't waste her words, nor flower them up to save her feelings.

'No, he's not having a ball, he's been injured.' She rushed to Molly who by now was reeling from side to side. If Clara hadn't held her up, she'd have fallen off the chair.

'He's been burned, there's this new deadly weapon they've released, and he's been caught up with getting burned and gassed.'

'Oh! No!' Molly's sob rang across the room. She put her hand over her mouth after hearing the tragic news. 'Issac's been gassed! Oh my god, Clara. Will he live, is he still alive? Tell me everything Clara please, from the start. Your mom and dad, they must be in bits.' Her voice was coming out in rasps. 'They must be going through several kinds of hell. When did you find this out?'

'Tell you what; come round for tea, after work. It's only that he made it clear to let you know he was asking about you, and wishing he was back home. Old rascal asked us to come right here and tell you. Trust me to arrive when you weren't here.'

'How did you get to see him?' She wanted to know every minute detail, no matter how long it took. 'He was asking about me?' Her heart beat a little bit faster. 'He hasn't forgotten me then?'

'Listen, long story short; Someone I know… well, very fond of and know quite well, actually.' She twiddled with her hair, reminding Molly that she wasn't the only one with the love of her life in trouble. 'Anyway, he's called Reg, and he's driving the ambulances out there; which I'm hoping to do before long when they realise how much they need women to get out on the battlefield to help. Not only driving, but helping with tending to the wounded as well.'

She paused and patted Molly's hand. He's been relaying news back to us about how the Bloxwich and Walsall lads are getting on, and I told him to keep a look out for Issac.'

'I can tell you more tonight, when you come round to the house later, that way; you'll be able to hear news at the same time. Better than me keep on repeating myself, eh?' She attempted a laugh, but the two girls had stony faces. This war game was taking too many chances with ones they loved.

'That'll be good. Only I wish you'd tell me every single thing you know about my Issac, right now! I'll be ready to burst if I have to wait until later. Take no notice; it's been a horrible time, without him.' Molly leaned forward and sobbed into her hands, unable to keep her emotions in check.

'Oh, my word, Molly, love, I hadn't a clue… You mean; you're an item… you and Issac… You're together? I thought he was laying it on a bit thick, about letting you know he was alright, for now.'

She quickly pulled herself up and dabbed her handkerchief over her tear-stained eyes, then composed herself, as best she could. 'Ah, no, not actually, you've got it wrong.'

Clearing her throat, she looked at Clara and smiled. 'When I called him, *my* Issac, just then, well, in my mind he is, but there's nothing we've said, not properly, just yet.' She felt her face heating, and her legs were fast turning to jelly.

'It's that we were so comfortable together, maybe took the situation - relationship for granted. I did anyway; but he never told me he felt the same; maybe me getting grand ideas. I do like him a lot more than I knew though, even though I knew.' She gave a watery smile, that wasn't fooling anyone.

'I wouldn't say he didn't have feelings; from the way Reg told me he was talking. He mentioned your name more than once, as I said.

He made Reg promise I come straight round Paradise Lane and let you know - thoughts of you were keeping him going. Don't think he doesn't care. He's just, well…' She shrugged, and then smiled. 'He's Issac.'

Molly sniffed. 'He asked me to write. And he's sent me a few letters, but they don't come half as often as I'd like them to. I always write back, but it's as if we're both talking in codes, not able to put what we want to as the letters get read by senior officers. Kind of takes the shine off a bit, knowing you've got others reading them before we do.'

'Tell me about that. I'm the same, but we get to chat more personally with the ambulance drivers out there. I've had the parents on to me asking how he is. But hey, let's know he's still alive, and asking about you, and you, oh and you again. So, there's always hope, that's the message he's sending you, remember. Keep hoping and know he'll be back with you as soon as he can.'

'Let's meet later, at Oak Tree Grange, I'll make ham sandwiches and scrounge some overgrown lettuce from the kitchen garden so we can have some salad on the side.'

Molly relaxed and smiled at the thought of ham sandwiches with old lettuce, just like aunt Violet gave them. 'Oh, Clara, it's good to see you, and thanks for the news. You're so brave, going out there.' She threw her arms around the girl who she really hoped would be her sister-in-law one day.

'Woah, calm down, not exactly… I've been getting news from the battlefield; then from the hospital in Belgium, where our Issac was taken to. We're all doing the best we can to get peace restored, if ever that's possible.'

'Hope, you said. That's my watch word now. Keep hope in our hearts.' Molly would make sure when she went to the house of her Issac's parents later, she would get every scrap of news she could.

'See you later.' She waved her off, and took a moment to powder her nose and apply a slick of lipstick, before going to find Francesca and check on progress with hat production. Issac was still alive; and seeing as she hadn't heard from him for weeks; knowing that, was the best news ever.

***

Home time couldn't come quick enough. It was a task and a half, trying to convince aunt Violet she didn't want to eat, as she would be eating out at the Cartwright's house.

'Oh well, as long you're sure. I go to great lengths to find nutritional food for you and Janey remember. They'll probably have a dainty little cracker with a morsel of cheese, or some other fancy stuff you don't like. We eat traditional, basic food here, and there's always plenty for you to eat. I make sure of it. There aren't many households around Bloxwich as can say that.'

'If it weren't for Jack with his veggies and Danny the butcher, we'd be living on pigs' trotters with onion broth all week. Now why don't you eat some sausage and mash before you go?' Violet folded her arms across her chest and waited for her reply, giving a defiant glare while she stood waiting.

'I wasn't moaning about your food aunt Violet, it's the best. You know that. Only, Clara, you know, Issac's sister, she called in at work, as I told you. She's going to update me on all she knows. He's still alive; she's had news from an ambulance driver she knows, who took him to the hospital. There's hope, and he was asking about me, telling them to let me know, he's thinking of me.'

Molly glowed like the hundreds of lanterns lit up in jars, during the autumn lights of Walsall Arboretum.

Her enthusiasm wasn't lost on aunt Violet, nor Janey, who was looking at her now with much interest. 'So, are you going to marry him when he comes back then, our Molly?' Her eager face looked on in wonderment 'if you are, can I be a bridesmaid? And my friend Nadine would love to be one as well. The twins could be page boys…'

'Who mentioned that?' She looked from her sister, to Violet and then back again. They both had a knowing look, and waiting for her to say more. 'Hey, I'm going over there now, to get more news on how he's going on. I'll freshen up first.' As she walked past Janey, she gave her a side glance tutting… 'Bridesmaid's indeed.'

She got her jug of hot water and took it to her room, where she changed into a clean vest, under her blouse, and pulled her favourite warm knitted jumper over the top. The walk would be good to calm her nerves. The news could have been worse. She had to find out more, and the sooner she cleared away her wash things, the quicker she'd be gone.

Dashing down the stairs, she carefully carried her dirty wash water through the front room and out of the scullery to the back yard, where she emptied her water jug into the drain outside the kitchen door, and rinsed it under the tap. She placed her water jug upside down in the back kitchen, on the sink, to drain.

'Hey love…' Aunt Violet pulled at her arm as she leaned in to kiss goodbye. 'We're behind you all the way, and any news is good news by the way. 'I'm rooting for you.' The look on her aunt's face showed how much she cared.

Molly smiled. 'I know. I'm sorry if this brings back memories, for you. He's on your mind all the time, isn't he?' She knew without asking that she didn't go a day without thinking of Uncle Albert. 'I'll be back as soon as I can, but don't wait up.' Even though they promised not to, as she walked out the gate and into the street, she knew they would stay awake, until she got back.

***

Evenings were getting darker and colder now; they were counting down the weeks until Christmas at work. She didn't hear the van pull alongside her as she was so deep in thought, remembering she had to ask Francesca about coming round for Christmas dinner.

'Hey, fancy me seeing you here. Going anywhere nice? Danny Glover pulled up alongside her and wound his window down, dragging her out of her thoughts.

'Only a family meeting, Issac's family, that is. They've heard news.' She could have sworn his face clouded over for a second.

'Great, let's hope he's not been damaged too much to live a normal life then, eh?' His guttural chuckle made her shudder. 'He will.' She met his gaze, and held her head high. 'And until then, I'll keep the business ticking over. I must get on.' She continued to walk along the footpath, ignoring the obnoxious man.

'Don't forget my offer, if you need any help. Speaking of that, jump in, I'll drop you off. Don't wear yourself out.' He'd jumped out of his van quicker than she could say, no thanks, and had the door open ready for her.

'I'd rather walk, won't take me long.'

He was persuasive. 'Listen love, I've known your aunt and you girls for longer than I can remember, get in - take a kindness where it's offered. You'll get there quicker, like I said.

Knowing he'd tell aunt Violet she'd been rude, and wanting him to go away, she found it easier to jump in the van and tuck her shawl around her shoulders tightly, than it was to stand arguing with the little man.

'There you are. Off to the Cartwright's humble abode we go then.' He shuffled himself in his seat, and revved up his new van that already smelt of raw meat that made her want to be sick.

'There's news on Issac; his sister's had news of him. She's going to let us in on all she knows. It's the best thing I've heard since he left.' She couldn't hide the smug tone, but had to let him know unkind things he'd said about Issac weren't true. Other than that, she didn't want to make small talk along the journey.

'I know, you said. And remember my offer; giving you advice on the business, and a lump of cash to help out if yer need it. And I bet you do, with all that's happening.'

She stiffened in her seat. The cheek of the man, to think she'd want anything from him at all. 'We'll be alright. I'm going on the markets next week. It's in the family. My Cousin Isabella's on Dudley, but we're going to have a stand on Walsall. And she's offered me some space on the Dudley patch as well. So, any thoughts of helping me are a waste of time, *thank you*.' At least he couldn't blab to aunt Violet she'd been surly and rude. Glad they were getting nearer her destination, she felt herself breathing more easily.

'Listen, you might not know it, but hats aren't essentials anymore.' He craned his head to look at her. 'Oh, I know they want them out in the war zones, and to go with the uniform and such. But I get down to London, talk with the politicians, and find out what's happening.' He shuffled in his seat, and puffed his chest out. He was making himself sound more important than he really was. 'I know you're not that interested. But you should be.'

Molly turned, pretending to be listening to what he was telling her.

'I had lunch in the Regent Palace Hotel, with Prime Minister Asquith, seems they have Walsall on their radar. The saddler's business; they'll want many more than we're producing up here. Oh, yes, you might be surprised that I've an interest in politics.' He gave her a smug look. 'But it's good to know what's on the horizon.

Reason I'm letting you in on the information, is that they'll be looking for more premises, the saddlers, and you've got the business

132

there. Why don't I call down one evening, after you've finished work, and we can chat about how you can make more money renting out the business than making hats that nobody wants?' He patted her knee.

She quickly moved it to one side and grabbed the door handle. 'Thanks for the lift, and I'll have to think it over, but I don't see Issac wanting that to happen. And, as far as I'm concerned, a new wave of fashion hats is due to be released from our cottage industry as soon as you can say 'women get the vote,' they're placing orders every day.' She hadn't a clue where the little white lie popped up from. It was to shut his dirty mouth up; and didn't all the suffragettes wear the most elaborate hats from what she'd seen in the newspapers.

He huffed, not wanting to listen. 'You need to get real and think what you really want. He's not here, and you don't know how he'll be when he comes back. I've seen it all before, and trust me; you'll need all the money you can get. I'll be back here in an hour if you want a lift home.'

'No, I'll be ages here yet. Clara promised me a lift home.' She jumped out and slammed the door a bit harder than she intended to. This cad was making himself a pest. As if she hadn't got enough going on in her life to worry about. Without looking back, she ran through the black gates of Oak Tree Grange and up the drive. She rapped on the door eager to get inside.

***

Gertrude, more familiar with her now, and maybe happy because Clara was home, was more relaxed and friendly than she'd been in the earlier days. Molly smiled and wanted to tell her how good it was to see her, but knew she wasn't one for gushing emotions, so nodded and simply asked, 'how do you do?'

'I'm always alright when the kids are back.' She beamed, and Molly knew then that she looked on Issac and Clara as her own

133

family. The sight that met her on entering the main reception room was inviting and she was glad she'd waited until she got here for food.

Sandwiches of ham, with lettuce poking out of the edges, looked simply delicious and a mustard pot stood nearby with a tiny silver spoon standing in it. If only Janey and aunt Violet could be here with her. They'd love it, even though it was a completely different world to her own, they were friendly, and welcoming. Never once did they make her feel like she was beneath them, quite the opposite.

Suddenly, all eyes were on her; naturally, they'd been waiting for her to arrive before they got all the details on Issac. Dragging her thoughts from the food table, she gave his parents an informal greeting, and then hugged Clara, who was showing her a large armchair not too far from the fire.

'Sit down, Molly. We'll eat later, glad you could make it; Now, I want to tell you all about the conversation my friend had with Issac. It's easier to talk to you all at once. This way, I don't have to keep repeating everything they said … mostly, he sends his love to us all,' she gave Molly a wink.

'We're all ears.' Her father cleared his throat and poured himself a large brandy. He offered drinks all round, but made sure they were small measures compared to his own, Molly noticed.

'When my, 'friend Reg,' told me he was going out to the front line in France, to help with the injuries from the Battle of Loos, and how he'd be transporting casualties to hospital…' She paused… closing her eyes and swallowed hard, then took a deep breath. 'I trust you've heard news about thousands of men injured and even killed by now?' She paused. 'Lots from Bloxwich and Walsall, and the whole of the Midlands have already been killed with hundreds and thousands injured, some really badly disabled with severed limbs.

Argh, sorry, you don't need to know, this is just me preparing you for the depth of the injuries you'll see on the streets when all the wounded soldiers come back; after been rehabilitated in hospitals and rest homes of course.'

'Yes darling, what did your friend tell you?' Doris urged.

'Well, I'd been talking to him, about my brother, Issac Cartwright, and asking him to relay any news if there was a man with that name. Then, out of the blue, a week ago, a friend of Reg's was talking to a man from the Walsall area, name of Issac, who had a hat business back in the Black Country. He told Reg, and the next time he was dropping off casualties, he called in. Anyway, turns out it's our Issac.' She waited, giving her parents time to take in the news.

He's been in Belgium, where Nurse Cavell and her colleagues were tending to the British soldiers; she helped hundreds of the injured lads get back home, when they were well enough. Setting them up with papers, and clothing, and everything they need to get over the borders.

She flopped down, head in hand. 'The worst part is that she's been arrested killed since then accused of being a spy. That's all the information I have anyway, but we don't know where he is as last time Reg went to the hospital, he'd been dispatched. We have to be really brave and wait for news.

'What about his injuries?' Stanley looked worried, he had to know, same as they all did.

'They've been using gas, spraying it in the trenches, poisonous chlorine, it irritates the lungs, and makes the eyes sting and stream… They're developing more deadly ones to be used next year. He'd found this out, but got caught with a shower and had his face blistered.'

She covered her face with her hands. 'It pains me to talk about it, that's why I only wanted to say it once. He's badly injured, but he's still alive, and if he was looked after in hospital, we have to pray hard, and know he'll be home sooner than later.'

She let out a long sigh. 'They've been using cotton wool soaked in bicarbonate of soda now, for the men still in the trenches. I only hope his dog isn't injured, but if I know our Issac, he'll get more treatment for the dog than himself.' She took out a cigarette and lit up, taking a long drag.

'Let's make a start on this magnificent spread mother; you and Gertrude have worked wonders as usual.' Letting the serious moment pass, she put an arm around her mom, hugging her tight. 'He'll be okay, you'll see, we have to keep hoping, and one day he'll walk through that door and he'll ask us why we're all moping about, so come on, let's eat.

It was while they were tucking in to the food, and saying it's not that long until Christmas, Clara informed her parents that she'd got leave over the festive period. 'They're letting me have five full days off. How that's happened I'm not sure, but I'll be able to come home for Christmas, if you'll have me!' She looked under her lashes, towards her dad, though she was teasing, Molly could tell.

Clapping her hands together, Doris looked towards Gertrude. 'Oh, we'll have a proper Christmas; … I hardly dare say it, but maybe Issac will be home, could be a matter of months; time to prepare decorations, a tree and all the trimmings. No war will stop us making a lovely time of it. And I know…'

She raised her hand to stop Clara talking about trivial details. 'A lot can happen between now and then, but we'd love to have you with us Molly, wouldn't we Stan?' She urged her husband to agree, with the thought of Issac being alive and hope of him getting back home for

Christmas. This had to be a celebration of the Cartwright family getting back together.

'I'll have to check with aunt Violet, she was going to ask the neighbours round to Victoria Row… they haven't got much and there's a few of them. Francesca's got her mom, daughter Nadine, and her twin boys, Oliver and Patrick.' Molly gave a half hopeful smile. 'She wanted to give them a Christmas to remember, for the kids.' She clasped her hands in her lap, waiting for Stanley to say, *maybe some other time then eh?*

'We'll have a houseful.' She smiled. 'I couldn't leave them; they'd want me to be with them, especially at Christmas.'

'Then you're all welcome, aren't they, Stan?' He nodded, knowing he was out of his depth with the organising, and if Doris was happy, then so was he.

'Well, I can ask her, thanks, but she may have already made arrangements.' Molly simply couldn't see her aunt or Moira wanting to come here, but for certain, she could ask them; and if Issac was making his way home sometime soon, what better Christmas present could she wish for?

Chapter 15

They were waiting up for her, like she knew they would be, as she nipped in the front door.

'Only me, I'm home!' She hung her coat up and joined her aunt and younger sister as they sat watching the embers of the dying fire, waiting for her.

'I'll get some tea.' Violet busied herself, asking her not to start until she'd joined them.

'It's all good, I think…' Molly was busy relaying all the news. 'He's getting better, after being burned and gassed with some chemical spray they were supposed to use over the German trenches.' She sipped her tea aunt Violet handed her, and watched the patterns in the fire as she whispered more news.

'It didn't work though as they used it blew back over onto their own men as well, by mistake.' She closed her eyes at the thought of Issac getting burned with poisonous gasses.

'Anyway, turns out the ambulance driver's friends with Clara. She's heard he's been looked after, and could soon be on his way home if he's strong enough to get through the journey.'

'Oh, my giddy aunty, I can't believe it, burned and gassed the poor lad, oh love.' Violet was having a turn. Janey poured her more tea.

'Come on aunt Violet, get some tea down yer and if Issac has passed word he'll be home soon, then we have to be glad. Don't we Molly?'

'That's right Janey. We have to keep hope in our hearts, remember?' Molly held her close, and knew that if her little sister ever fell in love, he'd be the luckiest man on earth, and she prayed that he didn't get posted off to war.

'I asked Moira today, if she and her lot wanted to come to us for Christmas. I mentioned how we'll have a tree, all the trimmings and plenty to eat.'

Violet calmed down as she began talking over her Christmas plans as she absentmindedly picked up her knitting and began working on the latest pair of socks she was working on for sending abroad. Going in rounds with four double ended knitting needles kept her hands busy and her mind focused.

'Its ages away yet; plenty of time for Christmas arrangements;' Molly felt crossed wires coming on.

'It's only just autumn; we've not been round the Walsall lights yet, have we? Though I bet they're cancelled all because of the stupid war.' She spoke to Janey more than aunt Violet trying distraction tactics.

'I've got some taters need lifting in the next week or so. Come and help me if you want.' Molly smiled at her sister. Getting her involved with the gardening would give her something to do as a change from the sewing and reading. Apart from she'd be glad of her help. She was turning into a good worker. It'd keep her busy and she'd make new friends.

Most of the land girls took a younger sister or brother to help. 'The girls have been saving jam jars, to fill with candles; we'll be able to make a lovely display. It'll be a picture. You could come down and have a look too aunt Violet.'

'Watch you don't light the place up as a target for the zeppelins; they've bombed Dudley, Tipton and Walsall once already had you forgotten? Don't let us be targeted again, if you please. You wouldn't mind, but I heard from Danny Glover, they were supposed to be aiming for Liverpool; it was only because of the smog and smoke in the Black Country air that they hit us by mistake. I tell yer, they've got no sense of direction them bloody Germans.'

'Well, let's hope it doesn't go on much longer.' Molly fixed her dark-blue eyes on her aunt. 'How come you and Danny were talking about the war details? You'll be having tea at that new hotel in London next. He told me about it when he gave me a lift.'

'Afternoon tea with the prime minister, or lunch, something like that he said; and that they've got an eye on Walsall for the saddle making. He's asked me about renting part of the business. I told him no!' She was breathing heavily, waiting for her aunt's reply. For once in her life, Violet was silent. Only her mouth was open and moving but no sound coming out.

'You'd do well do avoid that man if I were you.' She turned away, pushing her tea to one side. 'Janey, you pop along to bed now, love eh. Look at the time, we've waited up, and now we know Issac will be home one of these days, when he's better. See you in the morning, love.' She gave Janey a kiss on the cheek, and took her cup and saucer into the scullery.

'I was going to keep talking a bit longer, our Molly. I'm not tired yet.' Janey looked where her aunt was tinkering around and didn't budge.

'Listen, I'll be going to bed as well in a minute. Let's talk more tomorrow, shall we?' She pushed her sister gently, and gave her a kiss and hug goodnight, before shutting the door behind her.

'Janey's gone up; I'll be following her in a bit. You don't have to hide at the mention of Danny Glover you know.' She stood at the door, to see Violet wiping tears from her eyes.

'It's nothing, love. Honestly… When I heard that your Issac is still alive, and being looked after,' she sniffed then broke down. 'I'll never know what my Albert went through.' Sobbing her heart out, she turned to Molly and wept. 'Even if I'd heard he'd been blown up on the battlefield would be something. It's just the not knowing, nothing. As if he just went off to war and vanished. Oh love, don't take any notice of this silly old woman. I'm happy for you. Issac will be back. You have it all to look forward to.'

Molly held her aunt close. For now, she had to drop all talk of the lecherous butcher and his stinky old van. Even if he kept popping up, she could ignore him or just stay on the right side of polite. She did understand how much her aunt depended on his charity. Yet how much charity was she giving in exchange for all the perks she knew she and Janey benefited from?

***

With the weather getting chillier, Janey and Molly wrapped up warm and put boots on in readiness for the mucky job ahead. Spending time together was a rare thing these days, and Francesca and Nadine joined them on the short tram journey over to Walsall arboretum, on the next Sunday in October. There was a gang already there. Making plans to start digging up the late potatoes, wheelbarrow ready with strong hessian sacks and gloves to prevent them getting too many blisters.

'I'm going to dig up the most spuds.' Janey beamed at Nadine as she strode ahead of the gang. The young Irish girl overtook her in great strides shouting back to the older girls. 'Oh no she isn't, you'll see who gets the most spuds in her sack then. It'll be me.'

'So glad they are not touched by this war like we are.' Francesca linked arms with Molly and leaned in for a cuddle. 'We'll have us a family Sunday, let them enjoy being out and helpful. The twins are with Ma, and they've got a football game going on in the back garden.' She pointed to where the girls were diving in. 'Look at them.' She laughed at the sight of Janey, skidding in the mud before she'd even picked up a spade.

'Oh, lord, maybe I should have given her a few gardening tips before we left. Like, keep on your feet and not on yer arse.'

Molly giggled, glad of getting out from under the watchful eye of aunt Violet and her unspoken relationship with Danny Glover. They had to have the conversation sometime, yet it was just there, lurking in the corner like a great giant of an issue she wasn't happy about.

'Hey, Janey, Nadine, grab yourself a spade from the shed over there, and follow me.' She gave a wave to the other families who were already working hard to lift the clusters of healthy-looking vegetables.

'I'll put the flask of beef tea, and sandwiches safe in the back of the shed. We'll have a break in an hour or so.' Francesca organised the refreshments for when they'd worked up an appetite.

The grounds were looking a picture. The usual flower beds now had cabbages, carrot tops, wafting in the breeze, along with long sprouts coming along nicely. 'I found beetroots over here, Molly, shall we pick some?' She put thumbs up, and smiled at her sister's enthusiasm, glad of the help and company of the younger family members. If only this happy feeling could stay with her all the time, and the war would end soon. She could only hope, but today was for having fun. Janey and Nadine were proudly showing off their latest harvest. Holding the giant stalks high over their heads.

'Those sprouts will likely be on every Christmas table this year. Oh, that reminds me… Molly turned to Francesca.

'Violet wants your ma, you, and the children to spend Christmas with the three of us.' She raised her eyes skyward. 'And here's the dilemma, would you believe it? 'All of us, and by that, I mean, your household, and our household, ma and Violet included, have been invited to Issac's parent's house, Oak Tree Grange, over Pelsall. It's a dream of a home. You can just imagine how aunt Violet's taken that offer now?'

Francesca put down her fork, and tucked her red hair back under her headband. 'You're kidding me, Jesus, Mary and Joseph, tell me that's a fib you're making up to give me a laugh?' She doubled up, finding the double invites quite hilarious. When Molly shook her head, and reassured her it was no joke, she caught her breath.

'Imagine my ma though?' Francesca placed her hand on hip to rest a while, and recover from the laughter that had her in stitches. 'Oh hello, Mrs Cartwright, I'm Moira from that little county of Donegal, North Western Ireland, so I am, do you know it at all? We had a farm there; near the port you know. Really busy port it was as well.' She placed a hand over her face and shook with laughter.

'Oh, goodness, I'm not sure how that'd work, really, I don't. Our ma doesn't get out much, and when she does, she could talk the back leg off a donkey.'

'No, aunt Violet wasn't struck with the idea either, but you know what? It would be a good way for me and you to see all our loved ones together. And that's what Christmas is all about after all, isn't it? We'll make the executive decision and tell them, it's where we're going.' She folded her arms, and stamped her muddy boot on the soil.

Francesca nodded. 'I agree. And if your Issac arrives on time, it'll be celebrations all round.'

Molly could only hope, and she did, with all her heart.

***

A week later, Molly saw the butchers van again. He pulled up outside the house. They were about to sit down to tea. Aunt Violet had made some stewing steak with carrots and cabbage. Her gravy was a taste of heaven, and when Violet twitched the curtain back to the sight of him marching down the path, she wiped her hands on her apron; 'What the bloody hell's he doing here now?' She hurried to the door, and the muttering got louder until, Violet screamed…

'What's going on?' Molly left her meal, and rushed to find out what the commotion was about. 'Danny, what's the matter, why are you here?' She wondered how often he was here if Violet was alone, but aside from that… 'What did you say to Violet?'

'It's bad news love. I wanted to tell you before you hear it anywhere else. She's been killed.'

'What are you on about Danny? Who's been killed?' From hot to cold, she felt frozen on the spot. 'Why are you calling here?'

'That nurse, the Angel from East Anglia, she's been killed.'

'I already know that.' Molly looked at Violet. 'I just didn't have chance to get round to telling you.' She looked apologetically to her aunt.

'You need to leave, but thanks for calling.' Violet pushed Molly away before ushering him out the door. 'We'll have a chat, me and Molly, you go home now, Danny, please. I'll see you next week.'

Molly felt angry, disappointed, and weary, with the horrors of the war creeping closer to home all the time.

'D'you think Issac's on his way back?'

Violet sighed. 'I can't say, love. It's hard to know but why could someone who was doing so much good, end up being treated like a criminal? They called her a spy, and that's why her fate was to die, he said. It's horrible, and why did he have to call when you already knew? Now this lovely food is going to waste.'

'Don't be daft Aunt Vi, it's only gone cool, that's all, we can still eat it, there's nothing going to waste.' She ate her food then began clearing away and knew it was time to ask.

'Violet, I've been wondering…' Molly stood, arms folded, her face like stone. 'Can you tell me how is it that most families live on broth and ox tail all week, and yet we have plenty of meat on our table, coal on our fire, when I buy only a fraction of it, and our best clothes? We aren't in rags like most folk around here. You're not telling me your old age pension stretches to all that, even if you include Albert's war fund.' Once Molly had opened up the floodgate the words wouldn't stop.

'What are you suggesting young lady, and I'm your aunt if you'd remember, not next door's cat's mother.'

Janey stifled a giggle. 'Next door hasn't got a cat, aunt Violet.'

'Shut up, Janey. I'm talking to her.' She pointed a finger in Molly's face, her own going a shade of purple.

'The ungrateful young madam, who thinks my life's a bed of roses. Welcome to the world; it isn't. Now I'm going to bed; and I want no more talk like this in my house, or there will be a price to pay.'

She barged out of the room, leaving Molly and Janey staring after the large empty space she'd left behind.

Chapter 16

Issac felt a pain like he'd never known. He heard it from the man in the next bed. The death of Edith Cavell was all over the newspapers. They'd know about it by now, back home. He was in no fit state to write letters, let alone try and run away. He lay back, eyes closed, the pain behind his eyelids stinging. His body trembled, half in pain the other half in fear. Their escape route had already been laid.

As soon as he was well enough, they would be given, passports, papers, clothes and money to make the journey home. He couldn't talk to anyone, he didn't know who he could trust so, he trusted nobody, left off from writing letters and with professional nursing care, got a little stronger each day.

He'd been told, multiple times, dogs weren't allowed in the hospital. Until one look at those big brown eyes, and Jasper, the German shepherd, war hero, worked his magic; the nurses provided him with food and water. The nuns walked him in the grounds, taking turns as they went on breaks. He knew Clara would have passed the word out as how he was by now.

When he slept, he dreamed of marrying Molly, and them having a little girl, who they'd call Edith, after the Angel of East Anglia. When he woke and realised it was all a dream, he began to shake, wishing he could be holding his Molly. He'd decided a long time ago, she was his Molly now. There was no other thought in his mind, apart from getting home, holding her tight, and spending all their time together. It was the only thing that kept him going.

***

'All ready for market tomorrow then?' Molly leaned on the gate, leading to Francesca and Moira's terraced house in Victoria Row.

'You bet I am, listen, come in. No need to hang around on the gate. You don't think Ma scrubs that front door step for you not to come and admire it now, surely?'

Laughing together, Molly pulled the gate open, and joined her friend, praising the clean doorstep as she stepped over it. 'I've been up to see the Cartwright's, had this brainwave, and wanted to see what they thought. Anyway, turns out, they're free to come to work tomorrow; so, if you get there early, load a few boxes of stock, onto the horse and cart, with Bobby, then get off to Walsall market, hopefully you'll get a pitch. Then I'm going with Stanley in the motor car, to Dudley, to see my cousin again. She said we could put some hat samples on her stall.

I'll buy some fabric off her while I'm there as well. Doris will hold the fort, seeing as me and you aren't there.' She gave a great smile, and hugged herself in anticipation of good times ahead for the business.

'Woah, that's a lot of thinking and planning going on there, girl. Issac will have to promote you to upper under manager, or summat similar.' More giggles and hysterical laughter ensued.

'I'd rather be under the manager more like. But, on second thoughts, how about, call me, 'Molly-do-it-all from Paradise Lane.' Tutting, she looked over to where Moira was brewing up a lovely strong cup of tea.

'Will yer have a slice of home-made bread pudding with it, Molly, love?' She had already cut a chunk for each of them, and plated up with a steaming cuppa to wash it down with.

'Now how could I refuse such a wonderful treat?' She noticed how welcoming Moira was, and really hoped they could all spend Christmas together. 'You're a real treasure, do you know that?' Molly put her arm around the lady, in a sideways hug; she was the rock of the family, just like her aunt was with them.

'Oh, they let me know I'm half useful sometimes, so they do. Family is everything Molly, that's all I know, and I'm grateful of your friendship with our Fran, you know that darling. She's happier here now, since finding the job, and having you for company. Mind you, think on, there's still a world out there, and me and Violet were chatting together, only the other day, over a cuppa, you really should make the effort … Get yer glad rags on, both of you… get yerselves out a bit - you know.'

She stuffed her face with a great mouthful of her home-made bread pudding and slurped her tea in satisfaction of telling the young ones how to live a bit.

Molly looked at her friend, then back to where Moira was munching on bread pudding. 'Go out? Where were you thinking of? We went potato picking at the arboretum remember? And we see each other at work.' She shrugged. 'Where else is there?'

'Oh, my goodness lord, save my soul…' She looked heavenwards, and crossed herself. 'Have you never heard of dancing you girls? You don't have to act like a pair of nuns just because the men are away you know. There's no rule I see where it says you work your backsides off, and mope around every minute of the day.' She looked from one to the other of the girls.

'There's a dance at the town hall up in Bloxwich, haven't you seen the posters around? For goodness sakes, get yourselves dolled up and go and let your hair down for once. You're only young for a short while you know. And when the men get back, they'll want looking after. Men always do…' She nodded, affirming she was right. 'Me and Violet will look after the younger ones. The girls look after themselves, any rate. You think on, and start living a bit, before it's too late and you're old and grey like me.'

How could they argue? And she was right. Molly looked down at her dreary clothes. She'd been wrapped up in the business, Issac, his family. Men who wanted more than she was willing to give, she had forgotten that she was young. Francesca was doing well at work, but they did need to have more fun. 'Tell you what; I'm up for it if you are.' She looked to Francesca, who gave a great smile. 'You're on, and if we do well on the market, I might persuade Bobby to join us.'

Oh dear, what had she started with getting Francesca together with the dreamy looking lad from Birmingham. Hopefully they could stay as friends. Yet the lively Fran did get an extra twinkle in her eye every time she spoke his name.

***

They walked the canal route to work, leaving earlier than usual to make sure Dolly had her refreshments, and the boxes of hats lined up for Walsall, were packed neatly as possible on the back of the cart.

'I'll fasten the boxes down with some rope. I know how-to do-good knots; my uncle comes back from the navy from time to time. He's got swallows tattooed on the back of his hands, and up his arms, he's got a mermaid. She got the biggest tits on her you've ever seen on a woman.'

Francesca blushed, and covered her mouth to avoid laughing. 'Can you not be talking about tits, we're here to sell hats, not talk about naked females.'

They got along like a house on fire, which was before they'd even left the yard. Molly wasn't sure whether to have a word to Fran about her being married, then thought better of it. Who was she to tell anyone not to have a laugh? If she didn't have the hots for Issac, she'd have been interested in the handsome Bobby dazzler herself.

'Just try and focus on what you're doing. Like, selling hats, and getting a regular pitch.'

Bobby jumped off the cart, and shoved his string into the bag he had strapped around his waist. 'All safe and sound; I've got this money bag and hopefully come back with it bulging.' He patted his pouch, and winked at Molly, who turned away, not getting into his wicked ways.

'Just do well, and Fran, take my apron from the kitchen, to help keep your clothes clean, and you can use the big pocket for the cash.'

She nodded, and pushed Bobby out of her way. 'Get up on the cart; I'll be there in a jiffy. And, I bet you didn't bring any food. She chided her new business partner.

'Oh, there'll be a chip van there, don't worry about that.' He climbed up and took the reins.

'No need, I've got my ma's bread pudding and a bottle of tea. It's hot at the moment, so we can have a swig when we get there to keep us warm, and the bread pudding fills you up like a meal, the size chunks she cuts.' She held up her holdall, full of provisions, and gave a huge smile.

As she waved them off, Molly couldn't help thinking – if Moira thought Francesca needed to have some fun, she was in store for a whale of a time with that dream boat Bobby. It hadn't taken them long to get into the banter. They were two of a kind, and she had great faith in them to shift a good deal of hats if they were lucky enough to get a pitch on the market in Walsall.

She'd only just stepped into the kitchen office, when the toot of the motor car pulling into the yard made her turn. It   was only just after seven o'clock in the morning. Her new sales team had gone out on the road, and here was the jalopy, with back up staff on hand, and on time; she filled the kettle, and lit the fire under the hob.

'How about a cuppa before you start?' Molly greeted Issac's parents with a brief hug and peck on the cheek.

'Aye, I'll always time for a brew.' Stanley puffed out his chest, and pulled up a chair. 'How much stock are we taking then lass?' He stroked his chin with his hand, and his frown showed that he wasn't quite sure about the idea.

'It's only an experiment. Thing is, we don't have to pay rent. My cousin, she's offered to let us have a space on her stall, so we don't need a lot. More samples, then if we sell any, I can make arrangements on how much we share with her, or even think about getting our own stall there, in time.' She wanted to reassure him, there was no risk attached to the Dudley market idea.

'Mm, now what was it you were telling me about Danny Glover's news, about the saddlers renting space off us?'

'He's coming here to chat to you later, there's so much he wanted to explain, and it's easier to hear it from him, than me. Shall we get this tea down us, and then I'll load up the few boxes we need.' He nodded.

'I'll keep an eye on the workers, while you're gone.' Doris looked like a woman on a mission. 'It brings back memories.'

'You sure you don't mind?' Molly wanted to know she wouldn't feel overwhelmed with being in charge of the boisterous workers.

'Not at all, Molly, love, it was my grandfather William, who started the hatting business in his back shed, down there, remember?' She pointed to the yard where stables and store rooms held vital stock, and the loyal horse Dolly. 'When he expanded to create all this, he bought the house next door, then his daughter, my mom, Amelia helped and eventually took over.'

'She'd go round knocking on doors, spreading the word about hats. I went with her sometimes, and used to spend all my school holidays here, helping to box up hats, and stitch on flowers and often a trim of lace. I often missed school to help get orders out on time. And do other little jobs, fetching and carrying, making tea. Don't you worry about me; it's a pleasure to help you.'

'The business was mine before I handed over to Issac, remember?' She gave her a smile; that told Molly, she really was glad to be left in charge, while at the same time putting her firmly in her place.

'That's the lot.' She threw the last box into the back of Issac's beloved motor car, and pushed them down safely. She put a pen and ink in her pocket, for writing prices on the boxes. 'Are you driving, or shall I?'

'No, love, I'll drive us into Dudley. You can have a drive next time, eh?' Stanley was adamant.

Secretly pleased at not having to drive under his watchful eye, she pulled her skirts up and gathered them underneath herself as she settled in and slammed the door.

'Here we go then, hang on to your whatsits!' With a toot and a bellowing of the exhaust, Stanley took to the wheel, and breezed out of the yard, waving goodbye to Doris as he went.

The Bloxwich and Walsall hatters were hot on the trail of sales on this bright and chilly autumn morning; and Doris Cartwright was back on familiar territory – her beloved hat company.

Chapter 17

Doris pushed her sleeves up and marched briskly to find out what was happening on the production front. It had been a few years since she and Stanley had taken a step back, knowing how Issac and Molly worked so well as a team. They'd come to the decision to let him take over, run the business his way. It was after all, his inheritance from her mother. It was Amelia's last wish for Issac to run the works one day.

Stanley never questioned or begrudged their son taking over. He gladly retired to enjoy his newspaper, the garden and occasional trips to the races, or the seaside when the mood took them.

Issac made it known, and gave his word, without it being official; any gains from the business would be shared with Clara. If either of them had a family, then it would be reviewed.

The hissing and spitting told her she was near the steam room. Jack pushed down on the pressing machine, sending a great cloud of hissing mist, hiding him from view. He was working on felting fabric, for the peasant style hats used by farmers, for themselves and their farmhands.

'Hello, Mrs Cartwright, good to see you – they left you in charge then?' His infectious smile gave her a lift. 'Back where you belong eh?'

'That's the plan, yes. So how many of those have you to do this morning then? Please call me Doris.'

He went on to show her the pile of hats he was getting through. 'We haven't got the orders for these yet, but they'll go. Always do and hopefully they'll all do well on the market. Oh, and call me Jack.' His smile lit up her morning.

'Yes, let's hope so, eh? I'll be back in a while, shout me if you need any help.' She left him with a smile, and promised to check in on his work. Mostly she was only here to oversee any miss-haps, which she hoped would be minimal.

Next, she heard chatting and laughter from the cutting room. Three rows of girls were measuring, laying felt, cutting away and making sure the patterns were right. She saw Rita helping one of the younger ones. It seemed like Issac had a good balance of workers, who got along really well.

She wondered what her old grandad would have made of the scene. He'd be proud she knew, yet couldn't help wondering when better days for hats would come again. If it weren't for the dratted war, she knew stylish hats would be highly sought after in all kinds of circles, from the gentry to the working class.

She knew from her circle of friends, who'd put in an order for a bespoke hats when she'd first started out. The trilbies for the London gents were never out of fashion either, nor the bowlers.

'How's it going here then, ladies? She walked among them, happy in the company of so many competent women. 'Who says it's a man's world eh? Let's show them how we can do anything just as well as they can. Well, we'll let them load up the horse and cart maybe, but keep up the good work.'

She watched as they cut and placed shapes ready for the next stage of production.

She finished her rounds, checking and chatting as she went surprised that it was almost dinner time. They'd mostly brought in their own sandwiches, only one or two of the lads went to the chip shop up the road. Issac had told her how they'd sometimes get one extra-large bag of chips then shared them. She boiled the kettle and dug out the giant teapot that Molly often used, for the staff during tea round.

'Oh, Doris, let me help you with that, it's a sight for sore eyes, and that's a fact.' Rita took hold of the huge pot and filled cups that were pushed forward.

'Have you got milk over this end or shall I get you some from out the back?'

'It's alright; we keep a bottle, out in the store. It's not everyone wants it any rate. They often take the tea black. It keeps warmer longer.'

'There's some in my kitchen, so don't go short, come and knock on my door. Now then, I'll leave you with the pot, Rita. Drink while it's hot. I'll be round this afternoon, to see what we've got to show them when they come back.' She trotted off; full of motherly authority.

'I hope Molly isn't going to be away all the time though.' One of the younger girls looked forlorn. She helps me with the patterns. I know you do an all, Rita, but Molly is more like a friend.'

'Oh, shut yer cake hole,' Rita chided. 'Molly's only trying to get more money in for us, and you know how hard she works. She ain't going ter be on the market every day you pumpkin. Eat up yer sandwich, and let's get back to work.'

* * *

Bobby pulled Dolly to a halt, secured her reigns, to the wooden standing post, near the water trough, and began lifting boxes from the cart. 'Leave me to unload, you just stand there a minute, looking pretty and we'll get us somewhere to stand. Just leave things to me.'

'Alright, you said that once, I'm not deaf, man.' She threw him an irritated glance. Francesca was determined to pull her weight, not stand around like a spare part at a wedding.

'Right, watch the stuff.' He nodded to the stock on the cart. 'I'll be back in a minute.' He strode over to the man with a brown saddle bag

155

over his shoulder. 'Hey up…' he whistled - the man looked over the handsome young lad striding towards him.

Francesca heard him ask, 'Hiya, mate. Got any casual slots, we're selling top quality hats all designs for every occasion.'

After words were exchanged, and pointing to the corner of the market, Bobby rushed back, face flushed, ready to begin.

'Well, what's happening?' Francesca looked, arms folded across her chest, waiting for him to tell her the news. 'Are we on or what?'

'Dolly can be tethered over there, where we can see her, and for this week, we're selling off the cart. Good job I put that tarpaulin sheet on the wagon that you got. We have to provide our own cover if it rains.'

'It's off a mate of my hubby; he gave it me for nothing. Good to know people who know.'

'Yes, well done there.' He smiled; looking like a man who had just been reminded he was with another man's wife.

'Come on then, I'll lead Dolly round, you put the boxes back on the cart. I wouldn't fancy it if it was chucking it down though, would you? Glad it's a decent day,' she glanced at the sky.

'You'll get used to it; if we turn up every week, we'll have a proper stall soon, a regular pitch. That way, we throw the tarpaulin over the stall, and we're undercover. We can always bring Dolly a coat as well.'

She led the horse to the corner of the market. Secured the reigns, and helped Bobby unpack the stock, putting the hats on display on top of the upturned empty boxes.

He searched the sky where clouds were parting to let the orange glow of morning sunrise poke through. 'We'll just chuck the tarpaulin over the lot. You don't pack up at a few drops of rain, you stick it out. That's how you get to be a true trader.'

He grinned. 'Now then, watch and learn.' He took a step forward and shouted. 'Come on missus; get yourself a fine hat for the dance tonight. Or summat smart for the wedding. Come and have a look, have a feel, sniff out the quality.' He turned and winked at Francesca who could only raise her eyes, blush and turn away.

'It's the only way to move this stuff, go on, your turn.' He stood back, resting against the cart and lit up a woodbine, then threw the match to the ground. 'We need to do well, there's no way I'm going back until we've sold at least half this stuff.'

Francesca reached out and stroked Dolly's nose, kissed the horse, and whispered, 'we'll show him, watch me.'

She swung round to face the oncoming public who had begun to trickle around. Two ladies approached the cart. 'Good morning to you, fine ladies. We're here every week, if it goes well today.'

She smiled and encouraged them to look more closely. 'All hats made by our team, in the Bloxwich and Walsall cottage industry; local work, all handmade. If there's any style or colour you can't see, then I'll make a note and we'll try our best to please.' Francesca smiled and passed hats from the back of the cart, for them to look at, and made sure they saw everything they'd brought with them.

They had a feel of the hats, encouraged by Bobby, who had quickly distinguished his fag when they saw how interested the ladies were; they tried them on, asking each other how it looked, and Francesca made a mental note to bring a mirror next time.

'How does that one feel?' She asked the younger of the two ladies who had pulled on a pale pink pill box hat with a feather to one side, and a delicate lace veil attached to the front, which could be worn scrunched up, or pulled down, she told them.

'It's comfortable, and I'm going to a christening in a few weeks. How much is it?'

'Two shillings and sixpence, cheap at half the price,' she crossed her fingers behind her back. This was one of the smaller hats they'd brought with them. Other more elaborate ones would be double that.

'I'll take it…' She reached for her purse.

Bobby passed some tissue paper they'd packed in boxes to keep the hats clean. 'Here's some wrapping, and we have some spare boxes, hang on my darling'.' He delved around and found her a small box, suitable for the hat.

Gently, Francesca wrapped the hat in tissue paper, and pointed to the ribbon stand nearby. 'Do you need any extra ribbons? We have a variety of colours and widths.' She chose a paler shade than the hat.

'I'll take a strand of that; it'll come in for a blouse I'm making.' She gave Francesca a smile, and handed over the coins, with an extra two pence for the ribbon. 'I hope you'll be here every week. Can you get any lace?'

'We certainly can get you some me love.' Bobby joined in the chatter, and promised they'd be here next week, with a selection to show them.

When they'd gone, he gave Francesca a playful punch on the arm. 'Well done you, selling some lengths of fancy ribbons as well. But who'd have thought they'd want lace?'

'Why wouldn't they you berk.' She punched him back. 'Next time, we need to be more organised and have a whole load of haberdashery. Buttons, embellishments, if we use them, they would an all. We can do better prices than the shops, and we only have the rent and our wages to knock off.'

'Come on now ladies, feel the quality, try before you buy.' He was in his glory, shouting his mouth off. And when an old lady placed a white feather on the stall, he didn't falter.

'How can I help you, my darling? You want a bit of ribbon to go with your feather there? Or something else tickle your fancy?'

'Why haven't you signed up? Gone to fight for your country? There's a name for men like you.' The sour puss wouldn't budge, and Bobby quickly moved to stand beside her.

'Let's put it like this… I have a weary old mom at home, who looks after my grandma, who lives with us by the way. And she's confused most of the time, waiting for her husband to come home, who died years ago.

There're five other kids, all younger than me who are working hard in factories – same as me, keeping things ticking over at home, while the brave lads are away.'

He turned to Francesca, who nodded and shouted. 'That's right, you tell her Bobby.' She glared at the woman who was picking her feather back up. 'Oi, and you can take your feather and stick it where the sun don't shine – go home and bully someone else.'

Bobby directed her, the way past their cart, 'Oh, and to let you know. Our boss is lying burned and gassed, in a Belgian hospital, we're working our backsides off to keep his business going; keeping it there for when he comes back. And his replacement is over on Dudley market, selling quality hats to more good Black Country folks. Now, I'm sure you have other innocent folk to go and hound into submission. Fucking ald witch,' he muttered under his breath.

The lady put the feather away in her bag, muttering to herself. 'Youth of today, back in my day…' She turned to take one last glare at them.

'Thank you for calling, maybe next week you could look at the haberdashery selection we'll have on show.' Bobby gave her a salute, and clapped his boots to attention, then turned and pulled a silly face at Francesca. 'Can't please em all, can we?'

She was long gone, and Francesca pulled Bobby into an embrace. 'Listen, you.' She tidied his jacket and dusted some bits off his front. 'You take no notice of that scatty old biddy. They're hateful bullies these white feather brigade; she hadn't a clue about your situation. Where the heck to you sleep by the way, with all those family members in the same house?'

'Well,' he tapped the side of his nose. 'Maybe I added an extra two siblings in there. Mum and gran share a room; me and our Peter share, yet he's never there, he's in the army. The girls share the back bedroom and we all get along fine. Just makes me wonder if I should be going off to war. Thing is, mom has enough worry about, with our Peter travelling around, God knows where, and gran getting more dependant and confused by the day. I feel I'm in the right place for what I should be doing. I'm the main earner in the family. They need me here.'

She hugged him again. 'You are well and truly needed, let's get on; we'll put it behind us and sell more hats.'

The day went well, and before the market ended, a farmer on the fruit and veg stall, took half a dozen peasant hats for his land workers. Two sisters bought matching hats for a day in London they were looking forward to, and a man visiting from Willenhall, took a pile of flat caps for his pigeon fancier mates. By the end of the day there was hardly any stock left.

The toby ambled over. 'How're yer done then lad?'

Francesca felt like telling him she'd done okay, thanks, but left Bobby to chat and hand over the rent money from his pouch, which by now was bulging. She went and tended to Dolly while the men talked men's talk.

'Give us two shilling for today, and then when you get a proper stall, it'll be a cartwheel, you happy with that?'

Bobby paid up and nodded. 'Five shillings sounds fair to me.'

'Why didn't you barter a bit and say we can only afford three shilling.' She handed him a sandwich from her bag. 'Get this down yer, we've been too busy to flipping eat and I could down a bag of chips if I'm honest.'

'Keep him sweet. You don't go arguing the toby on day one.' He gladly took a bite from the sandwich. We'll get some chips on the way back – an extra-large bag to share out, then they can't moan we were skiving, can they? Anyways five shilling's not a bad price, considering how much we've took.'

'Hey, Bobby, you didn't take notice of that bullying old biddy, did you?' She put a hand on his shoulder.

He loaded the last box onto the cart, and reached for Dolly's reigns. 'Did I heck, don't you worry about me. If yer wanna do summat useful, go and lead the horse to water, then we can hitch her up and be on our way.'

She led Dolly to the trough, feeling so angry he'd been faced with that. She let the horse drink, and then fed her the rosy apple the green grocer had swapped for a bag of ribbons. All in all, she'd enjoyed the day, and the thought of sharing chips with the gang, in Paradise Lane, would round off the day a treat.

Bobby clicked his tongue, 'Tch, tch, giddy up there Doll, homeward bound gel, hup hup...' He pulled the reigns round to the right, and took the road homeward. One or two of the other stall holders, still packing up, gave them a wave. 'I think we've earned our wages today, Fran, what d'ya say?' He turned and gave her a smile.

She nodded, and pulled her shawl around her shoulders, enjoying her day out right up until the end. 'Wonder how Molly got on with her cousin and Stanley?'

'We'll soon find out. Got any more of that cold tea and bread pudding left by the way?'

Chapter 18

It was a tired Molly that got out of the motor car, back in Pelsall, at the Hat works. Doris was at the door, eagerly waiting to see how they'd got on.

'Phew! Didn't realise how busy that Dudley market was. And talk about hard work. That little wench on the fabrics stall worked her damn socks off.' Stanley stretched his back and shoulders to loosen up.

'My cousin Isabella has been on the market for years. I hadn't seen her for ages, until recently. My Uncle Tom set her up and now she's the main earner in the family. His injuries from the Boer war make it hard for him to get about much now.'

'Well, how did it go with the hats? Did you sell any?' Doris wasn't listening to the family small talk; she was looking out to where the motor stood empty of hats apart from the few empty boxes left there.

'Cleared the lot, didn't we, Moll?'

She smiled at the new name he'd chosen to give her, and wondered if she'd still be Molly if they hadn't done any good. 'Absolutely, cleaned right out; mind you, we did only take samples. How did the other two get on?' She started to make her way through to the business.

'Same…' Doris wiped her hands on the tea towel nearby, and filled the kettle. 'I bet you'll need a brew. And, you're in luck, there's some meat pie left for you.'

'Definitely, I'll say yes to that cuppa love. And did I hear you say, meat pie?' He was looking at his wife as if she was having a funny turn.

'I most certainly did. Danny Glover paid me a visit. He has a new recipe and wanted to see what the workers think. Free samples would you believe. They went down a treat with them lot.' She gestured to the workshops. 'And, would you believe it? Bobby and Francesca only came up trumps and brought back a family bag of chips, plenty of salt and vinegar as well.'

'They've played a blinder on the market. Taken orders for caps, wedding ideas, and they're panning to take more ribbons, lace and accessories next time. They got lucky.'

Molly pulled up a chair and drew her jacket and shawl around her shoulders to keep herself warm, glad to get back inside the kitchen office where it was warm and cosy, and she could listen to all the information about the Walsall market; she absent-mindedly brushed all news of Danny Glover calling round with free gifts. Doris had kept the fire glowing under the aga. Molly warmed her hands that were almost frozen to icicles, from being out all day without her gloves.

'What d'you mean, they got lucky?' She rubbed her hands and knew she'd be wearing fingerless knitted gloves like Isabella if she went again. 'Did they have to pay rent?'

'Oh, lord, yes, but I think Bobby wangled it to pay a bit less until they get a permanent pitch. They were on the corner of the aisle. So rather than being out of line with the others, they told me they had customers coming from all sides. Whichever row they walked up, theirs was a pitch they couldn't miss?'

'My word, that's flipping wonderful,' Molly beamed with pride. 'And they got on alright, together, no arguments?'

Doris raised her eyebrows. 'Mm, nothing said, so I wouldn't have thought so. She'll be telling you all about it no doubt. He's a man who knows how to handle a situation, so she'll have been in good hands.'

Molly nodded, and knew Francesca could give as well as she got with Bobby, and would be well and truly in safe hands.

'So how was Dudley?' Doris looked from one to the other; Stanley was holding his mug of tea, but she gently removed it from his hands as it was in danger of being spilt as he was dozing off.

'Amazingly we were fine. Isabella gave us a quarter of her double stall. So, that gave us half a stand; more than enough room for what we needed.' Molly glanced at Stanley, and whispered, 'he went a walk around town, met up with a few old chums in the tavern.' She smiled while putting a finger to her lips, urging Doris not to tell him off. He'd been like a schoolboy on a day out.

She only raised her eyes upwards, and tutted, 'Doesn't surprise me.' She looked at her sleeping husband with affection. Obviously, she trusted him and they were secure in their love. A great team, she hoped one day she and Issac would have chance to be the same, then she would be contented with her lot.

'What did Danny Glover want, surely didn't come over here just to give out free meat pies?' She had her suspicions, though waited to hear what Doris knew before she blabbed her mouth off.

'He's got this idea to rent out the business, or part of it to the saddlers.' She sniffed and crossed her legs before wiping her nose with her lace handkerchief. 'Can't understand why he's so concerned to be honest though.' She took a sip of her now cold tea. 'Think he wants to put his proposal through to us all, and then move the Walsall leather workers in to our space; feels a bit like pushing us out of our hatting business.' She finished her tea and placed her cup on the side; 'Or trying to.'

'I think it's best to wait until Issac's back. We have lots of new ideas, which so far seem to be going well. Imagine, if we did as well every week as we've done today? There'll soon be many more hats being produced and we'll be back on track. And we could set up a retail shop in the front room of the original house, like Issac's grandma had, he told me. Oh, and I'll need to ask Stanley if he'd mind taking me to the fabric merchants in Nottingham to cover the orders you say they've got.'

Francesca walked into the office kitchen, giving a light knock on the door. 'Sorry to interrupt. Hey, how did you get on, fellow market trader?' Francesca gave a giggle, and rubbed her hands together, before warming them on the glowing embers of the fire.

'We practically sold out. Bobby's a natural, but I outdid him in getting the orders from the ladies. He'll tell you otherwise though, saucy sod!' She chuckled to herself, and Molly couldn't help notice the twinkle in her eye. There was no mistaking the spark between the two of them, but Molly knew to leave it be, they were only human, and both special to her.

'Glad you did well; same for us. I was only just saying to Doris, I'll need Stanley to drive me to Nottingham, unless he's busy.' She glanced at his wife; Molly couldn't take it for granted. 'I could always take Dolly and the cart.'

'Don't be daft, girl.' She looked shocked. 'It's giving him a new lease of life, look at him. Sleeping like a baby. Hasn't had so much fun for years. And I love it being back here. And if the Danny Glover thinks he can push us out to get his saddle making mates in… Well, he can think on.'

Francesca frowned at Molly, and mouthed silently, 'what's he said?'

'Oh, he thinks a free meat pie will buy us. He's asking to put the saddle makers in here, and they pay us rent of course. Making out he's doing us a favour. Imagine what Issac would say… Me supposed to be keeping an eye on his business and just let it go while his back's turned.' She crossed her arms in front of her and tapped her worn out old boots on the slate floor.

'What's that, who's letting the business go?' Stanley sat up with a start, wiping the dribble off his chin and almost knocking himself off his rickety chair. 'Who's doing what our Doris? Why didn't you wake me up?'

They all burst out laughing, at Stanley blinking and being rudely awoken from his slumber.

'Nothing that you need worry about, love; we were just saying, that butcher, he's got links with London… Good to keep in with him, he's always down the Old Smokey keeping up with the Asquith's the Astor's, Lloyd George and his cronies.'

'No more than I would have if I had a mind to be driving around all the time, wasting time. How he keeps his blooming butchers shop going is a mystery; he's got another side to him if you ask me.' Stanley straightened his clothes. 'How can you have a different recipe for a meat pie? Surely, it's always got to be meat in pastry. What can you do different with that? You tell me.'

Molly listened to the calming voice of Issac's mother, telling her husband, 'It was probably a little herb added or a bit more spice.'

Stanley wasn't convinced. 'He's got enough spice, what with his womanising. You want to watch out for that one.' He sent a warning in her direction.

If only she could tell them what she knew. But for now, she had to keep her mouth shut. Loose lips sink ships. Wasn't that the motto of the moment?

***

'You know, your ma has some great ideas, but for me and you to go out dancing… well, I have to say she's an amazing woman.' Molly linked arms with Francesca as they made their way up Field Road, and cut through the cemetery, to take the short journey to Bloxwich

167

town centre. 'It's at the Central Picture Palace. Normally the flicks, like you know, but they're putting on a band to cheer us all up, I think. We've only got to turn right, when we get to the other end of the cemetery, and we'll be there. I hope I can manage to get through there with these heels. I usually only wear my boots; these are quite fancy though.' She held her foot up to show off her T-bar shoes. 'You wouldn't mind, they're not even mine, they're borrowed from aunt Violet.' The girls laughed and made their way through the cutting to the town.

'Well, I'm glad you know where it is. You know my ma and her ideas. Anyone might think she just wanted rid of us. I sometimes think she forgets I'm a married woman. I can't forget him though, and it feels wrong going out without him.' Francesca gave a shudder.

'I'm not officially with Issac, but it feels like I am, and the parents are being so good to me, it feels as if they're already family.' Molly sighed. 'It's not normal, us not being with our men, or the one we want to be with in my case. She glanced at her friend. 'Did you tell Bobby you were coming here tonight?' As if she had to ask.

A small smile played around Francesca's lips. 'I might have mentioned it – only once. If he turns up it don't mean anything; only that he wants to have a bit of a rest from the work and more work. There's summat I need to tell you, but don't mention it to anyone, you have to promise me, Molly, its top secret and he'd be mortified if he thought you knew.'

'What the heck?' Turning to see if she was having a laugh, she wasn't, Molly held her hand tight. 'Listen, you know about my attacker, and I know you won't repeat it to anyone. What's the matter? Tell me.'

'It's Bobby, he got white feathered, at the market.' She looked under her lashes, almost afraid of what she'd say.'

'Oh no… don't say that… How can anyone treat a decent human being like that, working hard, for his family, his old mom depends on him, and the rest of the kids, a bit like me?'

'That's what I told him. He played it down, you know how he is, laughed it off. But I'm sure it hurt his feelings. Just thought you should know, I think I convinced him to put it out of his head. Anyway, let's get on and enjoy the dance.'

As they neared their destination, piano music rang out into the street. It's a long way to Tipperary, belting through the small open windows of the Central Palace. The sound of brass accompanied the pianist. The girls made their way inside, glad of alternative entertainment, other than digging up potatoes, selling hats, and watching old black and white silent movies.

Chapter 19

The pianist had more musicians join her, and a soloist. They were playing a great rendition of By the Beautiful Sea. Glancing around, it wasn't long before a familiar face waved them over. Bobby had a mate with him, a small dark fellow, with a friendly smile, and twinkling eyes. 'My mate's tagged along, Sid who makes saddles, so I'm not lonely. This is Molly our boss, and I've told you about my market trading pal.' He gave Francesca a cheeky wink, and Molly hoped they weren't trying to set her up with the friendly saddle maker.

Bobby didn't waste time in waltzing Fran onto the dance floor, even if they were making it up as they went along. His friend took her arm, 'Let's dance… My name's Sid.' Molly found herself being twirled and swirled, glad she'd put on her fuller skirt, to swish around in. From the other side of the dance floor, she spotted Fran, looking happier than ever, smiling up at Bobby who was whispering something in her ear making her laugh.

'You're the hat boss from Paradise Lane, then?' Sid gave her a lopsided smile, and she noticed he had a gap at the side of his teeth as he twirled his hand over her head, sending her reeling once again. She tried hard to stay standing, definitely no smooching going on here with this one.

'I've been left in charge, if that's what you mean.' She had to shout louder than usual; Molly didn't want to get up close, fearing he might get the wrong idea. 'The real boss has signed up for war duties. Not that he had to; he wanted to join the others.' She raised her eyes upwards, and did another twirl. Getting breathless from all the energetic movement, she leaned over and shouted. 'For me, I reckon he was more useful back here. It's a job and a half keeping a business going.'

Her dancing partner nodded, and his dark fringe flopped over his eyes, 'same for me; we're overrun with work, saddles and bridles are needed more than before. I'd have thought the hats would still be needed an all, though. Best not worry, eh?' He twirled her around and did some fancy footwork that made her laugh, then came back in front to waltz a bit more.

'You're right, this is the first time I've been out in months, apart from work, or church, and digging up spuds in the Walsall arboretum.'

'He made big eyes, and sung along to the next song. Moonlight Bay, singing about the girl he met in the bay. When it got to the part about hearts yearning, and when we're returning, he gave her a smile and whispered. 'Let's sit down a bit? Come on, I'll get you a drink. I'm not coming on to yer, gel; only being friendly. I can see you'm sweet on the boss man.'

Thankful he didn't make a move on her, Molly sipped her drink. He'd bought her a gin and tonic; not having the heart to tell him she didn't drink gin, she sipped it slowly. She wasn't responsible for Fran, and there was enough to think about with Issac, and work, her aunt and Janey, without being a nanny to her impulsive friend. If she wanted to have fun, who was she to go and lecture her, live and let live?

'Hey, look who the cat just dragged in.' Sid was looking towards the door.

'This is where you get to then; yer dirty little stop out.' Danny Glover teased Sid, making out he was a regular at the dance hall. In reality it was new for them all.

'I was only keeping a pal company if you must know.' He looked across to where Bobby and Fran were getting pretty loved up with the next song and nodded in their direction. 'Looks as if he's got a different kind of company in mind to me;' He laughed with the man who'd decided to join them.

'How's yer aunt Vi, today then, Molly?' He gave her a knowing smile, which gave her the creeps.

'Alright last time I saw her, thanks' Keeping polite, yet looking round, she would leave these two chaps talking if she spotted anyone she knew. There were too many good things in life to be doing, without getting social with Danny the dirty butcher.

'Excuse me; I've just spotted a couple of the girls.' She jumped up, 'Thanks for the drink, Sid.' She clutched her gin and tonic agreeing with a smile, when he suggested, they do it again sometime. She left the two men to chat.

She had spotted a couple she knew from work. Even if they wouldn't normally mix with she who gave instructions, it was better than leaving the Palace, or getting Fran to leave Bobby this early on in the evening.

'Hey, girls, fancy seeing you here? Now, who's dancing to this next one?' She was glad that Marlene and Rita were both up for dancing, and they were alone, so no men were objecting to her barging in amongst them. A sly glance over her shoulder, back to where Danny and Sid were sitting, told her they were engrossed in conversation; more than likely about the leather works. At least she'd got rid of him, and she wouldn't be telling Violet he was asking about her either.

The music went on, and the girls chatted and laughed. More drinks were drunk, and when Sid came up to ask Marlene if she wanted to smooch to a slow song, she didn't hesitate to take his hand and let him lead her to the middle of the dance floor. On her way, she turned and made big eyes at them and looked happy fit to burst. He'd made her happy even before she'd seen his special kind of dance moves.

Bobby and Fran were back seated now. Danny Glover had moved on. Rather than she and Rita being on their own, Molly said, 'let's sit down with the gang, we'll call Marlene over when she and Sid, let go of each other.' Giggling, at the famous dance moves from Sid and their friend, they made their way across to the seats around the edge of the room, where she and Fran had started off, earlier that evening.

'Hiya, Bobby;' Rita gave him a full-on smile. 'Great to see yer out of the work hours…you do enjoy yourself sometimes then?' She was flashing her eye lashes and flirting with him. He was definitely a magnet for the ladies, and everyone knew Francesca was married, so it wasn't as if she was being catty.

Fran kept her hand close to his under the table. Molly hoped this wouldn't turn into a, 'who wants Bobby the most,' competition. He was incredibly good looking, and the girls all swooned out of his way whenever he went up to get more drinks. He was the stuff of movies.

He nodded to Rita, and looked over to Sid, dancing with her friend. 'Looks like Sid got lucky, eh?' He gave Fran a nudge and winked at Rita. 'You'll find the right one for you, if you stay long enough.' Bobby encouraged her to keep looking. He was all wrapped up in Fran, who wasn't giving him any signals to stop.

'I need to get back and see to the twins.' She stood up after a few more tunes from the band, and made her excuses to get back. 'You don't mind if I leave early, do you, Molly. Only ma will be getting tired. You know how these old ladies are?'

'Look, I'll walk yer home, Sid's occupied; you two have each other for company now don't yer love.' He smiled at Rita, and nodded to Molly.

'Didn't yer ma expect you to be coming home with me?' The unexpected situation threw Molly for a moment; *Holy cow, from being on the market, and having a smooch, now they were walking home together!* 'If you're sure that's what you want.' She glared at Fran and would be having words with her in the morning. Yet, she was a grown woman, one with three kids, and married. She didn't want to cause a scene, and Fran would be sensible. Yet, who knew what being in love did to your head? She wished she knew.

'I'll tell her we were together, that's all she needs to know.' Fran made knowing eyes to her best friend, expecting the loyalty she knew she'd get from Molly.

Bobby held Francesca's coat, then pulled on his own jacket, and then they nipped out; not before he sidled up to Sid and whispered something in his ear.

'Well, there's a turn up for the books!' Rita folded her arms and leaned back in her chair. 'Did we just see the new girl, married new girl by the way, walk out of here with Bobby Reynolds, the Blond Brummie Bombshell - in broad view of everyone?' She gave an exaggerated laugh. 'Well, that's the way to do it. I've been shoving me knockers in front of him for weeks, and he isn't even noticed I have a pair. I'd better start asking the great holy Francesca there for some tips on getting a man. Why look, even our Marlene is having a rare old time with Sid the saddler.'

She huffed. 'He's not bad looking in a wonky kind of way. It's always the quiet ones you have to watch. Mm, I wouldn't push him away on a cold night, would you?'

Molly couldn't help smile, and she knew Rita was right. All this coupling up made her want to be with Issac all the more. Why was she even here? Only from Moira and aunt Violet going on about how they should get out more, that's why. Maybe Moira sensed frustration in Fran at home, but she wouldn't have encouraged her if she knew she'd left alone, with a work colleague.

Shaking herself, back to the moment, she was glad when the local farmers' handyman joined them. He delivered milk to Paradise Lane; she knew William, and welcomed him with a smile.

'How's it going gels? I'm Will, and your name is?' He was only looking at Rita, which gave Molly the opportunity she wanted.

'This is the lovely Rita. And if you want to know more, she's happy to chat.' Molly leaned forward, gave Rita a hug, and whispered. 'I'll leave you to chat, love. Will's a good lad; he'll be interested in having a dance. See you at work tomorrow. I'll try and catch up with Fran.'

Rita didn't discourage her to leave, and Will was still swooning into Rita's eyes. Molly had enjoyed the company, and drinks and music, but she wanted to get back home herself. Hopefully, she might find Bobby and Fran outside on a bench chatting and they could walk home together. If not, she'd have a word with her tomorrow, and see what was going on, like if she remembered she had a husband, who could arrive home any day.

The night was dark and cold. Molly pulled her coat around her and began the walk to the end of the street. Wondering now why she'd worn these ridiculous shoes belonging to Violet. Her flats would have been better to walk home in. It wasn't far, to the cutting beside the cemetery, leading the short walk home.

'Going my way, gorgeous?' He stepped out of the shadows and into her pathway before she could speak. Molly felt her feet scrape the floor, as he dragged her into the dark alley, between the empty buildings down the road from the Palace. Before she could scream out, he'd clamped her mouth, with his hand.

He wore black leather gloves. They stunk of meat, and him. Her attempts at biting his fingers through the gloves came to nothing, apart from hurting her teeth.

'I've heard as yer like to bite. Had all the details from Eddie Bradford; said you didn't want to play at letting him get up here.' He thrust his knee in-between her thighs, parting her legs wide. He heaved his knee higher up and rubbed against her, pressing his hard lump into her exposed thigh. 'Feel that… how about you try it for size?' He laughed, and held his hand firm across her face. 'Listen, we can do this, either ways; come with me, have a good time in my big warm bed, try my length of cock, or yer get it rammed up yer here.' He was mocking and talking like an idiot. She was stuck, no way out from his grasp.

'Now, personally, I'd rather treat yer like a lady, same as I do with Violet, in a bed. But knowing you being the slag you've proved yourself to be, pushing your tits in the face of a delivery man, you'll want ramming up the wall. Same one the chaps and dogs piss up after a skin full. And I bet I'm right.'

Molly gagged on the rough hand thrust across her mouth where his fingers groped her tongue. She could scarcely breathe, and retched when he moved his hand and grabbed a chunk of hair, pulling it until it almost ripped from her scalp.

'Listen to me, whore, you shout out, and the whole hat factory, and them Cartwright's will hear about how you came up this alley willingly. Come quietly, and we'll talk it through. You'll be more than gagging if you refuse me. I've had my eye on you for a while now, and that little sister of yours has started budding out as well. You can come with me now, or maybe I'll give her a go instead. Violet has had her time now, she's been great, and it's surprising how these war widows forget their blokes, when they've got a red-hot cock inside 'em.' His throaty chuckle made her sick. She couldn't speak, only tried hard to whisper.

'Don't you touch our Janey, and leave me alone. I don't believe you about Violet either, you're an ugly pig!' She choked, and began coughing from the smell of him breathing over her.

'Well, you're not listening to what I'm saying. Now I know you want it right here.' He took off his gloves, and shoved them inside her mouth, blocking her throat, she spluttered and gagged again.

He lifted her skirt, and pulled her knickers to the side, not bothering that he'd ripped them. By now, his trousers were around his knees, and he pulled her hair back until she heaved and wretched on the gloves, coughing and spitting them out to take a breath. His fingers were so rough; she made a noise that even she didn't recognise. With his hands, he hoisted her up and pressed her naked backside on the cold hard wall. With an animal like gleam in his eyes, he entered her, and pushed into her until she tried to scream and then she retched again. He muffled her screams with his wet hand from probing her. He laughed as he jerked himself again and again until he grunted like a pig and flopped like a rag doll and then told her she was all he'd been expecting, so she'd better get used to it.

'Hey, Molly with the big tits, I'm going to look forward to doing this again, and again.' He grasped her breasts and squeezed until it hurt her; she couldn't make a sound now, from shock. His smarmy words taunted her. 'Think how your little sister and aunt will be kept in food, fuel and comfort, now you know what you have to do to get it.' He pressed his tongue over her exposed breasts, and bit on her nipples. 'Perfect, and now let's get you dressed and cleaned up. You're coming home with me.'

Everything was a blur, for Molly, as he looked back and forth up the street, then bundled her up in his coat and into his van, then calmly drove back to his house and removed what was left of her ragged underwear and began to wash her private parts with his hands and warm water.

She gasped, and then fully aware of being on a bed, with him, tried to sit up.

'Stay where you are my love. I'm cleaning you up. Can't let you go home to your aunt Violet with my love juice over your legs can we? Must say I'm disappointed it wasn't your first time, with Danny Glover, your lover. Still, I always knew you were a whore.' He put his face close to hers and she was so fearful he'd try to kiss her she kept absolutely still, frozen in time. His fingers entered her again, and thrust up and rubbed. 'Only making sure you're clean. You're skirt isn't bad, and if you wash your face, then I'll drop you back, before she starts sending out a search party.

'Good idea of the old ladies to encourage you and your friend to go out, eh?' He laughed. 'I was remarking only the other day, the pair of you don't seem to be living a life, and amazing how the old dears, get an idea in their heads, when I offer em a bit of extra beef steak.' He smirked.

'You gave them the idea?' Her voice came out as a hoarse whisper. 'And then you came and followed us.'

His eyes gleamed. 'I'll expect you to come and see me, one afternoon, every week. Make it a Thursday or Friday. After all, that's your aunt Violet's time. She's gone past it now though, like ramming an old sheepdog.'

He ran his finger along her lips. 'If you don't, I'll put it out about that it was you, first leading on the delivery man, Eddie, who told me all about you, pushing yer big tits in his face, then not letting him do the business.' He rubbed his hands together. 'If you don't comply with our little agreement, I'll go after your sister. Wonder what she'd do for a couple of hours of fun with Uncle Danny?' He rubbed his bulge and Molly was suddenly afraid.

'You leave my little sister out of it. She's a child.'

'Oh, you reckon fourteen is too young? You want to ask the clients I meet in London when I go down there. They'd pay me good money for an afternoon with little Janey, don't you bet on it.'

Molly couldn't think straight. Everyone had let her down. She only had herself in the world to trust and believe in. If she didn't go along with this deceitful man, she'd be out of her job, her home, and she and Janey wouldn't survive. If she had to do what he threatened, she would only be doing it for her little sister, and her own good name. One day she would get her revenge, but for now she had no choice.

'But why would I be coming to see you? What would people think if they saw me leaving work, to come and meet you?' She tried to talk him out of the ridiculous suggestion, yet it wasn't easy to believe he wouldn't make her stick to it.

'That's all covered, I'm going to let Violet know, there is a possibility that Albert is alive, and I couldn't keep calling if there's a chance he might turn up. And you, my little love bird, will tell everyone, we're business partners. I'm going to put money into the hat business, and in time, we'll get the saddler's in and stop making hats.' With a satisfied smack of his lips, and getting things tidied up, he nodded, hardly waiting for her to reply.

'I'm not happy to say that… Issac left me in charge, and the business is going well.'

'Well, you say we're discussing options, and working on the figures.' He looked her over. 'It's up to you, Molly Marsden. Either way, I'm having you, and you can work out your own story. I'm only giving you suggestions. Other than that, say I'm getting banged up with my boyfriend, the butcher. Get your face washed; I'll drop you off.'

She did as she was told, and felt wobbly, not in control of her own thoughts. How could she face her aunt and Janey after what happened tonight. And whatever Fran wanted to do with Bobby, she didn't care anymore. All she wanted to do was go to bed and cry forever. Nothing would ever be the same again. She had no choice but go along with Danny Glover's agreement; his threats were far worse than what she had to do. Now she would remember the night of the dance at the Palace Picture House, where her world ended.

Chapter 20

Following a restless night, after going straight to bed, Molly had scribbled a note for her aunt, saying she had lots to catch up on, so gone out earlier than usual. The reality was she couldn't let her see how her face was swollen from crying into her pillow all night. She couldn't face food, and wanted to be alone, along the canal.

Early in the mornings, it was more peaceful; if it weren't for Janey, she'd have jumped in the cut and ended it all. The cold air and smell of wood smoke from barges further up the canal soothed her broken soul.

'Our Janey, may you never in your life get some of the horrible things happen to you, like I have.' She looked to the sky where the clouds were parting to reveal a red glow promising early morning sunshine; the moon lingered high above hedgerows, the whole place taking on a silvery gothic look. She stood for a while, taking in the magic of the changing sky.

'You about to turn into a werewolf or just spending half the night out in the dark?' A voice made her jump. She hadn't seen the long barge moored up on the near side of the canal, a few feet further up the tow path. 'Yaw got summat on yer mind gel, if so then you'rm in the right place.' With a swish of skirts, Agnes appeared, ghostlike beside her.

'Oh, crikey, I didn't know you were there, just having some quiet time. You know how it is, when you need to think things over?'

'Feeling sorry for yourself? That's what it looks like it to me. I've got some mint tea on the go, guaranteed to solve whatever it is that's bothering you. Come on, you'll turn to a stone out here.'

She led the way to her barge, and parted the thick velvet curtain that hid the entrance, revealing a glowing wood fire, and a cosy chair with crochet blankets draped over it. 'Sit yerself down, and we'll share a cup of grog.' She placed a kettle on the fire, using a thick glove. 'It's a mint and herb mix. Guaranteed to cast away dark spirits, I feel you need that right now.'

Not disagreeing with Agnes, Molly smiled. The warmth of the fire and the promise of a tin mug of grog sounded just what she needed.

As the kettle boiled, and Agnes picked leaves from the windowsill of her kitchen in the barge, she added a pinch of ginger powder from a jar nearby. 'This'll warm yer cockles, now then.' She reached into her pocket and pulled out a big pack of cards. 'We'll consult the tarot, the answers are all here, cos if you carry on along that tow path, and off to work, with a face like that, they'll all shut up shop and go home. Leave it with me.'

She pulled a couple of mugs from where they hung around the quaint kitchen space. The leaves went into a silver tea pot, and then she stirred and set the pot to one side. 'You pour when it's had chance to brew.'

Shuffling the cards, she placed them on the table in front of them. 'Cut them in two, and make a wish, like how you want your future to be.' She watched while Molly took her time to cut the cards.

'That's grand, now you pour us a cuppa, and then I want you to put them into three piles.'

The mint tea filled the air with a refreshing smell, and it cleared the air, and helped clear her head. She put the three piles in a row on the table.

'Now then, you're a strong woman. The mothering card is here, showing how you're a loving type who wants to look after everyone. It's showing what a good mother you will be, when the time comes.'

'Not yet a while, there's nobody…' Molly couldn't finish the sentence, dawning on her that after last night, and with the threats from one nasty individual, it wouldn't be surprising if she was up the duff, as her mom used to call it.

'That's as maybe, but my cards are never wrong. Now, what else do I see? She shuffled and turned over the piles, and The Devil card sat in front of them, mocking and goading. 'You have to be careful. There's someone around wishing you harm, but you know that, don't you?' Agnes sat back, and listened, as Molly sobbed silent tears slowly at first, and then gushier, until her face was a mess of pouring tears and more snot and snivel, like she'd ever known.

'It's not easy, trying to run a business, with the main man away, and no word coming from him, other than he's been injured.' She took the handkerchief from Agnes, and wiped her tears, suddenly embarrassed. 'I didn't plan to break down here, in front of you, Agnes, what must you think of me?' She picked up her grog and drank it all down in one. 'Woo, that's potent, and warming.'

'You'll be alright now, and listen,' she turned the third pile of cards over, where the Star and World shone back at them. 'You close your eyes, now and imagine how you want your future to be, and in your dreams, you'll sort things that are bothering you out. Trust me on that. And when the World card turns up, you have it all to live for. Don't get bogged down with other people's problems. You are the one with the world at your feet. Within the next year, all will come well. There will be a pathway to walk, among the smog and the dregs. Find the rose petal pathway my love, and keep on walking and smiling. It's what you do best.'

She gathered the cards, kissed the pack, and placed them back safely in her apron. 'Now, hadn't yer better be getting along to work?' Agnes patted the back of her hand and gestured for her to leave, and get on her way.

'Thanks, Aggie, you've helped a lot… I think. There's so much to sort out, yet in a way there isn't. You've given me a confidence boost. Do you sell that blend of grog, by the way? I'd love to have some on hand.'

'Aw, get away with yer duck, take this.' She passed a small pot of mint, and wrapped it in a brown bag. 'Keep it watered on your windowsill, and then don't forget this.' She added a heap of ginger powder to the bag, 'Only a pinch, mind. Take some every day, it'll help no end. Oh, and, Molly, love…'

She turned; Agnes pulled her shawl around her shoulders, and cradled her black cat. 'If you need to talk, anything at all, you know where I am.' The Romany lady sent her a warm smile, and waved, then disappeared, like the Cheshire cat in Alice in Wonderland book she enjoyed reading to her sister.

Taking a deep breath of crisp morning air, she knew this wasn't going to get her down. Who was she to be feeling miserable and sorry for herself; she had her Janey, the sister who was fast becoming a young woman. She would protect her with her very being. Nobody would harm her, how they were trying to do with her.

She would expose the lecherous butcher, but not sure how. Not as if she could go to the papers, even though she felt like it. He was so well connected, that was his plan - getting in with all the right people, in high places.

Molly stood tall, held her head so high she turned her face to the sky. 'Listen up, mom and dad…' She hadn't spoken to them since they'd passed away. Afraid it would make them being gone, more real. Often praying, before bed at night; and at church on Sundays, that the Lord God keep them safe, that was all. Now she had a purpose to talk – and she knew they would be listening.

'Don't you worry for one minute, about me nor Janey; We'll be okay, stand up for ourselves, and not be downtrodden, you'll see.'

'As for mothering, I'll look after Janey as a sister and guide, but not a mother. If it happens one day, with Issac, that'll be grand, if not, well, God will decide on that. We'll be together one day, I'm sure of it. And now, I'm off to work, and remember mom and dad, I love you both every day – just as if you were here with me. As I know you are.'

She felt glad of the solace along the curly Wyrley canal, her homeland and haven. Nobody would drive her away, nor frighten her. She made her way to work with a spring in her stride and a song in her heart as she clamoured off the tow path, across the fields towards the Old Town, and into Paradise Lane.

***

It was still early, when Molly unlocked her office door. She was buzzing from her encounter with Aggie. She'd never read her cards before, nor been given her such sensible advice. Whatever Aggie's gifts, their meeting had left her feeling good. There was one or two of the workers arriving. Some liked to have half an hour to prepare the work that was lined up for the day. She often wondered if some preferred to get away from their home life.

To round up her morning observations, she needed a tipple of Stanley's brandy. Opening the desk drawer she felt a bit naughty but being the boss, why not? She felt for the bottle, to the side of the petty cash tin. Under the tin something jutted out; she hadn't noticed it before - a white envelope. She delved in and retrieved it, along with the half bottle of brandy, and the special cut glass they drank from. Opening the envelope, a flurry of white feathers floated to the floor. Molly held her breath, and opened the white note paper. She read the scrawled attempt at writing. It looked familiar in a creepy kind of way. This was an illiterate writer, with a spidery poison pen, she'd seen before.

Cowards don't go to war, Hero's do –

Time yaw went to foot for yaw country, or are you always gown to
be

A Coward of the Black Country –

Issac Cartwright.

She turned the envelope over. Same scrawl with post mark -
Nottingham, dated a few months before Issac decided to go and sign
up! Her blood ran cold; this was a bullying white feather letter,
goading him. How hadn't she seen it before? She crumpled the
offending item up and thrust it into her pocket, but took one more
look at the writing. Tonight, she would compare it with the one she'd
had pushed through her door. They were almost surely written by the
same person.

The brandy tasted warm and soothing, reminding her of Issac, and
his family. Had they seen that spiteful note? She prayed they hadn't.
Whoever it was wanted him out of the way. Now she was more
suspicious than ever and she knew the crooked butcher must have a
hand in all this. He knew what had happened with Eddie the delivery
man, and used it to his own advantage. Yet, she'd seen on the
butcher's delivery notes, he had script style writing, as if he was well
educated, and yet, he was round here, bribing them with free meat
pies, and trying to get them out of the buildings in his roundabout
way. As if she couldn't see through his tricks.

Francesca bustled in with a coy smile across her face. 'Morning,
Molly, hope you had a good time after we left. I don't know what
came over me.' She tried brushing past the fact that she'd gone off
with Bobby. At that same time, the man of the moment swung into
the yard, then dismounted and wheeled his bike to the sheds, where
they secured their modes of transport for the day.

'Well, I hope he's worth it, and don't cry to me if it goes wrong. It's
your life, Fran, but you have other responsibilities, remember?' She
gave her a side glance and pushed her glass out of sight. 'I'm not

going to judge you, don't worry, we have work to do. Just be careful, that's all.' She picked up the work schedule for the day, and asked Francesca to put the kettle on.

***

Danny Glover had a busy morning. Considering there was a war on, he was more in demand than normal. Liver and kidneys were all sold out, pork belly was popular with the housewives, and when he looked them over in admiration, none of them had objected when he'd asked them if they wanted a bit on the side. There were several options open to him, but for now, he was obsessed with Molly Marsden.

From her dark blue eyes, to the full rounded tits that stood out just waiting to be fondled, she was the beauty of the back streets, and no mistaking it. Trust that Eddie Bradford to have got his hand in there first. He'd put a stop to that well and truly. Now he'd made it clear to the wench how the deal would pan out. And he was certain she'd turn up. He was looking forward to Thursday afternoons now, much more than before. The thought of lying naked next to the softness of her skin gave him a tingling in the groin area.

He had his rounds to finish before going round Violet's to put her in the picture. He had a story to tell her, and in his mind, it was so real, he believed it himself. Her Albert was only a boat ride away from being home by her side. How could the local butcher call on her anymore, and make out he was educating her on politics? She loved the gossip more than anything, he knew that.

'Just can't be doing it and it breaks my heart to say it, Violet love. It's been great while it lasted, you've been a tonic and that's a fact. But all good things come to an end, and what with news of your Albert being found after all this time; Aye, it's nothing more than a miracle he survived on that small island off North Africa. Who'd have thought it, eh?'

'Where did you hear this from?' Violet clutched her neck, and had to sit down. 'You know I've never given up on him returning, but why now?'

'Listen, love, don't get yerself in a pickle over your supplies, extra meat and stuff. You'll still get your bills paid and anything you need, like a lift up the town, anything like that. I'm not dropping you in it, just that with a husband on the horizon, well, you can see how it looks, can't yer?'

Violet sat, trancelike. Hardly believing what she heard. 'I'm glad of course, just in shock, and who told you. Give me more details, please? And don't talk to me about money and gifts, I never asked for any of that if you remember? We were managing alright, me and our Molly between us, without your offerings.'

He rattled out a few important names he knew would impress the woman who he'd been visiting for the last few years. She'd been a great distraction at first, lovely to look at, warm in bed. But lately, it was Molly who had taken his eye. He'd been keeping a watch on her, and it was worth keeping in touch with Violet for that reason. Now was his time to make a move. If he left it any longer, others would step in for sure. She was going to be his; and his alone. When Issac came back, if he did, which he doubted, the way the German's were advancing, he'd be a shallow shell of the man he was before.

In the meantime, he'd make her his woman, and a fine one she'd be. He'd give his sister a call next week and let her know his plans. Oh, yes, there were profitable times ahead, with the toffs over the border not wanting to spoil their tight tiny bodies being stretched having babies, and willing to pay great sums of cash for a new-born. He'd see to it that she got caught from him, sooner than later, and his Lavinia would do the rest. Oh, happy days. Danny Glover, you have landed well with this one.

'So, I'll keep you informed, and get any other news I can, love.' Danny left with a wave and promise of Albert's upcoming arrival. Smirking to think she actually believed him: 'Silly cow,' he muttered under his breath as he left her alone and hoping.

Chapter 21

'Issac, come on. It's time.' Sister Wilma who had lovingly brought him back from the brink after he'd been brought in on a stretcher, after being burned and gassed in the rat infested, muddy trenches, helped him dress into his new clothes.

'These are your civvies for now. You're a farmer's labourer; if anyone asks. If they don't ask, say nothing. Your kit bag will get dropped off at the station.'

Issac nodded. Hardly daring to hope he was getting away. 'My dog …' a glance at the clock, told him it was early hours of the morning. 'Jasper, he'll need to pee.'

'Already done, he's been over the road and through the trees. He'll go with you, but in the cab with the driver, my brother. They're more inclined to be distracted with the dog than asking too many questions.'

Issac pulled on baggy trousers and oversized jumper. She passed him a brown overcoat that covered him neck to ankles.

'Put this on, it'll keep you warm, and you won't be picked out from a crowd.' He placed the cap on, and glanced down at himself, wrapped up like a parcel ready to go to the North Pole.

'Keep covered; at least you'll be inconspicuous. Boots, size 8, well worn.' She smiled, and from the moment she'd come in to wake him, her shoulders dropped, visibly more relaxed. 'You're strong enough to be on the move now.' She stood back to look at him. 'I hardly recognise this handsome farm worker; to the wounded soldier they bought in a few weeks ago. Sooner or later this horrible war will be all over, and you can say you were tended by the best.' She crossed herself and let out a huge sigh.

'I will always remember, without question.' Issac nodded. 'The Angel of East Anglia will never be forgotten; I can't wait to see my girl, and only hope nobody jumped in and kept her happy while I was away.' He was trying to hold it together, yet he felt the shakes coming on and his chest burned like fire; he gasped for air. He knew he was a mess, and the Sister was being kind.

'Hey, come on, be strong now; we all have to be. This isn't finished until it's over. There'll be two of you. In the next fifteen minutes, the wagon delivering our potatoes, will leave us two bags, then you and Sammy will be settled, near the cab, but on the back of the wagon, and then we're going to pile the other sacks of spuds around you. My brother's the driver; he's a farmer up in the hills over the border. He's always driving around, so he won't attract any attention.'

Issac trembled, half with anxious thoughts of the event, and mostly excited. He was on his way back to England, and his Molly.

'Are you listening, Issac. You'll be met and given your papers, and instructions. From there, you'll catch up with the war train, taking other injured soldiers on the way to the port of Rotterdam, then, homeward bound, across the North Sea, dropping you off in North East coast of England.'

An impromptu hug, threw him off balance. 'Hey, you'll have me wanting to stay here, Sister. All this loving care is something a man could easily get used to.'

He smiled, making light of a heart wrenching situation. Again, the trembles inside began, until she physically pushed him out of the door.

As sister Wilma had described, he and Sammy were given breathing room, yet surrounded by hessian sacks. Now he could see why their coats were the same colour and almost identical material as the bags of potatoes; they blended in quite well. Especially seeing how she had taken some dirt from the potatoes in the kitchen and rubbed it over their faces. It was around quarter to five in the morning when they left the hospital by the side entrance, completely hidden under the vegetables, and if anyone was watching, all they saw was the lorry that had delivered the goods, now leaving.

There was space for the two men to talk if they wanted to, yet both were silent, other than to reassure each other they were comfortable, as they began their journey to freedom. Into the unknown was scary, but for Issac, nothing could be worse than he'd seen over the past few months. The fear in the eyes of brave young men who had been only too willing to fight and die for England was something that would haunt his days. Getting burned and gassed had damaged his lungs, but after building up his energy, and knowing he was strong as he could get, he knew the time was right to be on his way.

When he was picked up from the battlefield, on a stretcher, he'd fallen to exhaustion. Jasper remained by his side. Then it was after the medics kept chatting to keep him conscious, he heard one calling his name, and telling him he worked with Clara. He was a friend and colleague of his sister.

The field hospitals were full of soldiers needing more urgent attention than he was. Some had lost limbs, crying out for their loved ones; battle worn, clinging on to life. He was devastated to see the young folk, completely unrecognisable.

Some bandaged all over, nurses holding their hands, a priest giving last rites to others. It near broke his heart and he passed out at the horror of it all. The ambulance and stretcher staff was told to move him on to a recovery hospital, being burned and gassed was bad, but he would survive and needed nursing care.

They took him to Belgium - the hospital where he would be cared for until he was well enough to be posted back home. Sisters and nuns were working hard to build the broken soldiers back to health.

'Hey, mate.' The man squashed in opposite him hissed. 'Issac… you awake?' As if he could ever be relaxed enough to sleep; holed up in the back of a potato wagon wearing a coat five sizes too big.

'No, course not, what's up?' He wriggled slightly to get a look at his travelling companion's dirty face.

'Do you believe in god?' His inquisitive gaze studied Issac's expression.

'As it goes, yes, I do. And I've prayed more times these last months that I ever have in my life before.' He watched the lad opposite him nodding.

'Why, do you?' He watched him taking time to think it through.

'Well, I'd like to say I did, but how could any God let all the things we've seen be happening in this day and age.' He sniffed, holding back a tear. 'I mean, we've lost mates of a life time. And all they were doing was what they thought was right for friends and family. King and country, all that jazz.' He looked down hearted, and as if he was about to break down.

'I've thought about that an all.' Issac looked him in the eye. 'They say the lord moves in mysterious ways. But for the life of me, it's hard to know why he lets folk with young families die, and the likes of me, who's on his own make it out.' He swallowed hard. 'A mate of mine got shot, next to me. One minute he was talking about getting home to his family, next, lifeless.' Issac shuddered.

'Hey, listen. Let's lighten up. And if there is a God, we'll be back in England for Christmas, and I'll buy you a cuppa when we land on the home shores.' After a second, and seeing the disappointment etched on his face, Issac whispered. 'I'm kidding; we'll have a couple of pints in the town.'

Sammy smiled, and nodded. Gloomy moment over, Issac settled back to dreaming about Molly, with her feminine curves and deep inviting indigo eyes.

Chapter 22

'We'll have to get Christmas organised, Molly. Did you tell your aunt Violet yet, we'd love to have you all round at our place?' Doris was busy tidying the desk in the office of the hatting factory, Stanley was dealing with the post.

'I've mentioned it, but nothing definite has been arranged.' She stuck her tongue in her cheek, and busied her head with the order book. They'd come on a surprise visit, Molly was on edge.

'Has Clara heard any more news about Issac?' She looked to where his father was huffing and going through papers piled in front of him.

'Here's something that surprises me…' He cleared his throat and began reading. 'I'm writing to thank you for the cheque received, and wanted to say it's been a while since we delivered to you, after you cancelled all further deliveries from us, I'd like to have a chat if it's convenient for me to drop by, as I'd like to see you in person. Or if you prefer to call in and see us, that would be equally acceptable. Looking forward to your reply - Yours sincerely, Rufus Peacock. Esq.' Stanley stroked his chin, gazing out of the window, deep in thought.

'Funny that - he's always been our main supplier I know you said the quality wasn't up to scratch, Molly, love. But he's clearly upset. How about we take a drive up there, say tomorrow?' He threw the letter on the desk for all to see.

If her heart could drop any further down into her toes, it just did. 'Erm, if you think so, but do you need me to come? I have a lot to get on with here, with organising the stall, and things.' She'd risk bumping into the letch who'd hurt her, but there was no way she could tell them about that. Not in a million years.

'I'll cover. You go with Stanley; it'll be good for you to be there, Molly. You're running the place, after all, remember.' Doris smiled reassuringly.

It was a long night, for Molly. The next day, while they rode along, Stanley at the wheel, in Issac's wonderful charabanc, Molly accepted in her heart - some days, things just had to be faced head on. This was one of those days. Hadn't aunt Violet always said? 'What's meant for you – won't go by you.'

Seems like a lot was meant for her and one day, they would have a chat about that. For now, she focused on the job ahead. Why should she feel ashamed or embarrassed? She never asked to be assaulted. God help her, if ever Issac found out; he'd be mortified. Likely to go after him if he found out who he was.

Some days, she could so easily pack a bag and run away. Then it was always Janey, who came to mind; she couldn't leave her alone with an aunt who carries on with the local butcher.

'Penny for 'em then love,' Stanley raised his bushy grey eyebrows and gave her the side eye. 'You've been deep in thought for the last twenty minutes. Now, you like looking round at the scenery, but if there's summat churning around in your mind gel, then you can tell me.' His nonchalant shrug, told her that he wasn't expecting her to let him know what she was thinking, yet it jolted her into being a bit more chatty to the kind man taking her up to see their long-time supplier, who hadn't done anything wrong, and needed some kind of explanation.

'Nothing special, mundane things; how I'm grateful, having my job that helps me look after my family; more now than ever. It's quite a responsibility, you understand.' She held her head high, and gave him a smile. 'There's the three of us… my aunt and younger sister. And thank you for the invitation for Christmas dinner by the way. I'll do my best to see that we all get there…'

He nodded. 'I know, it means a lot to our Doris. She goes on, and like a flipping mother hen at times. And we all know it's just because she misses her babies. Never mind they're grown-up ones, who are busy on the front line of the war; or were, in the case of our Issac.' He revved the charabanc up the hill, which took them over the border, into Leicestershire, heading north east. The pull of the incline caused the motor to chug and splutter a while, until he got onto the straight road again. 'Bloody potholes, excuse me mouth love only you'd think the Roman's had only just left with the state of these so-called roads. More like blinking dirt tracks if you ask me.'

Molly chuckled… he had a knack of making her laugh. It occurred to her that other than Stanley, there weren't many men she could chat to, about Issac. 'I'm glad he's due to be getting on his way home. Do you think he'll have a safe journey?'

'It's like our Doris says, we hope and pray every day they'll both come through this and be able to live a normal life one day soon.' He gave a sigh. 'That's all we want, some kind of normal for us all, eh love?' He cranked the gears, and the car jolted sideways, causing them to lurch over to the side of the road, through a pot hole.

'Bloody hell; let's hope we can get through this flipping journey in one piece, what say you, old girl?'

Molly knew it was his way of talking, and he was so used to being with his wife, she couldn't mind him calling her old girl. She was only twenty-nine after all.

That's when it happened… the motor bumped and jumped, limping along, like a clown's car in the circus, kangaroo hopping down the road, just before they reached a cross roads, with a lopsided sign post, showing the way towards Nottingham.

'Bugger and blast; darn things got a puncture. Would you honestly believe it?' He manoeuvred the motor, and swung into a gateway, pulling the motor car off the main road. 'One good thing, we're on

197

the main thoroughfare, someone will get us to a garage, maybe.' He looked more doubtful than he sounded. But mostly, better this happen when you weren't out alone in this thing.' He kicked the deflated tyre.

'Don't we have a spare?' Molly hadn't a clue - just that she remembered Issac talking about getting one.

'He always said he'd get one, but that day never came.' Stanley looked up all three roads, pointing back to Walsall, and over to Lichfield, as if a trained mechanical man would appear from nowhere. 'We'll just have to wait and see who comes by. We're not that far from Nottingham.' He looked up at the sign showing only seven miles and they'd have made it.

'I'll sit up here and keep an eye out.' Molly jumped up on the stile, pulled her skirts tight around her and sat, on the lookout for the next bus, horse and cart, fancy carriage or whatever form of human life might possibly come to their rescue. She had a feeling from the few travellers they'd passed on the way; they may be stranded for some time.

'At least we can thank your Doris, she handed me a pack of sandwiches before we left, and a bottle of tea.' Molly poured a cup of tea for each of them, and offered Stanley a gooseberry jam sandwich. 'They're a bit squashed, but all adds to the flavour, eh Stanley?'

'Oh, great; we might as well get our refreshments down us, keep the hereby genies at bay eh, love?' He settled his backside on a large boulder near the side of the road, in readiness of stopping the next passer-by.

'This might sound a bit impertinent, duck. But how do you feel, regarding our Issac?' He stuffed a sandwich into his mouth and munched as he looked directly at her, searching for an answer. 'Seeing as he's been writing to you, and we heard as Clara has said he was looking forward to getting back to you. Only, I'd hate for him to have ideas that'll come to nothing, with him being war wounded now.' The concern was etched clearly across his face.

She took a moment to answer, looking to her right then left, nowhere to run. And he deserved an honest answer. 'I love him, Stanley.' There, it was out in the open, and she felt better. 'He doesn't know that, we never spoke about feelings, only work. More's the pity.' Biting on her lower lip, Molly felt closer to Issac, voicing her feelings to his father. She hadn't even said this to aunt Violet, nor Francesca, though she guessed they both knew.

'I was devastated when he told me he was going away to fight.' She breathed deeply, trying to control her speech, not wanting to cry. 'He wouldn't hurt a spider. He always put them outside and never once killed one.' She smiled at the memories of him calling every creepy crawly, a lucky spider.

'He didn't even swat a fly either. Imagine, how should someone as gentle and thoughtful as that be fighting in a World War?' She shuddered, not daring to think of what he'd had to go through.

'I could swing for the cruelty of that white feather brigade. They want to go off and fight, if they're so concerned about being conscientious making someone a coward. There's more to getting through a war than being on the front line; What about him being needed to keep his business going, protecting female workers from them who stay behind and prey on the females?'

'The ones in the drawer, in the office you mean?' Stanley drank the last drop of his tea, nodding. 'I saw them. Couldn't bring me self to tell our Doris, she'd have been mortified if she thought he'd been pushed into going over the channel.'

'I only found them the other day. They're still there; I should put them in the bin. There's more to it than I first thought though, Stanley.'

Now she'd opened Pandora's Box. They hadn't seen anyone pass in the last half hour. Talking about Issac; and her feelings for him was a salve for her soul. After the hurt and unkindness, she found Stanley and she were more connected through their mutual love for Issac.

'What's that then lass?' He encouraged her to speak up.

'It's to do with why I didn't want any more deliveries from Nottingham.' Holding steady, she hardly dare continue, he was all ears.

'It wasn't Mr. Peacock on the last delivery day; remember I told you? He was someone different, just that one day, not too long after Issac had gone. Came with the cloth, but it wasn't the usual standard, and he was obscene from the off.' She reached for more tea, pouring them both another cup from the flask. I did tell you, if you remember? When I came round, but didn't go into details, it was too embarrassing.'

'What! The bounder touched you?' He swung round and his face reddened.

'More than that Stanley, he was really awful. If I hadn't acted quickly, he'd have taken me.' The words flooded from her tongue, and if she thought she'd be embarrassed telling him, she was wrong. It was as if she wanted him to know why she had so much loathing towards the company, and definitely didn't want to go to the place where she might see the rat again.

'He was sorry after though, definitely bit off more than he could chew with this female, or rather I bit off his dreams that day.' She laughed out loud when Stanley spat out his tea.

'Anyhow, that's not all.'

'Blimey, there's more?' His eyes widened, and his bushy eyebrows twitched as he glanced up the road, as if to find a way out of hearing more x rated stories from miss Molly Marsden.

'One day, around a couple of weeks after that, I had a note, pushed through the door at home. It was there when I got back from work.' He shook his head, she nodded. 'My aunt had put it on the mantelpiece for me; my first thoughts were *its news from Issac.* Unfortunately, it wasn't.'

'Go on…' Now Stanley was engrossed.

'Well, the writing, more of a scrawl, as if a child or an illiterate had written it. And, I haven't compared them up close, but I would swear they were penned from the same author. The nastiness in the way they wanted to hurt somebody, make them feel guilty and dirty, that's my feeling.' She smoothed her skirts, as if to rid herself of the horrible words, and the menacing threat behind them.

'The note indicated that someone saw what happened, and that they would tell everyone.'

'Goodness me, I can hardly believe it. You poor child, and you haven't been to the police with this?'

'No, but imagine. If the same person was hounding Issac to get off to war, out of the way. Maybe he knew I'd be alone, and then, took his chance.' She felt her shoulders drop, her head went back, and she felt the pain and guilt she'd been holding on to easing away.

'It's possible; but horrendous if true.' Stanley scratched his chin. 'We'll have to go to the police with this.'

'I agree, but let me get the two notes together. Take a look, and then decide. If it is the same writing, then we need to be sure it's the man.'

'Good thinking. And… are you thinking what I am?'

'I couldn't possibly know what you're thinking.' She looked at him, waiting to hear what it was he had in mind.

'Well, if we see this man today, when we eventually get there, let's get the bounder to write something down for us. Hold yer nerve, young lady, and if we play our cards right, we can get him to confess, just by writing us a material order out, summat like that. What d'you reckon?'

'Stanley Cartwright, I reckon you've just had a blinding idea. Get your cap ready now to flag this chap down.' In the distance a roar of a motor car engine approaching gave them both reason to jump up, wave and shout…

'Help, stop, we need a lift, are you going to Nottingham by any chance?'

Stanley was delighted when he pulled up and not only that, he happened to have a spare tyre on the back of his car, along with the tools needed to change it.

'Hold fast, old man. We'll have you back on the road in no time at all.' He threw a wink across to Molly, who wondered what it was that attracted men to her. There was only one in the whole world she wanted, and the sooner he got back in one piece, the better.

***

Up in Nottingham, they pulled into their usual suppliers, to find Mr Peacock waiting for them, and obviously pleased to see them both.

'Oh, it's been too long. And if I hadn't been off work, with my gammy legs, there wouldn't have been any changes to our delivery service. How are you both?' He held out his hand in greeting, being his usual jolly self. 'Come on in, I've been looking forward to seeing you, and let's sit down and have a chat before I show you our new fabrics.'

It was clear after an in-depth chat that Eddie Bradford was a ladies' man, and that was putting it politely. Molly had chosen her words to keep it brief, yet to let him know how serious she was taking the assault.

'I've had word back from other places where I normally drop off; he's made a pest of himself.' Old Mr Peacock looked extremely troubled. 'I must say Molly, lass, there is nothing I can say to apologise enough, other than to say he's gone… sacked, and had his marching orders. I can't employ a fellow who thinks he can up and grab hold of females, not in this day and age, when they're doing men's work in the war, and home on the land and in the factories. This is a real embarrassment to me.'

'You weren't to know what the bounder was up to.' Stanley noted. 'How can you take the blame when you've been doing your own deliveries for so long, then summat like this happens, it just ain't your fault.'

'There's only one thing I'd like to ask,' Molly interrupted. 'I was wondering if you have a sample of his handwriting. Were there any notes in the books, deliveries dropped off, or something for me to compare my anonymous hate letter with.' She encouraged him to find some proof of Eddie's writing.

He got up and reached for the ledger. 'Hang on a minute; he would have logged things in here, while I was away.' When he pushed the huge book across the desk and pointed out the scrawl of the attacker, it caused Molly to gasp. 'That's it! Look at this…' She pushed her note to where Stanley was gesturing to see it. He had an interest in this as well, with the hate mail found in Issac's desk along with the white feathers.

'I'd say that matched, wouldn't you?' She eagerly waited for his response.

His face turned red and his eyes bulged. 'Well, Peacock old man, if you hadn't sacked him, I'd go a few rounds with the blinder until he was screaming for mercy. He's one evil son of a bitch, that one.'

'Do you want me to involve the police?' Mr Peacock was a fair man and he could see the distress his casual worker had caused. 'He only stepped in while I was off me legs, and he came with references.'

'Who the flipping heck would vouch for a monster like that, I wonder.'

'Well, the butcher from Walsall for one, Danny Glover put in a word and said he knew him.'

Molly felt a rage inside her. Now it all made sense. 'They must be mates, and my aunt is a friend of his. I'll have to warn her he might not be as good as he shows himself to be.' Secretly she knew what had been going on with her aunt and Danny, yet she couldn't bring herself to think of it. And now Janey was growing up, she wouldn't put her in danger with the unsavoury meat man sniffing around. They would have to leave aunt Violet's, she'd already decided, no matter how afraid she was of what the future held, it was the only way to keep themselves safe.

Chapter 23

'What d'you mean, you're leaving?' Aunt Violet spun round and looked ready to faint when Molly told her of their plans.

'As I said,' Molly kept her composure and as she'd practiced all night long, repeated, calmly. 'Me and our Janey are leaving, moving on, going our own way. Any other ways you need me to spell it out?' She stared her aunt full in the face and refused to budge on her decision. The determination in her voice sent shock waves through Violet; from the look on her face, you'd have thought she'd just lost her life savings.

'But why, love. I'm here for you both. What's happened?' Her aunt sat down, and indicated for her to come and sit opposite her by the fire. Molly knew she needed to keep her head, and talk this through with the woman who had lost so much, and helped them both, yet she was angry that she hadn't found the time to speak to her as an adult, more honestly.

'Well, like Christmas for instance.'

Violet nodded. 'Moira and the family are coming here, like I told you. Aren't you happy with that? You know how you and Francesca get on so well, and you came home late after that dance, so you must have both had a good time. You didn't tell me much about it.'

Molly flinched at the memory of that fateful night. Irritated, she shook her head. 'And I mentioned to you a few weeks ago, we've all been invited to the Cartwright's home, Oak Tree Grange, over in Pelsall. Doris and Stanley want to make us all welcome, and you refuse to even discuss their invitation, let alone accept it! They've got family at war, not sure if Issac will get home or not, their daughter driving ambulances and she wants to go out to Europe, on the front line, as well. All they want is a nice jolly Christmas, and you won't even talk about whether we can change our plans?'

That was one of the things she had festering on her mind, off her chest, and it felt better. Lots of things were being spoke about lately that she'd kept to herself for too long.

'Why didn't you spell out how important it was to you then, love?' They've never asked us before; I didn't realise how close you'd got to them. If it means that much, I'll ask Moira, see how she feels about that.' Violet clasped her hands in her lap and looked into the fire, as if all the answers lay in the flames licking hungrily around the coals.

'How about you tell, Moira, we're all invited and it'll be a grand Christmas all of us together with them. It's not as if we've got that much room for the Murphy's and old lady Doolan is it?'

'Watch your mouth, young lady, what's got into you lately? You're always on edge these days, snapping at me every minute.'

'Well, if you really want to know - I heard about your arrangement with Danny Glover.' She spat her words out and her tongue felt as if worms were crawling across it. She screwed her face into a hundred creases.

'He told me, you've been giving him favours, for whatever you need in return, and not only best cuts of meat, apparently.' Molly stood up and moved to the back of the chair. 'No wonder we're so well fed, well stocked with fuel and never struggle to find money for the next bill, like everyone else is on this street; even though I put in as much as I can for us. You didn't need to be entertaining him, unless it's what you wanted? He told me as much.'

Violet jumped up and pushed her fists into her side. 'You're so wrong, our Molly, love, and for all you're marching with these suffragettes, you haven't a clue how relationships work between men and women. You'll find out soon enough.

'A woman's place is in the home, making a safe place for the family she loves. And don't try and tell me about the Cartwright's having family at war. I had my lovely Albert at war. But I haven't had chance to tell you, what with you getting on yer high horse with me; Albert's been found, he's on his way home! So, for all I know, he and me might be having a private Christmas of our own, here.' She wafted her hands around the cosy front room.

'You go - and take your new friends with you. And when you're eating your turkey, think of those who have really cared, young lady.' She marched off into the scullery, pulled on her wellingtons, and retreated into the garden… her solace when things got heated.

Molly watched her checking the greenhouse, and then delving around in the small shed. That's where she kept her photo albums, and she'd be looking through them. She wanted to follow and tell her, the news about Albert needed to be from a reliable source; she had her doubts, but held back, for now.

Janey popped her head round the living room door. 'What's the shouting? Have you and aunt Violet fallen out?'

'Of course we haven't; you know how stubborn she can be sometimes. I was only saying to her, there'll be a time when we move on. We don't want to live here all our lives, do we? It's perhaps for the best, I start looking for our own place.'

'How can we do that?' The look on her face broke Molly's heart.

'Easy enough… I've been saving up, and working extra hours. We'll find somewhere, just the two of us.'

'What about aunt Violet though? She'd be so lonely, all on her own.'

Janey wasn't making this easy, and she drew her sister close, and stroked her hair, just like their mother used to do, before she passed away. 'Things will work out, they always do. If we just keep being good, help out around the house, and work hard. That's easy enough to do, for now, eh, don't you think?'

With a nod, and a frown, Janey went for a cup, and put the kettle on to boil.

'Anyway, how come you're not at school?' Molly put hands on her hips, and turned into their mother for the second time that morning.

'I could ask you, why you're not at work? But I think it's because you wanted to shout at aunt Violet about things.'

'It's my day off!' Molly could have swiped her little sister, who she noticed wasn't little any more, but getting wise to the goings on in the house. Only how much of the conversation she'd heard, she didn't want to imagine.

***

The journey in the truck had been bumpy, and uncomfortable, but after what he'd endured lately, it was a walk in Paradise Lane. He was counting down the days he hoped he'd be back home with his family, and the woman he was planning to take for his wife. Mostly it was the little things, a cup of tea, the smell of spring flowers and not hearing bombs going off around him.

Every little noise gave him the jitters these days; he intended to forget most of what happened. And first chance he got, he would go and find his friend's family, explain how he died a hero, with her name on his lips. Not something he was looking forward to but he'd promised and he intended to keep to it, if and when he got back to his homeland.

Issac felt the truck slowing down. Hearing voices, he lay low, and gave a nod to his mate opposite, hardly daring to breathe as they listened while Adam the driver gave his name and other details; Then jasper gave a bark, and the two men asking questions, laughed, and made a fuss of him, he could only guess. No prodding of the potato bags or lifting up the loose sacks, only jolly chatter, asking if the dog was the boss. It was a relief when that jolting began and they went on their way.

Only around three quarters of an hour later, they came to a halt. Both men stayed perfectly still, until Adam gave a knock on the side of the lorry.

'All clear, come on. I'll get you to the shelter of our farm for tonight. There'll be chicken stew waiting; only get a move on.'

Together they scrambled out, following instructions to the tee, keeping crouched and with black dirt from the potato bags, smeared over their faces. Heart hammering in his chest, and he guessed his pal was the same, Issac kept close to the ground, and keeping an eye behind him, as he was used to doing, they hurried to the shelter of the secluded farm house.

When they finally got inside, and gasped feeling thankful for getting safely this far, Issac asked where they were.

'Half way to Rotterdam, where we live, and all the farmland around belong to me and my wife Petula here.'

A lady putting a huge pan on the table, nodded. 'Eat up, keep your strength going, it's quite a journey ahead of you lads. We have workers in the fields, and if needs be, do some digging for us.' She smiled, as she handed them spoons. Ladling generous portions of her stew and dumplings into rustic bowls, Petula indicated for them to sit and eat. 'There's more if you want it. And for a while, when you're done, take a rest on the bunks in our back bedroom.'

'What'll happen to Jasper?' Issac worried they might take his dog, or want him for work on the farm. He was in no position to make demands, but he really wanted to take him home, all the way back to England.

'He'll sit with our dogs, they're in the yard, he'll be well fed and looked after.

'You'll have to excuse me but I'm feeling wary of everything and everybody. It's being so far from home, and seeing all the young lads getting killed. It's really got to me.' He tried not to break down, but he knew tears weren't far away. 'We're the lucky ones, having a chance to get away.'

'You'll be here for a day or so, and if any problems crop up, we can put you to work, and that way, you should be safer, as they'll assume your locals getting on with the job. As soon as we hear of the war train on the move, you'll be at the station, all set for Rotterdam, along with the other wounded men and women. And animals.' She smiled and he felt slightly reassured.

Issac was more afraid than he let on. The younger man was depending on him for guidance, and he needed to keep his head. He had to go along with what they told him; otherwise, the consequences could be dire.

Chapter 24

Janey sent a low whistle across the row to her where her friend Nadine was poking her head out of her mother's front door. 'You ready?' She'd heard Molly go off to work early, and after checking aunt Violet was down the garden, doing her usual tidying up among the fruit trees, gathering wind falls for apple pies, and Jack's pig, she quietly closed the door, and nipped out to greet her friend.

'Phew, it's a nightmare, pretending you've eaten breakfast when you haven't. Did you escape, without being seen?'

Nadine nodded. 'When you said we had a plan, I'm in. It's too boring going to school every day, learning the same thing over and over. I know tables like a parrot by now, and what use is spelling to us when we grow up?'

They shrugged and ran together, before anyone spotted them, up the street, and down towards the town.

'I wasn't sure if you'd bunk off with me.' Janey laughed as her friend danced along, swishing her skirt and showing her knees. 'I'm on the stage star of the show – watch me now, Janey. *When Irish eyes are smiling* she danced and sang her heart out in the early morning as they waltzed along into Bloxwich town centre, heading for the park and gardens, fully enjoying the moment.

'Aw, now I feel sad. My 'da always sang that to me and mammy when he was happy. I miss him.' She almost cried, and then looked to Janey. 'D'you miss yours? Oh, wash my silly mouth out, your poor daddy's dead, mine's gone to war and if I know how brave he is, then he'll still be alive.'

Janey, not to be out sung, and in no mood to talk about her family, took a deep breath, and belted out, *little yellow rose,* but then she couldn't remember the words. *Something about, cried when I left her.* Forgetting the words, and being utterly tone deaf, Janey had her best friend in stitches. They were happy as a pair of song larks, though in reality, they were scaring the birds away, and the ducks off the pond in the gardens, both missing the fathers' who'd idolised their young daughter's.

'Have you got any money?' Nadine linked arms with her friend as they marched on along the pathway leading to the shops, taking the scenic route into Bloxwich.

'Not much, a couple of shillings. Sometimes our Molly gives us a bob or two, but I've saved a bit by from me sewing jobs, for special days like these.' She gave her friend a linked arm hug.

'When me mammy does the market, for your Molly at the hatting works, she comes home with extra then I get a shiny coin. I've got a tanner.' She held the coin up and it glinted in the sunrise coming up across the fields. She says your Molly gives her a bonus if they do well. We can get some black jacks and a penny dip. Or some of them humbugs our nanna likes.'

'We'll have a look at the penny sweets in the grocery shop first.' With a shared grin and a giggle, the girls marched onward, happy wrapped up in their adventure.

'I might get us one of them Bakewell tarts from the cake shop to go with the sweets.' Janey had it planned out.

'One thing though, Janey;' Nadine chewed on her lower lip, a frown clouding young face.

'What's up now?'

'Say if the local bobby sees us, what shall we say – Y'know, about me not being at school, and you not being on yer errands?'

'Easy, we'll say we've been sent on a joint errand, and I'm accompanying you, to get medicine for your granny.' Janey smiled reassuringly; most grannies need medicine. But let's hope we don't see him, and if we spot him before he sees us, we run fast in the opposite direction.'

They linked arms, and enjoyed the walk up the street, browsing in the shop windows, choosing what they'd buy if they had more money.

'I just want to have a wander around town, chat with you, and then we can get some chips from the corner cafe, or I might get a scallop. Better not tell em we've been stuffing our faces back home though; we'll get a lecture on how scarce food is.' Janey warned, Nadine, and she nodded sagely, taking it all in.

The lady in the chippy on the corner gave them an extra scoop, with a smile and plenty of salt and vinegar. She didn't even ask why they were out and about, only told them to take care of themselves. They sat enjoying their lunch, on a wall, opposite the building site, out of sight from the main street.

'Mm, the chips weren't half tasty, and that vinegar fair stung me tongue, but we'll wash it down with a bottle of dandelion and burdock pop from that shop by Molly's workplace.' Janey wrapped the paper up, and put it into a bin nearby. 'Let's go and surprise them at work; we'll ask for a job. We'll cut through onto the canal and play skimming stones in the cut on the way back.'

For Janey it was such a relief, being out on her own, away from home and her arguing family. The raised voices from Molly and their aunt Violet scared her; it was horrible when they didn't get on, but she didn't know why.

'Does your mom talk about your dad, Y'know, being far away, and well…?' Janey got tongue tied. Nadine came to the rescue.'

'Whether he'll survive the war you mean? Janey nodded.

'She's a trouper, that's what our da always says. If anyone can keep the family together, it's our Francesca, that's what he tells everyone. And she will. But I don't want to talk about families.

They walked down the Wolverhampton Road, to where it joined Stoney Lane, they got onto the canal tow path and ambled along in the morning sunshine, chatting away as if they'd known each other a lifetime. 'It's great to have you to chat to, y'know, without having to worry you'll tell me to shut up or go to my room. They should treat us more grown up; I bet you get the same, eh?'

Nadine nodded… 'Have you got a boyfriend yet?'

Janey laughed. 'Are you joking, after what our Molly told me to expect.' She gave a cautious side glance to where Nadine was watching her eagerly.

'What, the monthly demon, you're talking about? The curse of womanhood, our granny calls it.'

'You know about that already?' Janey gasped, 'not that, well, that first of course, but how things work, like getting together and making a family. You've heard about all that have you?'

She shook her head, 'Yuck, no! From what my mammy told me, I won't be thinking about boyfriends for a while yet. I like being a tomboy, climbing trees and playing football.'

'Same as me, let's celebrate being tomboys and throw stones climb trees and do anything we want to do.' Janey ran ahead, whooping and galloping like a cowboy on horseback.

'Wait for me… That's what you say now, but you're a pretty girl, Janey, you'll find somebody nice one day.' Nadine caught up with her and held her side from running.

'I hope so.' Janey smiled at her young friend. 'But not for the moment. And have you got your eye on a smart young man at all; seeing as you want to know all about my non-existent love life?'

'I'm in love with our post man.' She laughed. 'He brings news from our daddy he's the only man for me.' Nadine went off into her dream world. 'He's handsome, kind, and tells me I'm his best girl in the world, after mammy. That's good enough for me.'

They made their way along, not noticing the Romany lady watching them from her barge window.

***

Molly knew she needed to let Doris know about Christmas; time was ticking on by, and she couldn't face being in Victoria Row with all that had been said lately. She could see her aunt's point of view, yet she'd rather go hungry than think of what she'd put herself through because of them. It made her feel so awkward, as if she was part of something she knew nothing about. Now he wanted to carry on the dirty deeds, but swap family members. And how long before he started getting his sights on Janey?

She shuddered, and got on with her order list. With Francesca and Bobby out on the market, it was quieter than usual. They were doing well, and got on like a couple of old mates. Though they'd both been really quick to tell her that; maybe a bit too quick, but who was she to intervene where relationships were concerned? All she knew was, she loved one man, he was away, and in his absence, she'd seen a sordid side to life.

Prostitution was commonplace, with the brightly decorated call girls hanging around outside the pubs, on street corners, all high heels and low-cut tops, looking for a quick ding-dong, for a few shillings. Why didn't Danny Glover get involved with them, and leave her alone? It wasn't their way, in her family, yet how aunt Violet had been going on, it amounted to the same. If her mother had known how things would have turned out, she'd be spinning in her grave.

Surprisingly, he hadn't turned up at her workplace, to confront her at all, considering she hadn't stuck to the bargain he'd demanded about her being expected round at his place. She knew he wasn't calling at Victoria Row anymore. There was something, niggling in the back of her mind. That's why she sat her sister down and made sure she knew about what happened when men and women got together.

It was a tricky conversation, but from the way she was fast growing into a young woman, she needed to be more prepared than she was. Without their mother being around to tell her youngest daughter, she felt responsible, and needed to put her straight; let her know she'd was there for her when men started showing an interest.

Her monthly was late – and she felt different, not in a good way. Her breasts felt hard, and they hurt. She would have to see the doctor to check. There was only one who could be the culprit. He had to know, he couldn't get away with it. She'd decided to go as soon as they got back from market, she'd make up some an excuse, about having to go and see the nail maker about his outworkers.

It wasn't such a great lie, as when she'd bumped into him last time she was in town, Old Desmond was telling her it'd be a good idea for her to get piece workers from home, same as he did; those jobs that didn't need the machines, only hand sewing, could easily be done by piece workers, they need less pay, and it would cut her wages bill by half.

Francesca and Bobby had another record day at the market, and were busy putting stuff away when she told them she had errands, and could they lock up?

'Of course, we'll see to it all, Molly – trust in us, and you'll be fine.' She laughed, and ran to put Dolly in the stable, with a bucket of food to restore her to fitness after the busy outing.

Seeing they were more than capable, and both engrossed in their jobs, she left to do her 'errands'.

To keep her cover, she knocked on the door of the nail works, half a mile from Paradise Lane. It was Desmond's daughter Ethel who answered.

'Adoo, Molly. Haven't seen you for a bit, how's things?'

'Oh, Ethel, I was going to chat with your dad, if he's around. He was telling me about taking on outworkers, how much you pay, and what type of work they do; but it can wait if he's busy. We'll get together another time; I know how precious your time is.' Molly hated fibbing, but having called and spoken to Ethel, meant she had an alibi, if anyone asked her where she'd been, and she knew someone would have seen her and tell someone who told someone else.

'Listen, you didn't have to rush off, but why don't we meet for a cup of tea in Walsall, next week sometime. We'll have a proper business chat, us being women in control.' Ethel laughed and folded her arms under her chest and held her head high.

'Oh, I'd like that.' Molly nodded. 'How about I meet you by Sister Dora's statue, in Walsall, next Tuesday afternoon?' Ethel agreed, and as she walked away, Molly knew she would enjoy the chat with her friend. Now she had a different kind of business to see to. Personal stuff, that she wasn't looking forward to, but he wasn't going to treat her like a common prossie and she not kick back.

That's how, a short tram- ride later, Molly found herself at the gate of the local butcher, Danny Glover. She had to get this off her chest. Coming here regularly, as his bit of entertainment, wasn't something she would even consider, let alone set up as a regular habit. She knocked on the back door, and listened as she heard him shuffling his weighty body to the door. His face lit up as he opened up and saw her standing there.

'Ah, you decided to stick to our little bargain, then? Good sort, Molly Marsden, I knew you'd give in sooner or later; what's up, run out of fuel in the coal shed and food in the larder?' His cruel laughter, turned her stomach, and she held on to the door frame to steady herself. She had noticed a sick feeling every morning as well, that made her stomach turn a somersault, especially being here. Yet, she didn't want to conduct the conversation out in the open. She'd seen a few curtains twitching already.

'Come on in, you can't get yer knickers of out there can you now, love, eh?'

'Well, that's the thing, Danny.' How she hated using his name, when she wanted to call him so many other things. 'I came to tell you; from when you assaulted me; you've put me in the family way. I've made an appointment to see the doctor.' She stood tall and refused to be made to feel guilty. 'And don't tell me to visit Nelly Crabbit; over the back end of town; I'm not going to risk getting her dirty obstacles anywhere near me; She left the girl from the tanners yard unable to have any children after that, almost killed her in-fact with the infection.'

'Hold yer horses, girl. What you gabbling on about, who said anything about getting rid of it, but you sure it's me that's copped yer, knowing how attractive your body is to the men. Probably any one of us yer've been with.'

'How dare you!' It was all she could do to stop herself throwing her fist into his fat face. 'Of all the damn cheek, you and your mate need to be reported to the police, and I've a good mind…'

'If you had a good mind, you should be flattered by my advances, speaking of which…' He traced his finger along her neck and pushed his hand over her left breast. 'We'll have a good time, then, I'll tell you what happens next.' He lunged forward suddenly, took her up in his arms, and marched her through into the hallway and though she was kicking and screaming, he gripped her like she was one of his animal carcases, and she couldn't believe it when he threw her into the bedroom and onto his big double bed.'

'I haven't come here for this.' She protested and tried to scramble off the bed before he reached her.

'Oh no, Molly, you should know better than that.' He was undressing himself, as well as placing his knee between her legs to keep he fixed in the same place.

'Are you mad? Didn't I just tell you? I'm with child, you'll damage me.'

'Well, I'll pleasure yer before I do that, now, come on, you'll get used to it.' He was groping and dribbling, and Molly gave a cry. 'Well, there's nobody around to hear you, so just lie back and let me show you how a real man takes his woman.'

'I'm not your woman, never will be, you have to stop this right now!' She wriggled to get away, but it only proved to excite him more. She couldn't overpower his advances, and through her tears, she knew, one day she would get revenge on this hateful man, and her child would never call him daddy.

'It's time I explained to yer what's going to happen.' This is how it'll plan out… He went on to tell Molly that when she began to show, he would drive her out to Shropshire, over the border, far enough away for anyone to find out.'

Molly was speechless, and sat quiet for fear of angering him and making him touch her again.

'So, as I was saying, you'll stay with our Lavinia, who'll take care of yer, and then when the sprog comes, it'll go to the best family you could wish for. No need for you to be involved after that. She knows all the barren women who crave a child; and the vain ones who don't want to be touched. Their husbands will pay any price to take the baby off your hands; only they'll be discreet. All you have to do is saying you're going away to rest, after the business is done, you'll go back to normal, and then we can get back to making more.'

He laughed, 'Money and babies, easy money, and all you've to do is carry the kid, and pleasure me into the bargain.'

He sat back and leered at her. 'Nothing for you to do, apart from open yer legs whenever I say; you've got the best end of the stick you might say.' He laughed and she sat numb, taking in what she'd just heard and couldn't believe her own ears. The room spun, she felt sick again. How could she spend time in his company, knowing now that he intended to use her for a baby making machine, only she was expected to give away a child she'd carried?

Everything was going wrong. She'd come here to tell him he had to be responsible for his actions, but not in this way. There was no way she'd play along with his sordid games. There had to be a way to escape his advances.

She had made an appointment with the doctor, after she'd left Ethel. He was going to see her the very next day. If he confirmed her condition, she'd have to tell him, exactly what Danny Glover had planned. That wouldn't be easy, as she'd come here today of her own free will. How would he believe she was afraid of him? Her heart was beating in her chest.

Pulling her blouse together, she adjusted her garments. Her hands were shaking, as she pulled her underwear into place; this couldn't be happening, not again. She knew when she left here, she had to talk to someone, yet who could she trust? At the moment, she didn't know anyone who'd be prepared to help her.

Janey and Nadine walked and talked, chatting about life, and families, and mostly how they should be treated more like adults instead of kids, they were growing up now, and both fed up of not being listened to, or taken seriously.

'Let's go and meet Molly out of work. She needs more workers, but can't afford to pay much; I heard her say that the other day, why don't we go and volunteer our services?' She turned to her friend. 'I mean me at first. You're too young, but you could put your name down ready, I'll speak up for you and suggest a Saturday job.'

Nadine shrugged. 'I'm easy, just out for fun with you, my friend.' She linked arms and skipped along. 'Won't Molly go mad at you turning up unexpected, like?'

'Naw, she'll put me on the pressing machine.' Janey knew all the jobs, and was determined to get herself in at the hat business. 'I heard her talking to aunt Violet. They need more money. It's easy for them to say I'm too young, but they don't see how useless I feel. They need me to help, but they're too proud to let me. I could scream at them, I really could.'

Nadine nodded, 'I know what you mean. Hey, look over there…' An old tyre swinging from a rope over the other side – let's have a twirl before we go job hunting.' She ran over the bridge, and tried to reach the rope. 'It's too high; you'll reach it better than me.' She stretched and gave up after a few tries. 'We need to stand higher on the bank, and throw it to each other.'

Janey leaned over the bridge. 'Is this what you're trying to do?' She reached over, stretching her whole length as far as she could, and pulled the rope towards her. Swinging her legs, over the top of the bridge, she held on tight to the rope, and jumped up to wrap her legs tight around it grasping on tight with both hands, sending herself spinning. 'Argh, I'm going to crash.'

Nadine laughed until she was fit to burst, oh you look funny. 'Don't hit the bridge, oh my lord, I can't look.' She covered her eyes and saw Janey stick her feet out to use as brakes, and stop herself bashing into the bridge with her booted feet. Gradually, she slowed herself down, and launched herself onto the bank.

'Oh crikey, that was fabulous. You have to try it. Hang on, I'll help you.' She went back to the top of the bridge, caught hold of the tyre, and dragged it to the wall on the bridge then called Nadine over. 'You sit up on the bridge, grab the rope and I'll lift you on, then like I did, have a swing and jump off onto the bank. It's not hard, it's like flying through the air, and you'll love it. Proper boys stuff for us girls who want to stay forever tomboys!' they spat on their palms, and shook hands to seal the deal.

Janey helped Nadine reach for the tyre, by lifting her until she wrapped her legs around the black dirty tyre swing. She gave her a helping push off, and next minute she was twirling, same as Janey was before her.

'Yay, I love it, look at me, and hey, I kicked the bridge and didn't crash, like you. Janey, I'm dizzy, it's so fun fun fun...' Ready now I'm going to jump, watch out...'

The scream followed by splash would have reached five miles away. Nadine waved a hand and pushed her head up in time to shout, 'I can't swim... help!'

Janey couldn't swim, but her friend was in danger and it was her fault for encouraging her to follow what she'd done. She let out an almighty cry; 'Help…' and again, her voice rang out over the barren land. Trying to scramble down the canal bank, she worried she might go under herself, and then wouldn't be able to help her friend. It was a short run to the hat works, there wasn't time, she must stay here. She kept screaming, hoping someone heard her cries.

Bobby and Francesca had locked up and started on the walk home, deciding to take the scenic route along the canal. 'Molly told me the lady on the red and gold barge reads Tarot cards, I want to ask if she can book me in.'

'I can tell you your future; let's look at yer palm.' Bobby took her hand.

'You're not taking this serious; Molly swore she was brilliant.' They were going up the lane that joined the canal when the piercing scream and shouts for help ran out…

'That's from the cut, someone's in trouble, quick, let's go.' Bobby raced over scrub land, jumping the brambles and gorse faster than the wind. He reached the canal bank as Janey let out another scream. She'd scooted down, trying not to fall, and then jumped in where she'd seen Nadine sink, and grabbed at the water where she'd gone down. She shouted again for help.

Bobby appeared, clearing the bank with one full jump, pulled Janey aside, and out of the canal, before going in himself; Head under the water he bobbed down like a fish, then he came up for air, gulped and went down again. He swished around, and with one almighty pull, dragged young Nadine to the bank, gasping.

Bobby turned the girl on her side, and rubbed her back gently, to check she was still breathing.

'Thank God, Nadine, talk to me, and tell me you're still alive. Come on.' Janey shouted. She shook her again. Nadine threw up all over Janey, and coughed then spluttered. Canal water trickled down her nose, and her hair hung like rats' tails around her neck. She held onto her friend as she wretched up more of the canal water, and tears trickled down her face.

'Nadine, is she Francesca's daughter?' Bobby's eyes widened like saucers, he turned to see his work colleague scrambling down the muddy canal bank.

'Me Nan's going to kill me, Janey I can't go home like this.' She sniffed and wiped her nose on her sleeve. The girl was soaked through to her skin. Holding each other tightly, it was only a second later when Francesca grabbed her daughter then held her tight.

'Never mind yer Nan; what about yer mammy, you pair of tearaways, what you trying to do; give me a blooming heart attack?' Frowning at Janey, she blurted out.

'What made you come along this part of the tow path? Does Molly even know you're here?'

'Sorry, we were coming to see Molly, and find work, to help our families.'

'Let's get you home, and we'll talk about it later.' She held her daughter close, and saw Bobby wringing the dirty canal water from his shirt. 'I think we all owe a thank you to Bobby, don't you?'

He shook his head, and waved his hand. 'As long as everyone's ok, that's all that really matters, isn't it? Look, I'll be getting off, unless you want me to…' He offered his arm.

'I think that would be good. A helping hand, getting these girls home, wouldn't go amiss; that's if you can spare the time, Bobby. I know they'll be waiting for you at home.'

'They will, but let's get this pair safe, and listen.' He put his arm around Nadine. 'Whatever your Nan or mammy may say… You being safe is all they want really. Just remember that eh?' He gave her a smile. 'And, tell me any kid who didn't play so hard, they got into trouble. Trick is, getting out in one piece.'

'Hey, whose side are you on?' Francesca gave him a shove, and then started to sing… 'Let's sing our way back home. Who has a song?' The bleak moment was gone, and Janey only hoped Molly would be as understanding as Francesca was.

Chapter 25

Molly couldn't face going home to Victoria Row. It didn't feel like home anymore. She knew time there was running out, for herself and Janey. She had to find somewhere else for them to live. Maybe then she could talk to aunt Violet and convince her to get away with them, but for now she had to think of herself. She ended up at the place she felt most comfortable, Paradise Lane.

Everyone had gone, and it was getting dark. She'd avoided the canal route, taking the tram back to work instead. The familiar surroundings, gave her a slight comfort as she lit the fire in the small grate, and put the kettle on to brew herself a cuppa at the Bloxwich and Walsall hat company.

She was going through the absolute worst time of her life. With Issac away, still no news and not knowing if he'd make it back home, her mind was in a whirlwind. Now, in the early stages of pregnancy, with nobody to talk to she thought her heart would break in two. It wasn't that she didn't want her baby; only that she wished it was Issac's.

Giving her practical head a shake, she knew it was too late to worry about that. And now it would be hard to imagine a future with the man she truly loved, when she was carrying another man's child. But it was her child and she vowed to love her little one, no matter what.

She drank the tea slowly, and pulled herself together; just in time, as the knock on the door gave her a start.

'It's you…' She looked into the face of Sid, the man from the saddler's business in Walsall; the one she'd met at the dance, with Bobby, on that night when… she cut the event from her mind.

'Can I help?' It was a job to know whether she could trust anyone these days. After Eddie the delivery man, and now, up the club with someone she'd thought was a family friend. Was Sid trying his luck now as well?

'Hi, Molly, glad I caught you. It's only on the off-chance – I know how you're here all hours; just an update on what we were talking about at the dance hall.' He stood, not being pushy at all, and she knew full well, he meant the saddler's having some space in her business.

'Come in, Sid; fancy a cuppa Rosie lee? I've just made one, the teapot's still warm.' She busied herself adding another heaped spoonful of tea leaves to the pot, giving it a good stir, and then using the strainer to pour the drink. She pushed him a mug across the table, and folded her arms.

'Ta, love. I'm not keeping you, I hope.' He took a slurp of the amber liquid and raised his eyebrows, wondering.

'I'll be here half hour yet, so I'm all ears.' She sat down, and indicated for him to do the same.

'We had a meeting at work today. About needing more space, for our production of the saddles and harnesses; they want to talk to yer; only I said seeing as I know you, even if only a bit, it's something we'd have to chat about. Just wondering how yer fixed regarding the idea?' He slurped his tea. 'Only we didn't go into any detail at the dance, obviously, did we?'

She bit on her lower lip, thought of Issac, Janey, and her little unborn baby. 'I'm not saying no, but there's Issac to think of. I'm only caretaker of his business, while he's away. When he gets back, it'll be his decision, though I could have a word with his family, they'd have an idea whether it's a flat yes or no.'

She put a hand to her head, suddenly slightly overwhelmed with all the responsibility that appeared to be gathering on her young shoulders.

'That'd be grand; if you could suss out the parents' they'd have an idea how he feels, I bet.'

She nodded. 'Come on, let me show you round. There's lots of space, and it's gone quieter, though we've started doing the markets, it's helped a lot.' She continued to guide him through the different workspaces, with rooms full of the equipment for a full workforce of hat production. Looking at it from a different point of view, she knew the trade was slipping, with the war, and folk needing money for more pressing things, like food and fuel, rather than hats.

'I've started designing some one-off hats, for weddings and christenings, something different to the drab stuff we're doing for the army and navy and the other branches of war personnel.' She put a hand on her little unborn child, wondering if she'd be able to get hers christened, without a proper daddy around.

'We're lucky to have the monopoly on the leather works, over in Walsall.' He raised his eyebrows and gave her a warm smile. 'Imagine all our lads riding into battle on horseback, with our leather saddles underneath em, and holding onto reigns, made in old Walsall town.' He couldn't hide the pride from his voice.

'Is it a family trade?' She picked up on his enthusiasm, and realised, she didn't feel the same about hats. It was the only job she'd ever done. Yet she was getting interested in making something more modern. She'd ask Doris what she thought of her idea.

'Yes, we've been creating leather goods for years. Still, you're the same; I know you told me they're all wearing hats from here.' He cocked his head and encouraged her to be proud of her work. 'I just wanted to check that you don't feel bullied into making a decision. They asked me to find out. Only that Danny Glover's been calling in. He's got shares in the business, and is keen to get as much of this place as he can... Haven't got a clue why,' he shrugged and shook his head. 'Only he's not the nicest of blokes.'

She froze, and looked him square in the eye. 'Oh? What makes you say that? I was led to believe you were pals.'

His face said it all. 'Good lord, you must be joking.' He drank the rest of his tea and put the mug down on the table. 'No, he's a nasty bit of work. You'd do well not to deal with him but don't repeat what I told you.' He looked uneasy, and reached for his coat.

'Well, I'll let them know you're making enquires and it's not a yes or a no just for now.' He smiled.

She wondered why she felt on the verge of tears. His kindness had touched a nerve, and he knew Danny was a dubious character. If only she could tell him just how conniving that scum bag was… Though it was doubtful anyone would ever believe such a story to be true, in this day of women supposedly having more rights. She nodded as she saw him out. The need to protect her unborn child overrode anything else at the moment.

Time for her to be getting along as well; she blew out the candle and made her way off to catch the tram at the end of the road. She must have missed the last one, and tired of waiting, she decided to take the canal route into Bloxwich.

As she neared Agnes's barge, the candle light gave off a welcome shimmer. She didn't want to disturb her as time was getting on; she walked without shouting her usual greeting.

'Cat got yer tongue or what?' The Black Country accent called out, and she turned, to see the friendly bargee, sitting quietly, on her stool, pipe aglow, on the end of her water home.

'Oh, cripes, Agnes, you made me jump. I didn't want to disturb you, how's things?'

'I was going to ask you that; how're the girls, after the events earlier? Good job the handsome chap took charge, eh?'

'What chap, and what girls?' She frowned. 'Agnes, I know you're a seer, and you have your crystal ball and everything, but can you talk in normal chat please?'

'You haven't been home then?' She looked under her lashes, and Molly began to have a feeling of dread go through her bones.

'I was called out, and then went back again later; I had private business to see to;' she waited.

'Of course, when I saw the young un's go past earlier, I says to me self, Aggie, there's going to be some trouble if you ask me, they ought to have work to do. Then again, you're only young once, can't blame 'em can yer?'

'Agnes!' She folded her arms, and shouted. 'What's happened? Tell me before I chuck you in the cut.'

'Exactly what happened? The girl went and jumped up, slipped off the tyre swing and fell in, and the good-looking fella, with the Irish lass, your friend Fran, he pulled her out. I'd seen em running, otherwise I'd have gone wading in. Think it shocked the pair of em more than anything. Thank heaven she's ok, though, so no harm done, eh?'

'They're all ok?' Molly took a deep breath. 'I don't know what to expect next. And I wouldn't have chucked you in, don't listen to me. It's been a long day. I'd better get home and find out the details.'

'No, love, you'll come on board and have a nice herbal tea, with me, and I can tell you all the details.' She wrapped her crochet shawl around her, held out her hand, and welcomed Molly up to sit next to her on one of the wicker chairs on deck of her barge.

Molly sat, stroking her cat while she watched her brew one of her herbal specials. 'Is that safe to drink?'

Agnes spun round as if she'd been prodded with a hot iron. 'Safe… My herbals… it'll be a darn sight safer than anything any other bugger's given yer today.'

'What if for instance someone was with child, then would it be safe?' She crossed her fingers, and was ready to say it was her friend, not Francesca, another friend she was asking for.

'I wouldn't give you anything to harm the baby.' She came and sat down next to her, placing a cup of yellowish liquid in front of her. 'It's a small jar of yarrow and honey. It's to help you relax, and if you want to talk, then I'm all ears; if not, I can wait.'

Molly looked at the drink, then the water gypsy. 'How do you know so much? Is there nothing you haven't an answer for, or an herbal drink that will cure it?' She took a sip of the warm tea and immediately felt better.

'It's alright love. If yer weren't, like that, I'd have given yer a tot of my rum. Best stick to that for now though, and worrying about things never put em right yer know; trust me on that. Getting on with things is always the best. I'm due to head off tomorrow, but we'll talk a while.'

'I'll miss you.' She meant it. Who else would produce a drink of soothing herbal tea when you needed it, and even know you were carrying a child, when she knew there wasn't a man in her life, and not judge? 'Not everyone thinks like you do.' She smiled.

'That's better. You're a pretty girl, got it all going for one so young. And remember, you wouldn't be the first to get put in the family way. Does the father know?'

'Oh, yes, I told him, and that I was going to the police.' She took a sip of the drink to steady her nerves. She knew nothing would be repeated from Agnes's lips. She held a confidence to her very soul.

'Bet he laughed at that one, love. Not to be unkind, but it's not often they want to be part of it all. Unless you're a woman of property and wealth, that is. And I'm not trying to make yer feel cheap, just being realistic.'

'Of course you are, and you're right. I've been used, and now he wants to carry on using me; take the little mite away from me. He ain't even given it chance to put in an appearance, that's the worst of it.' Molly put her cup down, and held her head in her hands. 'Oh, Agnes, I feel such a fool. But he was so strong, I couldn't fight him off.' She wept until she could cry no more.

'You get it out of your system, love. Bullies are like that, but you know something?' She put a comforting arm around her shoulders. The love for your little one will make you stronger. You've done yer crying, and now think of you and the baby. Drink up and calm yourself. He can't keep on hurting you, unless you're stupid, and I know you're not. Do they know at home yet?'

'Good lord, no, not yet.' How could she tell them, but she would have to one day; just not today. 'Thanks for the drink, and the chat, Agnes; everyone should have a friend like you.' She hugged the woman who was mysterious and mischievous, and tomorrow she'd be gone, until she came back again, which was who knew when.

The darkness didn't bother Molly at all, she continued to walk and walk, not knowing where she'd end up.

***

Still not in any mood to go home, she walked round in circles, head down, wrapped up, until she found herself outside the Cartwright's house. It was all in darkness, due to the great thick curtains they had, she knew that. They would be home, and all she wanted to do was talk to someone neutral. She'd ask if they'd heard any more about Issac, and then tell them, it would be great to be at theirs for Christmas.

Over half an hour later, Molly gave a huge sigh, her shoulders drooped and she sighed again. It just came out; she couldn't prevent it.

'Oh, dear me, Molly love. Did you have something else on your mind, other than Issac?'

How perceptive she was, maybe a woman's instinct, but she knew she looked a state, from the way she felt so washed out.

Stanley picked up his newspaper and made a polite exit. 'I'll be in the drawing room, with rum and cigar if yer need me, darling.' He gave his wife a knowing look and beat a hasty retreat. As if he too sensed something bigger than he wanted to hear.

They'd sorted the financial business out, to his mind. They were up to date on that. Mr Peacock had replaced the missing money from the petty cash, and the books were balanced. Women's talk wasn't something he wanted to listen in on. His rum and black was waiting for him, and that would keep him company while the ladies chewed over the fat.

Molly's head was in a whirl; not knowing where to begin she looked Doris in the eye. 'I'm having a baby.' She clasped her hands together under the table. Heat rose from her middle up to her neck as she whispered. 'I'm afraid; me and the baby are in danger. He's threatening to take it away.'

Her hands covered her face – before it's even born, and he doesn't want it.' Now the cat was out of the bag. She felt better, yet ready to face being told to get out and never come back.

Gentle hands reached for hers. The cool touch of Doris, clasping her hands and pulling them away from her face surprised her. There were no bad words, no shouting and not even a gasp of horror. She looked into the face of Issac's mother and saw only concern, and empathy.

'Listen to me…' She took her chin in her hands and looked her right in the eye. 'You need to start at the beginning. I'll get Gertrude to make us a fresh pot of tea, and we'll have a proper womanly chat. We've known you now for a long time, distantly, but more recently; you've become one of the family.' She put her hand up to stop Molly from protesting.

'Issac chose well, when he took you on as apprentice, and now the way he's left you in charge, shows how much he admires and respects you. And Clara likes you, so that's a good start, like I have an extended family now, with you all coming round for Christmas.'

Molly nodded and wiped stray tears that trickled down her cheeks.

As tea was poured, and the story unravelled, without telling it quite as bad as it had been. Molly refused to recall, every little detail, and even if she did, it couldn't be repeated to Issac's mother.

'So here I am, in the family way; it's hard to tell aunt Violet, we've had words.' Head down, she felt uncomfortable about the way she'd spoken to her closest relative nearest to a mother that she had.

'I wouldn't ask unless I was desperate, but would it be alright if I stayed in the spare room, at the front of the hat works, only for now. I need a place to be quiet; think over where me and Janey are going to live. My aunt needs her own space now, and we do as well.'

She hadn't thought it through in much detail, apart from that she'd need blankets and clothes. 'I would be safer there; in case the dreaded father of the child came knocking at Victoria Row. I can ask at the Red Cross place, next time I'm passing, about blankets, and any help available. Only it's not safe for me to be anywhere near that monster who thinks he can sell someone else's baby, just because he created it.'

'But what makes you think you'd be safe there, rather than at home? Surely your aunt would be your protector, just like she's always been.' Doris had tears in her eyes.

'No, I don't want to go and face her, or Janey. I have to stay at Paradise Lane for a while. It's the only way. They don't need the burden of me being in Victoria Row. Imagine the disgrace I'm bringing to the family.' Wiping her face, Molly stood to leave.

'I'm sorry to have troubled you with all this. It's taking some getting used to. I hadn't planned to have a child so soon, and definitely not with someone I don't even like.'

'I'll get Gertrude to make up a bed in one of our spare rooms. There's a choice of three, but you can have the one at the back… It looks out over the fields, peaceful and quiet. It'll do while you sleep of the trauma you're feeling. And I'm going to have a word with Stanley. He'll get Bart, our stable lad to go over and let your family know you're safe.'

'But, there's no way I could…' Molly began to protest.

'Listen. You're not leaving here until you've had some rest, and a bit of lamb stew. It's left over from our evening meal; you're going to get stronger and then we can make a plan. But it's only fair your aunt and sister know you're here. They might call out a search party and worry you've come into danger.' She led her to the kitchen.

'You sit down a minute, and Gertrude will sort you some food out. I'll get Bart to say you're working on those new designs you mentioned, earlier, with me. He'll tell them it's gone too late to walk home, and I insisted you stay, and you'll see them tomorrow.' She smiled.

Molly knew kindness, from her own family, and how she'd ended up here, was baffling, yet the way Doris bustled around, getting things ready for her to rest her head made her want to cry all over again. This pregnancy lark was something she'd have to get used to, and thank the lord for Bart. She made her way up to the room that was warm and inviting, with a fire already lit, flames licking round the apple scented log. Gertrude had told her to get settled and give the stew chance to warm through.

Bed covers plush and clean lifted her spirits, though she worried what Stanley would have to say in all this. For the moment, she sat on the wide velvet armchair, placed near the fire. When Gertrude entered, with a bowl of wonderful smelling stew, with a chunk of bread on the side, she accepted it gratefully.

'I'm in the room at the end of the corridor, if you need anything.' Gertrude stood, as if she'd heard everything. With an awkward smile, she bobbed and tilted her head. 'Don't forget. We're all here for you.' Then she disappeared.

Of course, she would live in, as she was always there. And now she was saying she was there if she needed anything. For a moment, she thought about Janey. She'd let her down, yet none of this was her fault. Life was taking a turn of its own. The stew was warm and fulfilling, it made her see things clearer, and she certainly felt safe here, yet she knew people like Danny Glover always had their own way.

As she settled down in the comfortable bed, making sure the guard was across the fire, she whispered a prayed for Issac. 'Please God, let him stay safe.' And tomorrow, she would go back to Victoria Row, and talk to Janey, and aunt Violet. She hadn't abandoned them, and would make sure they knew that. For now, she was glad to feel warm and safe.

Chapter 26

When Issac and his mate, Sammy woke the next morning, they were told it was time for the next stage of their journey. 'Get changed, there's bacon and eggs on the table, in the kitchen. You'll need to keep your energy up, and Petula has already made up a parcel of food. There's a war train going taking all injured soldiers across to Rotterdam.'

Without asking questions, he followed instructions to the letter. He knew it was the only way of getting back home. He'd prayed hard the night before. Something he did most nights, yet recently he felt the need to pray extra hard. Without being able to write, and not hearing from Molly, he felt lonely. Trusting in the help he was getting, and the company of his travelling companion kept him going. The last lap would surely be the longest, but soon he would be heading to Rotterdam and the journey over the sea, back to England, his homeland. He wondered if they'd be pleased to see him, or would he be seen as a failed soldier, the one who got gassed and hardly the returning war hero.

'What about my dog?' Issac couldn't leave him. 'He'll be with me all the time, he's a war hero too, delivering his message, and he'd have died without being rescued.'

'Thanks for all you're doing for us, but he's part of me now. And I promise when we get back safe, to England, I'll let you know, he's okay. As he bent down to stroke his dog, a huge tongue came out and gave his face a wash. As if the German shepherd understood his every word, and agreed, man and dog travelled together.

'Seems you're all for taking him, and I don't blame you. He's a cracking feller.' He stroked the dog's ears. 'Well, take good care of each other. There's a lorry coming along soon. You're in the back of a truck load of pigs today.' He grinned. 'You'll be used to this rich living by time you get back.' He told them the dog would travel up front, same as before.

They couldn't risk having him among the livestock, and they'd be under some hay bales, in with the pigs, until they got to the station. Issac knew this was the last push to get back to England, knowing that faithful black and tan Alsatian dog wouldn't be far away.

***

It was a subdued Violet and Janey having breakfast when Molly entered the terraced house in Victoria Row the next morning. 'Hello, I've come to see you – I had a ride in the pony and trap.' She couldn't think of anything else to say that wouldn't upset them any more than she wanted to.

'Aye, we got news last night you were staying over with the bosses.' Violet crossed her arms over her chest and looked more than annoyed, without saying a word.

'I felt rotten. Been a hard day, and it was late, so they offered.' Clearing her throat, she looked at the table. 'Can you spare a crust of toast, then?'

Janey jumped up and began slicing the bread.

'Glad to hear you and Nadine are alright after the tumble.' She gave her sister a gentle hug. 'You can tell me all about it when you're ready.'

'I've got things to tell you.' Molly sat down, and gave them a chance to reply. They were only staring at her, giving her more reason to feel deflated.

'There's been a lot going on lately…' She spoke slowly.

'You can say that again.' Violet couldn't resist having a jibe which Molly let ride.

'I'm having a baby.'

'How can you be, our Molly. You haven't married anybody, nor got a boyfriend.' Janey puzzled over her statement.

'Janey, can you go and check if the milk man's been round with the delivery pram yet, please? I need another cuppa.' Reluctantly, she got up and left the room.

'What's happened love? When did it happen?' Full of questions, Violet wanted to know every last detail.

'I can't say right now, only wanted to let you know. That's why I stayed away last night. It's complicated.'

'Who's the father?'

'That's just it; I'd rather keep it quiet for now. The Cartwright's are being reasonable, considering.'

'You've got my full support, our Molly. Just let's say nothing to worry little Janey, eh. Though you'd be better off here, it's where you belong.' She poured more tea.

'There's a man with a horse and trap waiting outside.' Janey was back with the milk.

'Stanley is waiting to take me to work. There's still plenty to do. A baby doesn't stop the world turning, and hats still need making, so I'd better get a move on and see to it they're cracking on with it.' Glad of escaping the ring of questions she knew Violet would want to ask, she made her getaway.

'Are you coming here tonight, love.' Violet followed her to   the door. 'Only Janey will want to see you.'

'I'm having a few days until… well, let's say, I need to keep a low profile, not be seen as such, you know. Better that way, until we come to terms with the situation. I don't want to bring trouble for you.'

'There are options; you know love, if you're not sure.'

'Not for me, I'm going to be late for work if I don't hop it, now. I'll be round soon.' She jumped aboard waved then held on tight, as Stanley swung the trap round in the road, and drove onward to the main road.

Christmas Eve 1915

'I'm so glad you asked if I could stay over with you, our Molly.' Janey was beaming, and she hugged her big sister. 'Aunt Violet is alright, but it's not the same without you around. And every time I see you now it's like there's a bit more of my baby niece in there.' She put her hand on Molly's thickening middle.

'Doris offered… I think she knew how much I was missing you. They're good people, I like them a lot. Anyway, it might be a nephew.'

'So, have you found out who the baby's daddy is yet then?' Janey looked puzzled.

'Oh, Janey; what can I say?' It's complicated, but all you need to know is, you'll be an auntie to this little one, and we'll love it more than all the stars in the sky. Agreed?' Crossing fingers behind her back, Molly could hardly breathe. She'd have to think how she would ever explain the virgin birth. Now, if the baby came tomorrow, that might be useful. But it was so far away yet, so with all the jollity she could muster, she nudged her sister.

'What if we go down and see if it's supper time. They told me it's Gertrude's home-made soup and crusty bread with cheese; I don't know about you, but I'm starving.'

'Yes, and I am. It'll be great to see aunt Violet and Nadine and all the family tomorrow, won't it?'

They scrambled off the bed where they'd had a heart to heart, and made their way down to the Cartwright's front room where a scrumptious Christmas Eve supper awaited them.

Chapter 27

Christmas Day 1915

Doris and her husband were up early, with Gertrude who was already peeling potatoes.

'I was wondering about a tree, Stanley… Would it appear ostentatious, seeing as war rages on; it's such a difficult decision, only with everyone coming round…'

'Already decided my love… me and Bart are off to collect a couple now; we'll have one indoors and one outside. He's got my saw and axe ready on the cart. You go and get all them traditional decorations out, the ones we all love. They always cheer us up. We're not going to sit here crying, you wanted to keep the British Spirit up, and keep it up we will, for all our special guests.'

He put his finger under her chin, and turned her face towards him. 'We'll get through all this, and our trees will be a symbol of strength and endurance; and when I've got the goose and turkey from Danny Glover, then you and Gertrude can get creating us a wonderful feast. I bet you'll have it all looking scrumptious and festive before the others get here.' He planted an affectionate kiss on her lips.

'Happy Christmas, Doris my love; and to our lad, wherever he might be. Clara said she'll make it over later, so you won't have chance to get thinking and worrying, about things, are you?' He gave an irresistible wink, leaving her so sure in his love, ready to face decorating tasks.

She frowned. 'It's only that I'm not sure we should … after, Y'know,' (she lifted her eyes up to where Molly and Janey were getting up and dressed) whether we should be having anything to do with him?'

'Leave it with me, love.' He tapped the side of his nose - eyes squinted like a man with a mission. 'There's more than one way to skin a cat.'

'What are you up to Stanley? Don't do anything you shouldn't do – promise me. I ordered the Christmas birds' ages ago, now things have changed. Just be careful.'

He was gone, after reassuring her, everything would be fine, telling her, 'Just look after the girls.'

She delved into the cupboard under the stairs, where she retrieved a huge box, and dragged it into the parlour.

'Janey, Molly, its Christmas! Fancy helping me to sort the trimmings out?' She hollered up the stairs, and it wasn't long before the two sisters appeared, and were busily sorting out the boxes of traditional Christmas decorations that had been in the family for years.

'We've got small candles to attach to the tree last of all, and Gertrude has come up with a wonderful recipe – small cakes, like miniature Christmas puddings, topped with a sprig of marzipan holly. It's going to look wonderful. I'll find my ribbon box, to tie them on. You can both help decorate it when Stanley comes back. In the meantime, there are Chinese lanterns, and streamers to fix up.' She turned in her tracks. 'No climbing ladders for you though, Molly, we'll let Janey do that.'

'How about I ask Gertrude to cook us up some coddled eggs, on crumpets, with a big mug of tea? If we have that and a bowl of porridge, it'll keep us going until later, when we have the main meal.' Molly and Janey nodded; engrossed in the task of sorting an array of decorations.

'Sounds delicious,' Molly remembered her manners, 'doesn't it, Janey?' She nudged her sister to acknowledge the hospitality offered to them both.

Doris stood at the door, watching the sisters revelling in their task. Laughter from the girls, crawling around the floor, sorting and comparing wooden soldiers, peg dollies dressed as angels with halos and a selection of home-made streamers, reminded her of how she and her own sister, Marie enjoyed Christmas so much, when they were younger. Then her Issac and Clara got just as excited when it came this time of the year.

A warm glow surrounded her, and she was so glad they were with her.

Some decorations were ancient; and some more recent... After she'd showed Molly which ones Issac and Clara made, instructing that these needed priority of place on the trees, she left them to share their sisterly moment.

She disappeared to find Gertrude, where they'd discuss stuffing recipes, handed down from grandmas and great grandmas, tried and tested, strictly never altered to this day.

Not before organising a huge pan of porridge, for everyone, followed with eggs on crumpets for breakfast. They needed a good wholesome start to what would be a long and busy day.

They discussed whether they'd stretch to brandy butter for with the pudding. The answer of course was a firm, yes. If there was one day Doris Cartwright could share her good fortune with others, who deserved it, this was that day.

Hearing laughter and having warm-hearted folk who worked hard, around her, was a tonic that she needed most. 'Happy Christmas, Gertrude,' she smiled at her most loyal worker who was more like an extra daughter than a worker at Oak Tree Grange. 'Did you ask your friends to come in and help you later on?'

Gertrude was already piling more logs onto the fire, in readiness, for heating the water in the pans she'd set on the hob. One for the porridge, another for the eggs;

She turned in surprise. 'Yes, thanks, as usual, they're looking forward to it. And a Merry Christmas to you as well,' her smile was one of genuine love that let Doris know, she belonged here, with the Cartwright family who meant the world to her. 'If the war generals think they'll dampen our spirits they thought wrong didn't they, Mrs Cartwright?'

***

Stanley and Bart were on the track to the forestry, on the Cannock side of Bloxwich, another part of the Cartwright's land, to find the best all round, suitable trees to be used for Christmas. 'It shouldn't take us more than an hour, Bart.' The deal with Danny Glover was a tree delivered for a goose and a turkey in exchange.

He'd keep his side of the bargain, and give this butcher who he thought was a friend, and idea of how the future was laid out. Stanley had morals and principals of a proud man who loved his family with a passion.

What he'd heard over the last few days had cut him to the core. His so-called friend, to come out with stories from the gutter, to feed a lovely young woman; the one he knew had strong feelings for his son. Whether their Issac felt the same he couldn't tell; he'd gone away before he'd said anything to them on the personal side of the relationship. He must feel something for the bonny wench; otherwise he wouldn't have trusted her with his business.

'Over here, sir, I've seen a row of decent sized trees. He stood up, steadying the reins, and leaned over to show Stanley the way to where he'd spied the trees they could use. How about we chop a couple from there?'

'Leave it with yer, Bart. As soon as we get them chopped, we'll deliver to Mr Glover and get ourselves back home. I want two for us though, one indoors, one outside. With kiddies coming, let's give em a show, eh?' He took the reins from Bart and drove the horse and cart in the direction he'd suggested. The lad was a great help with the horses, and proved as handy with the axe. Using ropes to steady the felling, between them they managed to saw three hefty, sizeable fir trees to the ground. In no time at all, the trees were chopped, checked for lopsided branches, then loaded and roped safely onto the cart.

'Well, would you look at that?' Stanley turned his head to the sky, where a flurry of snowflakes blew in a whirlwind of patterns. 'A white Christmas; just like the olden days.' He smacked Bart on the back, and reached for the rum bottle in his pocket. He took a slug and passed it to his helper, who knocked back a good measure, and replied, 'Merry Christmas, sir.' They made a dashing pair coasting along on the horse and cart, loaded with festive green branches dusted with snowflakes. They nodded and saluted everyone they passed, wishing peace and good will for Christmas. If it weren't for the absence of young men, you'd never have thought there was a war on.

'Left at the next crossroads carry on up to the end of the road then we'll be at our destination. Stanley had another swig from his hip flask.'

Pulling up outside the butcher's house, Bart tethered the horse to the sturdy gatepost, placing the nose bag over his head. With a flick of his penknife, Stanley freed one of the trees, and gave it a shake. Between them, they manoeuvred it to Danny Glover's back door. Stanley felt for his axe hidden deep in his overcoat pocket.

The loud knock on the door, and Stanley's shout, told Danny his tree had arrived. He was expecting his sister, Lavinia and her two friends to arrive shortly, for Christmas dinner, he was already ahead with his vegetables, and a goose was crisping up a treat in his oven. There weren't many men who could rustle up a feast like he did.

'Tree delivery… It's a big un; shall we leave it out here?' Stanley looked round for a suitable spot to deposit the six-foot spectacular greenery.

'Aye, drop it over there, by me shed, looks like a good un. And I'll get yer goose and a turkey like the lady ordered, swaps like for like, no cash needed?' Danny nodded, grinning, to check the deal still stood;

Stanley nodded sagely back to him discreetly handling of his weapon of choice. He inclined his head towards the pathway, instructing Bart to go.

'I'll meet you back at the cart you carry on and see to the nag, I won't be a minute.'

'It's in the shed, all prepared and oven ready, come and look at these beauties.' Danny whistled as he led his long-time friend into the darkness of the poultry shed down his back yard; you happy with these pair Stan?' He turned, reaching for the brace of limp birds dangling from the hook.

'Perfect for …what…' the butcher felt the bulk from his attack when his face slammed into the side wall of his shed. Stanley grabbed the back of his collar and rammed his knee up between his legs. 'How do you like being treated like this, eh? Tell me Danny Glover!'

From his pocket, he pressed the blade of his axe firmly against Danny's neck then dragged it slowly up his cheek, pushing harder as he spoke.

'Bit of a shock, is it? When someone you've known for years, think you trust, breaks that trust?' He drew the axe back down and pressed again, harder into the butcher's neck.

Danny screamed like a pair of mating cats. 'Take it away; I don't know what yam on about.'

'I think you do, so does all the family.' He threw him to the ground, and pinned him down with a body slam, sat astride him, and used both hands to cut a chunk of his hair from the back, by his neck in one neat chop. 'I didn't do time in the last war to be afraid of bloodshed, even if you butcher for a living.'

He held his captive's hair in front of his eyes. 'This is for Molly… And you're not the only one with friends in high places.' He bent his arm, and pressed the axe against his wrist, 'Go anywhere near Molly or any of her family again, you won't come out alive. You get me, Danny Glover?'

He dug the axe deep into his forearm, releasing a gentle trickle of blood that oozed along towards his wrist. 'Not the main vein, more's the pity. Always next time, though if I hadn't got a busy day ahead.'

'I hear you.' The surly butcher whimpered. 'Let me go, I've got family due any minute and there's a bird in the oven.'

Stanley grabbed the coward by his greasy hair and chucked him across the shed floor, kicking him into a pile of chicken shit, hard between the legs. 'You need to watch where you're putting it cock; else they'll be fishing you out the curly Wyrley cut.'

Stanley wiped his axe on the butcher's back, and calmly placed it back in the deep pocket of his overcoat, picked up his turkey and goose, then left the scene. He and the sleazy butcher had about finished their little chat.

'All set then Bart, mate?' He threw the birds on the back of the wagon, and then jumped up beside Bart giving him directions. 'Head home, pronto. The old gel will be waiting to get them cooking.'

Bart nodded. 'Everything go alright with Danny?'

'Oh aye all went just champion thanks… why?' He looked sideways to where Bart was looking up, watching the snowfall getting thicker by the minute.

'Only asking…' he gave a knowing smile to his boss.

***

There was a cheer from the girls when Bart fixed the tree in the huge porch way, making sure it was safe before standing back to admire what they'd brought home. 'And there's another one for indoors. I hope yer've got enough decorations.'

Doris clapped her hands, 'you've done us proud, love.' She turned to hug Stanley. 'And the birds will be first class. The oven's all ready and Gertrude's been busy, chopping all the herbs ready to sprinkle over them. We're going to have such a feast.'

Her husband picked her up and twirled her around until she was dizzy.

'Honestly, Stanley, what's got into you, you're positively lively. Bet you've been having a tipple from your jacket pocket, am I right?'

She bustled into the kitchen, without waiting for a reply. Vegetables bubbled, puddings steamed, and potatoes, some for boiling others for roasting around the birds stood in a huge pot on the side.

'Look at the snow; it's just perfect for a white Christmas.' Molly looked to the sky as she ran onto the lawn. 'Shall I go and get the others?' She looked at Stanley. 'If you've had a tipple, I mean. Then you can put yer feet up.'

'Take the motor, love, but it's still early, how about we get this tree decorated up first?' She agreed.

Together, Molly and Janey made the tree look spectacular with reds golds and green decorations, then tiny candles on the tips of the branches were lit, and small tangerines hanging from red ribbon finished the look.

Gertrude squealed with delight on seeing the beautiful sight. 'Oh, it's just like a proper Christmas. I need to get the table laid now.' A couple of her friends from the other side of Bloxwich had been called in to help out with the preparation and serving of food.

Molly noticed how much jollier she was with her own friends around her, and it was wonderful to see. 'I'll go and get aunt Violet and the others, now in case the snow sticks. I don't want her to have any excuses to change her mind.'

'Molly, get Bart to take the horse and double carriage; you take the motor for Violet and Francesca's mother,' Doris put in her thoughts, and then clapped her hands. She was in her glory, organising and all was going to plan so far.

'Hurry now, then we can get on with laying the table, and making sure everything's well cooked.' She waved Molly out and walked with her, to where the motor sat waiting to be used.

'Thanks so much, Doris.' Molly turned and gave her an impulsive hug. 'She was looking forward to seeing Violet and Fran; this really would be a Christmas to remember.

Over Bloxwich, Bart waited outside, while Molly rounded everyone up; 'Are you ready for a motor car ride? Come on aunt Violet, it's a day for us to be together. I've missed you.'

'Aw, our Molly, what's happened to our family? I miss you as well, love. Come here…' They hugged and both wiped away a few tears. 'Come on, Moira's here now, look.'

Nadine and the boys were dancing around in the snow, trying to gather snowflakes as they flurried and swirled all around them. Francesca stroked the horse, while Bart busied himself lifting the Patrick, Oliver, and Nadine up into the double-sided carriage. Lastly, he hoisted their mom up, much to the amusement of her kids.

'Oh, I saw yer knickers then,' screamed the lads.

'Shut yer mush before I shut it for yer,' she joked back.

'Hey, Molly, Happy Christmas, race you there.' Francesca waved and shouted, see you soon… Go get em Bart!' In the mood for fun, Bart clicked his tongue and Midnight their faithful horse took a wide turn around in the road, and trotted off, leaving Molly at the wheel, revved up and ready to go.

Violet and Moira stood watching the young ones set off. 'Ee, she's happy to be getting out for Christmas, and me an all.' Moira and Violet linked arms, and left Victoria Row singing of Irish eyes smiling.

The journey in the motor felt like driving through a winter wonderland; something you'd see in a picture. Snowflakes tumbled down, covering skeleton trees, and making the journey a slow one, yet Violet and Francesca's mother put Molly in mind of a pair of youngsters, marvelling everything they passed. 'It's a novelty to be going out for Christmas, isn't it?' They agreed… 'And no cooking.'

Down the Wolverhampton Road, they kept an eye on the horse drawn carriage, a little way ahead. The squeals of laughter rang out as they were clearly enjoying the horse and carriage ride.

Molly drove slowly, and everyone they passed, shouted out, 'Have a Merry Christmas,' reminding Molly of the Dickens story, with Ebenezer Scrooge, who suddenly realising his destiny, had a change of heart. She felt an overwhelming sense of gratitude; for her aunt, her friends, and the children, especially her sister, who would be looking forward to their arrival, waiting for them back at Oak Tree Grange.

As they pulled up the drive, the boys were hanging out of the carriage, and the second Bart drew Midnight to a halt, they jumped and ran to the huge front lawn. 'Let's make a snowman!' Patrick shouted, 'No, a snowball fight,' Oliver replied.

Janey ran out the front door, and hugged Nadine, grabbing her hand to show her the tree, filled with candles twinkling in the entrance hall, giving a proper black-country welcome to the Irish ladies, and the family. Molly swung in to the parking space, and looked at the two older ladies as they delighted in watching the children.

'How're you both feeling? Let me just tell you, Doris is the most down to earth person you'll meet, a bit like you two. It was her idea to have you all here for Christmas. She wanted your company, to get to know you.'

A scooter pulled up beside them, and when the rider removed their headgear, it was Clara, sat astride her new form of transport, smiling back at them. 'Hello, everyone… looks as if there's a party in the offing, lucky for me I've arrived in the right place.' She parked up, and ran across the lawn gathering a handful of snow and showering the twins with a cold ball of slush. The screams drew the attention of Stanley and Doris, who came forward to welcome Violet and Moira. They chatted together like old friends.

Molly shut the motor down, and took in the peaceful setting, now the youngsters had gone in, and the elders were talking about brown ale and sherry for the ladies; she knew instinctively, Christmas was all about family. She sent up a silent prayer, thanking the lord for the friendship and hospitality of Stanley and Doris.

The tarpaulin was secured firmly over the motor, keeping it safe for the night; she'd been told earlier, they would all be staying over, due to the weather, and not wanting to let new friendships end after the meal.

From the corner of her eye, she spotted a four-legged creature race across the lawn, and then performed a gambol in the settling snow. It lapped the lawn, and then stood still, watching her for a few seconds, before it scampered back the way it had come. She rubbed her eyes, and put a hand to her head.

Molly you're having hallucinations, holding her hand to her head she brushed her hair back from her face. The Cartwright's had a black and white Jack Russell. He was kept out the back and was a fantastic rat catcher. That wasn't him.

She looked back to the gate of Oak Tree Grange … the soldier, in full uniform, silhouetted against the backdrop of skeleton trees, all covered in snow. His army uniform giving him an air of otherworldliness, handsome, different, yet the same…. 'Issac…' She whispered; hoping this wasn't an illusion, wishing him here to the point of imagining it was him.

He moved forward, in time for Molly to see the horse and carriage disappearing from the bottom of the drive just as quietly as it had arrived when he'd been dropped off; how didn't she hear them?

He stood motionless; looking at her, eyes full of love. She ran to his arms. 'You're home, my Issac, oh my love. You made it home.' As she held him close, she felt his heart beat against her chest. He was back. He slumped into her embrace, gasping, taking breaths as if they were difficult. She broke away, and looked at him. 'They're all inside, are you ready for this?'

He nodded, taking her hand. 'With you by my side, I'm ready for anything, Molly my love. We need to talk.'

Putting her finger over his lips, she walked with him slowly towards the house, where they heard the family singing, '*Good King Wenceslas looked out*,' at which point, Stanley was in the front window.

He rubbed a circle in the steamed up the glass, then rubbed his own eyes as he peered, then shouted, his voice a wobble… 'He's home, Doris, our lad's back!'

'Issac, is it really you?' His mother ran out and fell into his arms, and they embraced for what seemed like forever.'

Clara gave a little cough. 'Erm, any change of getting a sister hug then, soldier?' He lifted her off her feet, and they cried into each other's shoulders.

Stanley glanced over to Molly, and raised an eyebrow before he whispered. 'Now our Christmas really has begun.'

Chapter 28

The celebrations were talked about for long after the Christmas pudding was eaten. Janey was persuaded to go home on Boxing Day, with aunt Violet, while Moira, Francesca and her brood were left in no doubt Molly and Issac were made for each other.

'I'm not surprised you're having a child.' Issac couldn't hide the sadness from his voice, when Molly took him his early morning tea, the day after Boxing Day; 'Look at you…' He studied her from head to toe. 'Was there ever a bonnier wench in the world, never mind in the black country?'

'It's not quite like that…' She couldn't bring herself to tell him about the rape. It would bring it all back, and she refused to even think of that, all she wanted was her child to be safe and well. 'It's me and the baby I have to focus on, and your parents have been so kind, letting me stay here for now, though it's only temporary, until I find somewhere.'

'It doesn't matter, you don't have a man around or you wouldn't be here; stay as long as you like. Now, how's the business… The folks said the saddlers are after it.' He smiled.

'Issac, you haven't told me how you got on. I know you were burned and gassed. It's taken its toll. And where did Jasper come from. There's so much I need to know. And I'm here to help look after you.'

'Molly, love, please don't ask. Other than to say, I met some really good people along the way, and proper mates, ones I'll keep in touch with. Others….' His voice broke and he slumped onto the pillow. 'There's folk I need to see, to tell them… He was next to me when it happened.' He cleared his throat, but not before she heard the sob that escaped his lips as he talked of his friend in the trenches. 'I promised to go and talk to Betty; he spoke about her all the time. I'd like it if you came with me. Only if you want to though, maybe she'd like to have a woman's hand to hold, given the stuff I have to tell her.' He took a great sigh, and looked ready to break.

'I'm so glad you're here.' He sat himself up, and sipped the hot drink. And, with you around, I'll be up and about in no time. Your friend Fran and her family are good people.'

'They are, all of them kept me going, and she was a godsend, having the idea to take the hats onto the market. That's when we turned a corner. And I've started designing some bespoke pieces. Your mom is a first-class saleswoman; she took some samples to her charity groups, and got me half a dozen of my own designs to get to work on.'

'Molly, love, come here.' She took in the sallow colour of his skin, how he'd lost weight since she'd waved him off at Walsall station. He was a changed man. He only wanted to hold her tight, spend time together, and having each other was enough.

'I'm here for you, no matter what, Issac. You'll come through this, and when you feel up to it, we can go for walks. I bet you could sleep for a month.' She tried to make light of the seriousness. That beautiful dog will need lots of canal walks, and maybe we can go over Cannock Chase, like you said in your letters. He'll be a great guard dog round at Paradise Lane as well. Imagine, nobody would dare to harm us, would they?' She only wished she's had jasper near when she got assaulted, but it wasn't worth thinking about either of those times any more.

'It's not the time or the place, but I want to marry you. Make an honest woman out of my Molly. I've loved you for as long as forever, but it took being out on the frontline in the fields of France and being injured and taken to a Belgian hospital to realise it. Now with the baby and all, you'll need support. That's what you need, and I'll marry you as soon as I've sorted things out with the vicar. That's a promise.'

He made to get up and then the coughing started.

She took his hand, almost welling up with the thought of him being her husband. Her little baby having a daddy as noble as Issac, the dreams she'd had of this happening, all the times she'd wanted to hear him say it and now… she hardly felt worthy of such devotion.

'That's not possible, my love.' She held his hand tight, and put her head down to avoid looking him in the eye. She simply couldn't use him, just to make everything right. He didn't need the pressure of taking on a child that wasn't his own.

'But you love me, I love you. I can see it in your eyes, Molly. We have to talk, properly, but I feel our love is as strong as it ever was; I know you do too. We're great together, always were. What's the problem? You've promised someone else, is it the father of your child?'

'No, never ever, it's not like that. It wasn't planned, and my baby will never see its father; it wasn't a mutual conception. That's all I ever want to say, Issac. Don't push me on it.' She swallowed hard, but had to let him know; even though she couldn't look at him while she told him.

'There wasn't one second when I gave him any encouragement, nor went along with the, 'event' that ended up with me like this.' She put her hand on the tiny life growing inside her. 'I can't marry you in these circumstances.'

She threw her arms up and looked around his room. 'You're vulnerable, from your time out there. It will take time, and lots of loving, I'm here for you, but I'm with child, and it's not what I planned, certainly not what *we* planned. There's nobody else, just that I can't marry you, Issac, please don't ask me again.'

She closed her eyes, kissed him on the cheek then left the room, leaving all her hopes and dreams lying there, with him needing more care and love than she could promise him with her future already set out before her. She'd devote herself to being the best mom ever to the little child who would never be sold for any amount of riches in the world.

He stared at the closed door, after she'd gone; all the nightmares of the battlefield rushing back. He'd assumed, taken for granted she, his Molly would want him, fall into his arms, just like before. He wanted her, she glowed. Never had she given off so exuberance, a love for life, looking so womanly now. How could he bear to look at her, and not be with her? Close like they were before. It was too much for his brain to take in. He drifted into a fretful sleep; sweat poured down his face on waking filled with a fear he was back in France. The familiar surroundings calmed him for a while.

As long as she was around, he'd get better, stronger every day. One day she would marry him; it was the only thing keeping him going, his main ambition in life. The hat works didn't mean a thing, and everyone else around, though they cared, his entire world was Molly. She'd always been *his Molly*; and as long as he was alive, he vowed to make her his wife. Keeping that thought close to his chest, he settled back to sleep, only to have nightmares and flashbacks keeping him awake all night long.

Later, in her room, Molly sobbed her heart out. How could it ever work? He needed so much care and nursing, she wasn't a nurse, and she could only love him from a distance. She needed support with the baby. Already there were people around her willing to muck in, do their best. That's what black-country folk did, look out for each other. She had Janey, aunt Violet, and Francesca and her lot had offered help on hand any time she wanted it. There was so much love around her, she was incredibly lucky, and she knew it.

How could she saddle Issac with a child that wasn't his? And what if Danny Glover showed up again? She wouldn't use the man she loved as a shield - she wasn't scared anymore. He being there was enough; it made her feel safe.

Becoming his wife was only a dream. As long as he wasn't far away, she'd enjoy each day as it came. There was too much to think about, and he had so much healing to do before he took on responsibilities that he didn't have to. He'd never spoken about children. If they had, it might have made a difference. There was no way she'd have her baby become a burden to anyone. The little mite was her little miracle, and she would love it with her whole heart, whether a boy, girl, twins or triplets. She smiled at her own crazy thoughts.

His family had been more than kind, she wasn't one to take advantage, and they couldn't be happy deep down for him to marry a woman carrying another man's child. Whatever they said, it would bring disgrace to the family name.

She'd be there for him, until he got stronger, then by that time, she'd be a mother of a baby who she vowed to cherish and love. She choked on her tears as she placed her hand over the little one growing inside her.

***

1916

It was a hot day in July, after a long labour, Molly pushed her baby daughter into the world. The midwife handed her a bundle wrapped up in the white shawl, aunt Violet had lovingly crocheted for her. Janey wanted a cuddle, and later that day, Francesca called by to say hello to the new baby. 'It's all go at work, Moll.' She rocked the baby back and forth. 'The saddlers are coming in, and Issac's made them sign a document … it's all in writing. None of us lose our jobs; we're all to be taken on, *and with a pay rise*!' Her joy sizzled like a firecracker.

'Me and Bobby are still on the market, selling all the leather tackle, and hats as well.'

'Have you thought of names yet?' She cooed over Molly's new baby.

'She's Lily Rose,' her name came to me earlier, as she's got rosy cheeks, and pure as a Lily.'

When aunt Violet saw her, she said, 'there's no mistaking who she belongs to, she's the spit of you.' She couldn't put her down, until Molly insisted, she let her sleep. 'It's alright if you want to come back and live with me, love; until you get on your feet.' She looked worried.

'I'm alright, renting the lodge for now. I'll be back at work as soon as I'm fit enough. And Janey's a great help. I wouldn't know what do without her to be honest.'

The lodge was in the grounds of the Cartwright's estate. It meant she could help with Issac's recovery, but he was much better now, back at work, and in charge just how he used to be. She planned to get back to work when Lily Rose was big enough to go with her.

'The offer's always there, remember that, won't you?' Her aunt kissed her cheek.

'I will.' She leaned back, glad of a rest when the visitors had gone. Janey had moved in with her, on the promise that it was only until she got on her feet with the baby. It gave aunt Violet time to herself, and the sisters grew closer and knew that they had an unbreakable bond.

'You've got one more visitor,' Janey poked her head round the door. 'You awake, our Molly?'

He whispered to Janey, that he'd stay even if they were both sleeping. She left the door open, and ushered him to where Molly was propped up on her pillows, feeding baby Lily Rose. He didn't offer to leave, and she felt perfectly comfortable, with him there. The white lacy shawl was wrapped around Lily's dark curls, and her rosy cheeks, glowed as she reached her tiny hand to grasp her mother's breast. Molly smiled at Issac, who looked at them both like a man in a dream.

'Hey, how're you feeling Molly, love? I've been sorting out stuff with the saddlers, and that Francesca is practically running the place. But look at your beautiful baby.' He came closer, and stroked her cheek with his finger.

'She's a miracle, aw, Molly. I'm glad to be here for you both. We'll make sure she'll have everything she needs.' He sneaked a look to check she wasn't offended with saying – we.

She smiled, and reached for his hand. 'Thanks, Issac. It means everything to us both, and Janey of course.'

He nodded, 'Of course, Janey – goes without saying. Like they say, family is everything, and this little one will never be lonely. Wait until my folks see her. Have they been over yet?'

'No, I think Janey said, they're giving me a day or two to get a bit stronger.'

Issac laughed. 'I'll bet if I know my folks, they're sitting looking at the clock, waiting for the time to tick around.'

'Do you want to hold her?' Molly held her breath. It was one thing, him visiting and promising everything, but did he really want to know Lily?

'Well, I thought you'd never ask.' He ever so gently, scooped up the little bundle, and Molly pulled her nightdress into place, while he focused on speaking to her daughter. She was amazed at how much love he had in his eyes at that moment.

For now, nurturing her new baby and spending special time with Janey became a routine for Molly, and having Issac and his family on hand made her life the best it had ever been. Some days, they'd take Lily in her pram over to see aunt Violet and the other residents in Victoria Row.

She saw Issac every day, and he never pushed her with going back to work, even though they went down with Lily Rose to say hello on a few occasions. He kept his word about having everything they need as well. She couldn't imagine life without him, but he hadn't spoken about them being married since the day she told him no.

***

The summer turned to autumn, and Walsall arboretum was a picture of gold and bronze leaves as they blew and rustled swirling to the floor. Lily Rose had begun to gurgle and coo, and by now she was smiling every minute for her mummy. Issac was besotted with her. The boating lake shimmered and sparkled - a turquoise haze, in the late October sunshine. They walked along, linking hands as easy as the day is long. Molly pushed the pram while Issac held Jasper on his lead; when he stopped, to tie his bootlaces, she waited for him.

He looked up as she turned to face him, still on one knee, and smiled. 'Molly, love, I'm asking, with all my heart. Will you *please* make me the happiest man in Bloxwich, and the world, by saying yes, to being my wife?'

He waited… 'I'm staying here until it's a yes, so don't let my joints stick like this much longer, otherwise I'll never get up. Molly, what do you say?'

She looked into his eyes and could see his very soul. There never was or would ever be anyone else. Now she could tell him, from the bottom of her heart.

'Issac… Oh, love, of course, I say, yes.' Her legs felt wobbly, and she almost collapsed. He stood and pulled her into his strong arms, swinging her round, much to the delight of passing strangers, who took Jasper's lead as he'd started barking in celebration with them.

'She said, yes! We're getting married.' The happiness in his smile melted her heart. This time she knew; she'd never let him go. They'd stand side by side; whatever life threw at them.

THE END

© Lydia King 2025

About the author

Lydia King is the pen name of Susan Jones, author of six romantic drama books with a touch of humour. This is the first of the Black Country Sagas; more contemporary romance stories are in the pipeline.

The setting of the story is the place I was born and grew up, surrounded by family, flowers and freedom. Often I would be sitting under the apple tree reading a book, with Judy dog, and Sister Sal, and Cousin Julie. Happy Days.

Acknowledgements

Thanks to all my readers and the carry on writing group, for your support and   encouragement. From a 1 - 1 meeting with my preferred agent who asked me to write a war time saga, any war in the style of the late great Meg Hutchinson. This is that story.

Jean and Josie, my two aunties, top fans of my books, thanks for being the best sister in law's our mom could have had.

My Husband Alan; so good I married him twice, thanks for all those cups of tea, and your love.